WYNTER'S BITE

Scandals With Bite

Book 5

BROOKLYN ANN

Cover design by Brooklyn Ann

Published by Broken Angels, an imprint by Brooklyn Smith

http://brooklynannauthor.com
contact@brooklynannauthor.com

Dedicated to Karen Ann
6-11-62 ~ 2-14-09
Every happy ending is for you.

Acknowledgments

Thank you so much to all of you who helped make this book the best it can be: Rissa Watkins, Layna Pimentel and Shona Husk.

Thank you to my faithful readers and newsletter peeps whose never-ending encouragement keeps me writing.

Thank you to all my friends and family who cheer me on.

Thank you, Bad Movie Club for restoring my sanity.

And thank you to Kent and Micah, the best guys in my life.

Chapter One

Morningside Asylum for Lunatics
Manchester, England, May 1825

Bethany Mead cringed against the stone wall of her cell. Greeves was guarding the female ward this night. She *hated* Greeves. The way he looked at her, like he could see through her shift, and the way he held her too long when guiding her back to her cell, both filled her entire being with sick dread. She'd been in this hell long enough to know what unscrupulous guards did to female— and sometimes male— patients.

"I've got most delightful news, love," Greeves spat through the bars. The man was incapable of speaking without emitting a shower of spittle. "The good doctor will be taking a holiday at week's end. That means we'll have more time in private to get to know each other better, you and I."

Bethany made a small, choking sound, but knew better than to scream. That would only get her thrown in the quiet room for at least two days. Doctor Keene wouldn't believe her. Greeves acted like a kindly Samaritan in the physician's presence. At least the doctor may have thus far kept her safe from being violated from his frequent unexpected checking in on her, but his prescribed treatments for her hysteria were agonizing. She was rarely allowed outside, never allowed to look at a newspaper, and could only read novels that the doctor had perused and decided they would not "overstimulate" her. She wasn't even allowed to read the bible, for Keene thought that the demons and bloody violence were too extreme for a lady of her condition. That resulted in very insipid reading material. The most passion she'd read was a kiss on a gloved hand. The most intimate touch, the hero lifting the heroine from her horse.

Never could she read of heated embraces that lingered in her memory. Never could she read of kisses that inflamed her dreams.

So Bethany often pushed the dull romantic novels to the side and accepted the equally dismal literary novels offered to her, full of bland musings, but no story. Though every once in a while, Eleanor, another patient, would smuggle gothic novels and stories to her. Bethany's favorites had been written by Alan Winthrop, who was reputed to really be the Duchess of Burnrath. The tales of ghosts and witches tickled her fancy. John Polidori's short story, *The Vampyre*, had also captivated her and she had been distraught when Dr. Keene caught her poring over its pages and tossed her back in the quiet room.

For Bethany was absolutely forbidden from speaking, hearing, or reading anything about the supernatural, especially vampires.

Never vampires.

That was what had landed her in this prison in the first place.

Greeves's sibilant voice pierced her musings. "That's what I like about you. Yer so quiet. I wager you'll be quiet when I have ye as well. But I'll try to get some noise out of ye."

Nausea roiled through her belly at the thought of Greeves's filthy hands on her body. She'd once planned on giving her maidenhood to a dashing, crimson-haired viscount whom she'd believed had loved her, a man of secrets and dark magic beyond her most fervent imaginings. Now, after eight years of hell, her virtue would go to this wretched lout.

Eight years. The words scratched her mind like a fork on slate. Had she really been here that long? The first four years hadn't been so bad, as her parents sent money to ensure she had a decent room and meals, and her mother came to visit from time to time. But as she increased her pleas for her parents to take her home, her mother's visits dwindled. And once Lord and Lady Wickshire had the son they always wanted, both the money and visits stopped completely. She hadn't even received a letter in over three years. And without funding, Bethany had been moved to the pauper's wing, subject to rougher patients and lecherous guards. Doctor Keene also refused her requests to free her and threw her in the quiet room when she'd vowed to find a lawyer. The one time she'd tried to escape, running off when the patients were herded to the chapel, the guards had run her down and she'd spent a week in the quiet room, so intoxicated from Keene's tonic that she couldn't tell up from down. After that, she'd not been allowed outdoors for two months.

Bethany cringed as Greeves leered at her. More than ever she longed to leave this place. Every day in captivity increased her fear of going mad in truth.

Tears burned hot on her cheeks and a strangled sob tore from her throat.

"Oh yes." Greeves clasped his hands together. "I like it when you—"

He halted abruptly when Doctor Keene came round the hall. "How is Miss Mead this evening?"

Greeves cast her a smirk before turning to face the doctor. "Overwrought, it seems. I tried to comfort her, but she won't have it."

"Oh?" Keene lowered his spectacles and peered at Bethany. "I'll see to her then. You run along and make sure the doors are locked before you return to your station."

"Very good, Sir," Greeves replied before tipping Bethany a wink on his way out.

Dr. Keene opened her cell door and approached her, brows drawn together with concern. "What ails you, Miss Mead?"

Bethany bit her lip. Keene had already dismissed her complaints about Greeves, and if he thought she was having hysterics, he'd lock her up in the quiet room for a day or two. She *hated* the quiet room, a small, coffin-like chamber that isolated her from all light and sound.

"Very little, Doctor." She forced herself to smile. "I am only missing my mother." She wiped the tears from her eyes. "I feel better already."

Dr. Keene regarded her with a skeptical frown as he patted her on the shoulder. "Are you certain? Your hands are shaking. Perhaps you should spend some time in the quiet room."

Bethany shook her head vigorously. She'd experienced inexplicable tremors and aches for the past year. This time, her shakes were justified, but Keene refused to believe her. "I only need some rest. I will go to bed now."

Keene smiled and reached into his pocket. "Yes, rest is the cure for many things. A dram of my soothing tonic will help you sleep."

She bit back a grimace. Keene's tonic was anything but soothing, making her feel off kilter and sometimes bringing her hallucinations and vivid nightmares if he felt a higher dose was necessary. But the doctor had neatly manipulated her into making a choice: the tonic, or the quiet room.

"Whatever you think is best, Doctor," she said as demurely as possible.

Thankfully, he only gave her one teaspoon of the bitter potion instead of two. One time he'd given her three, and Bethany had spent countless hours trapped in a barrage of bad dreams, unable to wake.

"I will look in on you tomorrow morning, Miss Mead," Keene said as he strode out of her chamber. "If you are calm, perhaps you may take a turn through the gardens with the other ladies. Won't that be nice? Until then, sleep well."

The door shut with a clang that reverberated through her ears with undulating waves. Already, the tonic was taking over her senses. At least Keene had the mercy to slide the privacy panel closed on the door so Greeves couldn't peek in at her. Bethany stumbled to the small straw-stuffed cot and sat down hard on the prickly mattress, rubbing her arms as a draft swept in through the small barred window. She'd forgotten to shutter it. But the sight of the full moon in the sky gave her comfort, reminding her that there was a world outside, a world she had faint hopes of rejoining.

Wrapping her thin wool blanket around her shoulders, Bethany twisted her fingers in her lap to distract herself from the dizzy sensations the tonic wrought. Counting back from when the patients had last went to chapel, it was Tuesday. Four days until Doctor Keene went on his holiday. That left her little time to come up with a plan to save her from Greeves.

She wished she knew how long Keene would be gone. If it were only for a few days, she could muster the courage to get herself thrown in the quiet room for that time. Only Nurse Bronson was trusted with those keys, so Greeves wouldn't be able to get to her there.

But a sennight, a fortnight? She shuddered, unable to fathom torment of that duration. Such a long time in the dark might break her. Yet what Greeves had in store may also drive her truly mad.

But her family had abandoned her, she had no funds for herself, and *he* never came for her like she thought he would. Justus, Lord de Wynter. Although she'd finally come to understand that he wasn't a vampire. Somehow she had imagined that part, but now it seemed she had invented Justus's ardent love for her too. From the moment she'd been committed to the asylum, she'd believed he'd come to rescue her, to marry her as they had planned beneath the boughs of the apple tree in her family's orchard. Even when Dr. Keene convinced her that Justus couldn't have been a vampire, Bethany still thought Justus cared for her.

But as days turned into weeks, then months, then years, Bethany's hope for Justus to rescue her gradually dried up like the last pool of water in an arid desert. He wasn't coming. He never cared for her. He'd just been a rake like her parents had insisted.

And Bethany had paid the ultimate price for falling in love with him. Her family had thrown her in the asylum and abandoned her. If only she'd obeyed them and kept her distance from the man who'd fascinated her from their first fateful encounter.

Swallowing a lump in her throat, Bethany pulled the scratchy blanket tighter around her body. She needed to bring her tormented thoughts under control before the tonic turned them into nightmares.

But the moment she closed her eyes, they came anyway.

Greeves grasping at her, the guards locking her in a tiny box, screaming, struggling to get out. The lid opening only to see Justus standing over her, laughing with blood-drenched fangs before closing the box, shutting her in darkness.

Bethany jerked awake and took several deep breaths, trying to think of Chaucer, of Camelot, of a book she'd read long ago about a Fairy Queen.

Just as her eyes began to close, a voice echoed in her cell.

"Bethany…"

At first she thought Greeves had returned, but then she heard the voice again, rich as marzipan, and achingly familiar.

"Bethany!"

The hairs on the back of her neck stood on end. It couldn't be!

She then heard a soft rapping on the bars of her window. Bethany turned and gasped as she saw a face peering in at her. Her heart clenched like a fist at the sight of crimson hair, pearl-white skin, and glittering green eyes.

A strangled cry trickled from her throat. She was dreaming of him again. "You're not real."

More than ever did she loathe Keene's horrid tonic. What kind of evil substance was it to inspire such heartbreaking hallucinations?

The vision made a noise that sounded like a cross between a laugh and a sob. "Of course I'm real." Arched lips curved in a small smile. "Look at me. Touch me."

Long pale fingers reached through the bars toward her. Bethany cringed back against the wall. How long would this drug delirium last? "Not real," she whispered again.

"Then take my hand and feel for yourself." The vision crooked his finger, beckoning her, daring her. "Come on now, I never before knew you for a coward."

That old, not quite mocking, slightly daring tone held the same compulsion as it had in real life. Without thinking, Bethany swung her legs over her cot and slowly shuffled towards the window. The bare stone floor felt cold beneath her feet. Moonlight reflected on his skin, turning it luminescent and casting an angel's nimbus over his fiery locks. If he was a hallucination, it was the most vivid one she'd ever experienced. Had Keene changed the recipe of his tonic?

With trembling hands, she reached out to touch his fingers outstretched towards her. Warm and firm, they slid across her skin with solid tangibility. Frissons of heat sparked at his touch, just as when they'd first met that fateful night long ago.

Once more, she dared to meet his eyes and study the face that had haunted her dreams. As if transported back in time, she saw the same love, longing, and touch of melancholy in his gaze that had lingered in those green depths the night he asked for her hand.

"Justus?" she whispered.

"Yes, Bethany." His lips curved in a broad grin. White fangs gleamed in the moonlight. "I've come to take you out of here."

Blood roared through her ears before the world went black as pitch.

Chapter Two

Rochester, England, August 1817
Eight years ago

Bethany stepped out of the carriage, eyes fixed in rapt wonder at Ellingsworth manor. Gossamer paper lanterns hung from the trees, lining the drive like stars from the heavens. Strains of enchanting music emanated from the house.

Her mother rapped her on the shoulder with her fan. "Don't stare! They'll know you're a green girl immediately."

"Yes, Mother." Bethany schooled her features into what she hoped was an expression of urbane boredom, as if mansions decorated like fairylands were a regular sight. As if this were not her first country party.

Her mother continued her lecture, straightening invisible wrinkles on Bethany's gown and fussing with her already overworked coiffure. "Remember, this is our best chance to secure a proper match for you. We cannot afford an elaborate come out when the Season begins, and besides, there will be even more attractive debutantes to compete with you in London. We must strike early, while the eligible bachelors have their guard down."

Bethany nodded, struggling to conceal her disgust. Her mother spoke of the resident gentlemen like they were nothing but hares to be flushed out and trussed with a snare. But Cecily Mead's plan for a preemptive matrimonial campaign was not simply due to worry about the more affluent competition for the Season. As her father had no sons, his baronetcy would be going to her cousin, Willis, and it was imperative that Bethany marry into a good family so that her parents would be assured of a comfortable future. To make the matter more urgent, the family fortune was dwindling away after two years of bad crops and a few gambling debts. Furthermore, Father had grown impassioned with politics and was determined that Bethany's marriage secured him the right sort of connections.

Unfortunately, her mother was right. With a modest dowry, only passable skills in ladylike pursuits, limited social connections, and what her father referred to as "irrational flights of fancy," Bethany was not the most attractive candidate as a prospective bride.

"At least your hair is blonde," her mother often said. "That is all the rage this Season."

As if her hair was the only thing about her of value.

Hiding her dejection behind her fan, Bethany followed her parents into the manor, keeping a polite, disinterested smile plastered on her face as the butler announced them.

As they made their way to the bottom of a sweeping staircase to greet the hostess, Bethany's mother whispered behind her fan, pointing out prospective prey.

"Willoughby may only be a squire, but his income is twelve thousand per annum. You must wrangle a dancing invitation from him at all costs." Her fan flicked in the direction of a stooped old man. "Lord Peabody may be a little long in the tooth, but he is an earl. Just imagine, you could be a countess! There's Lord Darkwood, a baron. He is possibly the best catch in attendance. We must endeavor to secure you an introduction."

Bethany followed her mother's gaze. The Baron of Darkwood was at least handsome, but something about his harsh countenance and emotionless dark eyes made her shiver. He looked all too capable of cruelty. Darkwood turned and said something to another man, who grinned and laughed. "Who is that gentleman standing next to him?" she whispered, captivated by the man's long dark red hair, russet brows, and brilliant green eyes dancing with merriment.

Her mother's lips pursed as if she'd sucked on a lemon. "Viscount de Wynter, a known rake and blackguard. Stay clear of that one."

"But a viscount ranks higher than a baron." Bethany frowned in confusion, trying to make sense of her mother's contrary logic.

"Yes, but the only proposals you're likely to receive from that one are the indecent kind. He ruins maidens for sport." Mother lightly grasped Bethany's upper arm to guide her forward. "Now, avert your gaze before he sees you looking at him."

Lady Ellingsworth greeted them courteously enough, though with hurried disinterest. Bethany couldn't blame the hostess, for she still had a long line of guests to greet.

Disinterest turned out to be the best reception Bethany received all evening.

Her first country ball was a disaster. Bethany started the contradance with her left foot, rather than the right. To make matters even worse, she stepped on Squire Willoughby's toes. He politely continued their dance, but from his flared nostrils and lack of invitation to dance with her again later, Bethany knew she'd made a cake of herself.

Then, after she was introduced to Lord Peabody, the man actually fell asleep when she was telling him about the songs she played on the harpsichord. A dull topic to be certain, but her mother insisted that she only speak of her feminine talents, not of her literary tastes, her love for her horse, or anything that made her resemble a human being with thoughts and opinions of her own.

She didn't fare any better when she was partnered with Lord Darkwood. Something about the man made her so nervous that she stammered every time she tried to engage him in conversation. His eyes were so black and cold, his hair dark as the devil's. While they danced, he barely looked at her as she twisted herself inside out to catch his interest.

Even worse was that after their humiliating dance, Bethany's mother took it upon herself to introduce them as if they had not just danced together. Bethany's face burned like a hot coal as she heard a few titters behind fans and Lord Darkwood stiffly uttered a curt greeting, not quite giving her the cut direct, but making it clear that he had no desire to further his acquaintance with her.

Dejected, Bethany fled to a far corner of the ballroom as soon as she was able. A small cluster of young women stood to her right. One of them, a tall brunette, met her gaze and smiled. Bethany shyly smiled back. Perhaps this group hadn't witnessed her gaffes.

The brunette immediately dashed those hopes. "Is this your first time attending a ball?"

"Was it that obvious?" Bethany replied, waiting for the mocking laughter, or for the girls to turn their noses up and walk away,

They did neither. Instead, the group surrounded her, the brunette even giving her a comforting pat on the shoulder. "We've all had our own horrid introductions to these affairs. Allow me to introduce myself. I am Lady Rebecca Chatterton, the blonde is Lady Mary Ellingsworth, and this raven-haired beauty is Miss Deborah Peabody."

"I'm Miss Bethany Mead." She curtsied, pleased that at last someone was showing her kindness.

"Your father is the Baron of Wickshire, yes?" Rebecca inquired.

Bethany nodded.

Rebecca cocked her head to the side. "Last I knew, the baron was leasing his estate to Mr. Bunting."

Bethany blushed at the reminder. Until this year, they had never stayed at their family seat, for it was much more affordable to lease the property and remain in London year-round while her father sat in Parliament and hosted political gatherings. But now that the Governor of Rochester was retiring, her father had set his eyes on a new goal. "Yes, well, Father thought it was past time we came home and took in the country air."

"And find a husband for you?" Rebecca prodded with a wry smile.

The heat crept back to her cheeks as she nodded. "Yes, but I'm afraid I did not make a good accounting of myself."

To her further embarrassment, Rebecca glanced back at her friends and nodded in agreement. "Perhaps I can help you."

Gratitude flooded Bethany's heart. "I would very much appreciate anything you can do to mitigate my predicament."

Rebecca leaned closer and subtly pointed her fan. "Do you see that gentleman with the dark red hair?"

Bethany's mouth went dry as she once more looked upon the striking visage of Viscount de Wynter. She'd been covertly snatching glimpses of him all evening. Something about him elicited a primal stirring in her belly. "Yes, I see him," she whispered.

"Persuade him to dance with you," Rebecca instructed. "Or even better, have him escort you out to one of the balconies."

Bethany frowned. "But my mother said I was to avoid him at all costs." Were these girls making sport of her?

Rebecca laughed behind the lace edges of her fan. "Although she is partly correct in that you should never let him catch you alone, there is benefit in having a rogue such as de Wynter pay you some attention. If the other gentlemen see that he is interested in you, they will then wonder what garnered such interest and will hasten to make your acquaintance."

Like a magnet, de Wynter pulled Bethany's attention back to his striking visage. A tendril of doubt curled in her belly. Why in heavens would he show her the any interest? She was a green girl, hopeless with social banter, a clumsy dancer, and worst of all, a little too plump. Slim, willowy figures were all the rage. But though Bethany listened to her mother and ate as little as possible, her breasts, hips, and waistline did not oblige her by decreasing in the slightest. Mother had tried corsets to see if they could diminish her curves, but all they did was make her resemble an overstuffed sausage.

Bethany hid a dejected sigh behind her fan. It was hopeless.

Yet she had to try. If she didn't do something to raise her esteem among her peers, she was doomed to remain a wallflower forever.

How would she carry this off? She and de Lord de Wynter hadn't been introduced, so she couldn't approach him and strike up a conversation. And introduced or not, she certainly couldn't ask him to dance.

As she slowly drew closer, unable to stop stealing glances at him— she'd never seen hair in such a dark shade of red— a tentative idea blossomed in her mind. He could still deign to ignore her, but if he did, he would look the cad, not her.

Bethany prayed he would at least look at her, maybe even smile, and not just because of her goal to gain attention from suitors.

Chapter Three

Justus de Wynter, Viscount de Wynter, and second in command to the Lord Vampire of Rochester, frowned as he heard the group of tittering girls making their malicious plan. With his preternatural hearing, he knew that the young misses of the aristocracy were not the innocent paragons that they painstakingly paraded themselves as. But he usually ignored their mean-spirited gossip and little pranks.

This time, however, the chits meant to include him in their scheme. Justus gnashed his fangs in irritation at their presumption to use him. He would not oblige them by dancing like a puppet on their strings.

Their vituperative words repeated in his mind.

"Silly little greenhead. Just wait and see what she does when he gives her the cut direct. I wager six pounds that she will cry."

"I wager ten that she'll faint."

Though it was true that Justus was merciless in driving away any unmarried female who dared to approach him, this time, he would be gentle with the poor girl. Instead, he would guarantee that the malicious misses lost their wagers.

His gaze swept over the crowd, landing on the target of the girls' prank.

She looked painfully young, likely barely out of the school room, a picture of innocence with her golden curls and large blue eyes. However, the curves of her breasts above the neckline of her snow-white gown chased away all thoughts of her youth. Tearing his eyes from that tempting view, he once more looked upon her heart shaped face as she made her way towards him with graceful, yet tentative steps.

A pang of worry struck his gut. She wouldn't introduce herself to him, would she? Or God forbid, ask him to dance? Such gaffes would render her a pariah.

The young woman licked her lush lips as if about to speak. But thankfully, she halted and merely stood near him, occasionally glancing at him over her fan.

Good. So she wasn't a half-wit after all. At this point, he could either ignore her presence and appear rude— something he did often— or have someone introduce them so he may engage her in conversation or ask her to dance.

For possibly the first time since he was Changed nearly two hundred years ago, Justus opted for the latter. Catching Lady Ellingsworth's gaze, he gave her a beckoning grin. She returned his smile and excused herself from the people she was conversing with and hurried his way.

"Would you do me a kindness and introduce me to that young lady?" he whispered.

Lady Ellingsworth glanced at the female in question and a line formed between her brows. "Although I've heard some tales, I have never seen you seek sport with a debutante."

"No sport intended." Already he was coming to regret his impending act of kindness. "I merely owe someone a favor," he improvised.

"Well then, if you are seeking sport…" She placed her hand on his sleeve.

Justus forced a tight smile. "I know where to look." He thought he'd made it clear to Lady Ellingsworth and every other woman he took his pleasure from that his liaisons were for one night only. He couldn't risk any human learning what he was, so he kept his distance.

The hostess gave him a slightly petulant frown before pasting a placid smile on her face and patting the blonde maiden's shoulder. "Miss Mead, have you met Lord De Wynter?"

The young lady blinked in surprise. "I have not had the pleasure, my lady."

As the introductions were made, Justus bowed and concealed an amused smile at her shaky curtsy. Nervousness emanated from her subtly curvy form in tangible waves. Even when making an effort at kindness, he still appeared to intimidate. Just then, the strains of a waltz began.

Perfect. This ought to sever the vipers' tongues.

Justus extended his hand. "Would you care to dance, Miss Mead?"

Her pale cheeks flushed the color of rose petals. Usually such blatant timidity was tiresome, but for some reason with her, he felt a tremor of delight. "Yes, my lord," she said softly, and took his proffered hand.

Even through the thin fabric of their gloves, he could feel the heat of her fingers intertwined with his. Shaking off the odd intensity of his reaction to her touch, Justus concentrated on leading her to the dance floor and maintaining a mask of indifference at the surprised glances cast their way at the sight of him dancing with a debutante.

Her steps were slightly off time, but for some reason, he only felt sympathy rather than irritation. "You're overthinking the dance," he whispered. "Relax and let me lead."

Her crimson flush deepened, but she heeded his advice and suddenly the dance became fluid, their bodies fitting together perfectly. Justus blinked in surprise. She followed instructions exceedingly well.

The scent of her skin, clean and tinged with the lavender oils she must have bathed in, awakened his lust even as the pulsing vein at the juncture of her neck and shoulder prodded his other hunger.

To combat the alarming reaction, Justus decided to converse. "Do you have any hobbies?"

Closing his eyes, he prepared for the usual prattle about needlepoint, the pianoforte, and watercolors. Not that he frowned upon any of these genteel pastimes, in fact, many young ladies produced admirably good paintings and played pleasing music. But the fact of the matter was that they were so boring to talk about.

"I like to read." An undercurrent of passion threaded through her voice.

Interest pricked at her answer. "I like to read as well. What are your favorite works?" Probably romantic novels, but some literacy was better than none.

"I adore medieval literature." Her eyes sparkled with enthusiasm for their topic. "Especially Chaucer."

Chaucer? Justus blinked in surprise. That meant she could read old English. Once more, pity welled in his heart. Women like her were always counseled to hide their intelligence. But she didn't have to hide hers from him.

"I enjoy Chaucer as well," he informed her with a grin. "My favorite is *The Book of the Duchess*. What is yours?"

"*The Canterbury Tales*." Adoration infused her voice.

He couldn't help but smile in understanding of her joy to speak of a favorite work. "But they were never finished."

"I don't mind. In fact, it leaves a little mystery to the experience of reading them, wondering where Chaucer was going, what else he intended." A dreamy smile curved her rose pink lips. "Unfinished stories fascinate me."

And she was beginning to fascinate him, despite his better wisdom. It was difficult to find someone whose passion for the written word matched his own. Justus's best friend, the Baron of Darkwood and the Lord Vampire of Rochester, had little time for books between overseeing his territory and attending scads of country parties. And since Justus was Lord Darkwood's second in command, all other vampires ranked below him, and thus were reluctant to engage in any sort of banter with him.

But he could not become close to this enchanting little reader. Women her age, by necessity, were only after one thing: matrimony, which he could not undertake without revealing that he was a monster and then transforming her into one as well.

As if to reiterate that their conversation must come to a close, the song ended with a poignant note on the violin strings.

The sparkle in Bethany's blue eyes dimmed, though she made a valiant effort to hide her disappointment with a tremulous smile. "Thank you for the dance, my lord."

Instead of escorting her back to her mother as he should, Justus found himself reluctant to part from her company. "Would you care for a glass of punch?"

Her face lit like the dawn. "That would be lovely."

As her slender fingers curled around his bicep, Justus once more experienced a tremor of pleasure. He tried to tell himself it was only because he wanted to continue their literary discussion. Oh, and tweak the noses of the chits who attempted to pull a prank on Bethany, of course.

Justus glanced in their direction and met their petulant scowls with a triumphant smirk.

"Do you only read medieval literature?" he asked Bethany as he fetched two glasses of punch from a passing footman.

She shook her head. "I read anything I can get my hands on. Greek, Roman, French…"

"Your nose wrinkled when you said Roman," Justus interrupted with a chuckle. "Why?"

"Because most of their works are veritable copies of the Greek tales, aside from changing a few names and placing extra emphasis on the 'glory of Rome.'" Her gaze tilted upwards as if beseeching the heavens to justify such nonsense. "For a nation that conquered half the world, they are shockingly unoriginal."

Justus laughed. "I've never heard a more accurate assessment. And what of the Greek classics?"

"Some of them are interesting, but I cannot help but think that most of the characters' problems wouldn't have existed if Zeus had not been such a philandering cad." She blushed and covered her mouth with a gloved hand as she realized what she'd said. "I apologize, that was inappropriate."

"Yet it is indeed the truth." Justus's shoulders shook with laughter.

Their conversation continued, each discovering what works they'd both read and dissecting the merits and perceived flaws of each. But once Justus realized they'd remained rooted to the spot, holding empty glasses for Lord knew how long, he reluctantly admitted that their time together must come to an end.

Bethany confirmed the sentiment as she looked across the ballroom and sighed. "I had best return to my mother. She's watching me and doing her best impression of Medusa."

"Then I must take you to her before she turns us to stone." Justus handed their empty glasses to a passing footman and escorted her to her mother's side. The murderous glare that Lady Wickshire cast upon him did Bethany's Medusa comparison credit and he had to bite the insides of his cheeks to hold back laughter. After sketching a quick bow, he hastily retreated.

Normally he would take pleasure in feeding from sour-faced matrons like Lady Wickshire, but out of respect for Bethany, he would spare the woman and seek other prey. Perhaps one of the mean-spirited girls who had attempted to humiliate his new friend.

Just then, he met the scrutinizing eyes of Gavin Drake, Baron of Darkwood. "What were you doing with that debutante?" the Lord of Rochester inquired softly. "You normally avoid the petticoat set."

"I was thwarting a malicious prank," Justus hastened to explain. "A group of debutantes thought to humiliate the poor thing by having her approach me and I did not care to be an instrument of cruelty, so I offered the innocent lady a dance."

"Ah." Gavin's dark brows drew together with suspicion. "And then shared a glass of punch for good measure?"

"We were having a stimulating discussion about Greek and Roman literature." Justus crossed his arms over his chest. "I do not see why that should be a problem. *You* danced with her as well." And why did the idea of Gavin doing so make Justus's stomach sour?

"Yes, her mother made certain to thrust her at me at the soonest opportunity. Soon I shall have to take another bride to fend off the matchmakers." Gavin released a weary sigh. Every fifty years or so, he had a female vampire pose as his wife to deflect suspicion at him remaining single too long. "But you typically hold them at bay with your reputation as a notorious rake and ravisher of maidens. If you give that yellow-haired Miss too much undue attention, you'll either ruin her, or find yourself caught in the parson's mousetrap."

"All right!" Justus held up his hands in surrender. "I'll keep my distance from the young lady."

But that proved easier said than done.

As he caught a glimpse of another eligible bachelor leading Bethany to the dance floor, he alternated between grinding his teeth in irritation and wondering what she thought of Voltaire.

Chapter Four

Bethany spent the rest of the evening in a daze of lightheaded happiness. Rebecca had been right. After Lord de Wynter danced with her, gentlemen did indeed pay her more attention, which placated her mother after she'd given her a furious scold.

After Bethany had accepted the first gentleman's invitation to dance, she'd cast Rebecca a grateful grin. The girl had given her a tight-lipped smile in return, yet her countenance had taken on a queer cast. Perhaps her new acquaintance was not feeling well, Bethany thought with a wave of sympathy.

Her dancing partner, a squire's son, was amiable enough, but she couldn't help but feel that their conversation was stilted and awkward. The man didn't enjoy reading, and seemed obsessed with gambling on horse races. Bethany just couldn't sustain interest, no matter how much she tried. It was nothing like her discussion with Lord de Wynter. As if conjured by the thought, she saw a flash of red over her dancing partner's shoulder.

There he was, talking with Lord Darkwood. Their eyes met, and Bethany's belly fluttered with the most alarming sensation. She'd been so afraid earlier, when she'd shyly made her way towards him on Rebecca's advice. There was something vibrant and dangerous about him, this man her mother had warned her away from. His hair such a deep red that it looked sinful, his eyes green and somehow reminding her of a great cat.

She couldn't stop reliving the moment they'd first touched when he'd led her to the dance floor. The rapid beat of her pulse roared in her ears as his hand rested on her lower back and she'd grasped his firm, warm shoulder. When their gloved fingers intertwined, how her breath caught as electricity seemed to surge through their palms.

He was a rake, she reminded herself. She'd even heard snatches of conversion that hinted at a past dalliance between him and their hostess, which made her stomach clench with jealousy.

Yet now, as he tipped her a wink before turning back to Lord Darkwood, all Bethany could think of was the patient way he'd guided her in the dance, and how they'd talked of literature until their punch was long since finished. When he'd at last escorted her back to her mother, she'd felt a sharp pang in her chest, as if she'd just lost a dear friend.

Bethany's lips curved in a self-mocking smile. First she'd regarded him as a dangerous rogue, and now suddenly he's a friend? Perhaps her mind was indeed addled from reading too many books, as her father insisted. Yet it had felt so good to talk about her great passion with someone who'd understood. Like she wasn't alone in the world.

Perhaps she could recreate the experience with a gentleman who could be a potential suitor. Ignoring her mother's advice, Bethany attempted to discuss books with her next three dance partners. Alas, every one of them eyed her with the same impatient boredom as Lord Darkwood had.

She cast Darkwood a quick spiteful glance. Why did de Wynter have to be friends with such a cad? As if sensing her scrutiny, Darkwood's black eyes suddenly whipped to hers. She shivered. There was something frightening about that man. He brought to mind a villain in a gothic novel.

For the rest of the evening, she caught de Wynter looking at her, sometimes even starting toward her as if to ask for another dance, but he never did.

Disappointment weighed on her as her mother packed her in the carriage shortly after midnight. Decent maidens never stayed until the wee hours of the morning, after all.

Just as Bethany was about to step into the conveyance, she spotted a glimmer of crimson. Lord de Wynter stood on one of the balconies. He raised his hand in a wave.

She couldn't wave back, but she flicked her fan in his direction, smiling over the lace.

Her father interrupted the covert exchange. "Did you enjoy your first ball, my dear?"

"Oh yes," she said sincerely. Unable to tell him the true reason, she spoke of everything but. "I very much enjoyed the dancing and Lady Ellingsworth was a capital hostess. And her decor brought to mind a fairy kingdom."

His eyes narrowed in displeasure. "Fairies are not real. What have I told you about speaking of fanciful nonsense?"

"I did not mean—" she broke off at his warning glare and bowed her head. "I am sorry, Papa."

As silence fell over the carriage, she scolded herself for forgetting Father's odd terror of anything that fell beyond the bounds of realism. It seemed to consume him so much that even when they'd arrived at home, he still regarded her with a worried look as if he expected her to declare that Pegasus had conveyed them here, or pixies were on the roof.

However, even his reprimand could not dull her happiness of this night.

Once tucked into her bed, Bethany closed her eyes and once more relived her dance with the captivating viscount. The feel of being in his arms, his charming smile, the delight and interest in his eyes as they'd discussed Chaucer.

And finally, that secret smile and wave from the Ellingsworths' balcony.

Perhaps he was interested in her. Perhaps he would even pay her a call upon the morrow!

But he did not. In fact, no gentleman dropped by the Meads' country house all morning. Between visits with matrons who came to call, Lady Wickshire cast Bethany censorious glares and admonished her to try harder to be charming at the next gathering.

Yet it was difficult to muster charm when her emotions were ratcheting back and forth between disappointment that she'd misjudged de Wynter's interest, and embarrassment for being so foolish as to think she would mean anything to someone such as him. He dallied with married women and never showed interest in green girls like her. Why did Bethany think she would be any different?

She tried to hide her desolation as she accompanied her mother to a musicale performed by Miss Chatterton, one of the girls who had dared her to approach Lord de Wynter in the first place. Her sadness turned to joy when she saw a familiar red-haired figure sitting with the other bachelors on the far side of the music room. Their eyes met and he tipped her a wink.

Her flesh heated all over even as she chided herself for responding to him. He could only be interested in one thing. Quickly, she averted her gaze, resolving to ignore him. But throughout Miss Chatterton's dull plinks on the pianoforte, Bethany could feel de Wynter's gaze on her. Even worse, she couldn't stop herself from glancing at him whenever no one was looking.

Blast him! How was she expected to find a husband with him distracting her? Rakes promised ravishment, not marriage. Suddenly, a vision of de Wynter holding her tight in his arms flashed across her mind. Of his lips covering hers, his hands caressing her bare skin…

Bethany bit back a gasp. What was the matter with her? Surely she did not want to be ravished!

When silence fell and the people around her began to clap, Bethany tore her attention back to her surroundings and rose with her mother to mingle with the guests and nibble on tea cakes. She would ignore him, not look his way again. She would—

A light touch on her elbow made her shiver. She whipped around to see Lord de Wynter smiling down at her. He held an old book in his hands.

"I thought you might be interested in this one," he said softly. "You may borrow it if you like."

Their gloved fingers touched as he handed her the slim, battered volume. Once more, an electric thrill coursed through her body at his touch.

"Thank you," she whispered, heart blooming with delight. *A book!*

He bowed. "I'm afraid I must go, but I do look forward to discussing that book in the future." Green eyes glittering with an unspoken intensity that made her pulse quicken, he gave her a teasing grin. "I do hope you're a quick reader."

With that, he departed, slinking away on soundless feet like a tiger off to the watering hole.

Bethany looked down at the book he'd handed to her. *The Faerie Queen* by Edmund Spenser. Just as she was about to open the cover, she felt a light rap on her shoulder and looked up to see her mother scowling down at her. "What did *he* want?"

"He loaned me a book." Bethany made sure to emphasize the fact that he hadn't given it to her. Her mother would have an attack of the vapors if a man gave her daughter any sort of gift without a formal betrothal in place.

Cecily's eyebrows drew together in confusion. "Why would he do that?"

"During our dance last night, we discovered that we share a common interest in medieval literature," Bethany explained warily, knowing Mother disapproved of her broaching such topics. "So he thought I may enjoy this one. Hardly the behavior of one with improper intentions. Look." She pointed at the far end of the room where Lord de Wynter was bowing to Lady Chatterton. "He's already leaving."

"So he is," Lady Mead murmured with patent relief.

Why *was* he leaving so soon? Bethany wondered. Had some emergency come up? Another thought teased her mind, filling her with such pleasure she grew lightheaded.

Or did he only come here for the sheer purpose of bringing me a book?

Chapter Five

Justus delivered his farewells to Lady Chatterton, praising her daughter on a magnificent performance, though to be truthful, he'd hardly paid attention. All his focus had been dedicated to discreetly slipping the book to Miss Mead in such a way that would not compromise her reputation. And, of course, ignoring that inner voice demanding why it was so important for him to give some debutante a book in the first place.

Lady Chatterton crooned in token disappointment at Justus's early departure, but her eyes were on Lord Darkwood as the most desired match for her daughter. She was hunting the wrong fox there, Justus thought with a chuckle. Unless she fancied the idea of her little heiress growing fangs and drinking blood.

Gavin would only marry other vampires once or twice a century. And those marriages were in name only, for the sole purpose of driving back match-making mothers. Justus much preferred to be the bane of said mothers, carefully refining his image as an unrepentant rake and ne'er do well. He didn't have time for a wife, as his duties as Gavin's second in command left little room for even the pretense of love.

Such duties awaited him now. First he was to meet with Benson, the third in command for a report on the south half of the territory, then together they were to round up all of the vampires of Rochester for a Gathering.

A scent drifted on the night breeze, making Justus's lips curve upward with grim satisfaction. Now it was time for one of his most important duties. With lightning speed, he dashed behind Chatteron House to find a rogue vampire lurking behind the stables.

The rogue took one look at him and his eyes went wide as saucers. He turned to run and Justus seized him by the collar of his ragged coat.

"I- I'm lost, Governor!" the vampire stuttered, writhing like a worm on a hook.

"If that were the case, you'd have asked me for directions instead of trying to run," Justus replied with a smirk. "All the same, I'll be glad to escort you to snug accommodations during your visit. That is, unless you have a writ of passage from your lord?"

The rogue struggled harder. "Piss off, you limey ginger!"

Justus cuffed his captive so hard the vampire spat blood. "That's enough talk until Lord Darkwood comes to question you."

As swift as possible, he dragged the rogue to Darkwood Manor, and after making sure the human servants were otherwise occupied, tossed him in a cell in the hidden dungeons. The rogue's curses echoed behind Justus as he made his way out of the dungeons.

Blasted curs. Rapists, thieves, and careless ones who broke the law and killed humans, rogues were vampires exiled by their lords when a death sentence seemed too harsh, or perhaps they simply lacked the stones to execute a criminal. The rogue could then become a citizen of another vampire's territory if they applied for lenience. However, such was rarely the case. Most Lord Vampires killed rogues on sight. Some threw them off their property to be killed by another. Lord Darkwood was especially prone to killing rogues, though at least he gave each one he captured a fair trial first. Only one had become a Rochester vampire as Gavin discovered that the vampire had only been exiled for courting a vampire in another territory without permission. Three he chased off when he was in a merciful mood. The other scores had been beheaded and taken out to the garden for the sun to burn away their remains.

Justus shook his head. The system and reasoning in dealing with rogues was impractical and often hypocritical. Far too many lords were opting for exile rather than execution. It seemed there were more rogue vampires about every night. Were Lord Vampires growing so lax they were failing to give death when deserved? Or were all vampires to blame for not being more careful on who they Changed? It was only a matter of time before efforts to prevent rogues from banding together would fail and someone would have an insurrection on their hands.

By the time he met up with Benson, the vampire was pacing around the oak tree in front of his house. "Late again," Darkwood's third in command snapped. "Don't expect me to keep that from His Lordship."

"Oh, don't trouble yourself, I'll tell him," Justus said airily as he tightened his grip on his struggling captive. "You see, I'd caught a rogue on my way to meet you."

Benson stepped back, flushing in embarrassment. "I see. Well, very good. His Lordship will be pleased." The corner of his mouth twisted in irritation. "Blast it, how do you do it? I swear, you've captured more rogues than Darkwood and I combined."

"In this case, it was sheer luck. The sod was creeping around behind the Chatterton stables. I merely caught him on my way out. Convenient, but hardly anything admirable on my part." Justus shrugged. "In other cases, perhaps I merely get lucky then as well."

Grudging respect glimmered in Benson's eyes. Taciturn and steadfast, he and Justus always clashed, although if it came down to it, each would die for the other. "See that you maintain that luck. Now, how fares the southern half of the territory?"

"Fairly quiet aside, aside from the rogue I captured."

Benson nodded in satisfaction at the thought of order. "Good. Things in the north region are peaceful as well, though I did have to have a word with one of the younglings about being more discreet in the hunt."

Justus held back a yawn. It wasn't that he wanted trouble in Rochester, exactly. But did things have to be so dull around here? Maybe he'd ask Gavin to send him on another mission to spy on his neighboring Lord Vampires. London would be good. The Duke of Burnrath, the current Lord of the City, always merited some scrutiny.

"Well, let us fetch our people for the Gathering," Benson finished and started down the dirt path illuminated with dappled moonlight.

As they walked, Justus attempted to strike up a conversation. "I just finished reading *The Monk.* Quite salacious. Have you read that one?"

Benson's lips curled down with a touch of derision. "I am far too busy to read."

Justus sighed and fell silent. Perhaps he should loan the book to Miss Mead. On second thought, to give a maid such a torrid novel would likely cause a scandal.

Benson didn't talk much as they rounded up the Rochester vampires, instructing them to go to the Gathering place, beneath the ruins of Rochester Castle.

Gavin awaited them, pacing on the dais, his hands behind his back. Benson and Justus joined him on either side, facing the incoming vampires with mild, yet stern gazes.

Once the chamber was full, Gavin raised his arms for silence and greeted the assembly. "Vampires of Rochester, it brings me joy to see all of you present and well…"

Although Gavin was called "Ruthless Rochester" under the breaths of the common vampires, he truly did care for his people. It was just that he had little tolerance for disobedience. If one were to be honest, no tolerance at all. Justus knew that Gavin had been brought up in the monastary, to train for the priesthood, and that something had happened to him to make him not only abandon that course, but had also made him overly harsh.

This Gathering was more sedate than others as no one had stepped out of line and thus no punishments were to be meted out.

Instead, Gavin related what information he thought his people should know, and then in turn listened to news and grievances from them.

Dull. Even his report of the rogue in the dungeon did nothing to liven up the evening.

"And to close this meeting, I am pleased to announce that it is Alexander's fifty-fourth year as a vampire. Alex has been a

Rochester vampire since the night he was Changed by Susan and...."

As Gavin went on about Alex's accomplishments, Justus's attention wandered. Against his better logic, his thoughts strayed to Miss Bethany Mead. Her inquisitiveness, her intriguing air of mixed innocence and wisdom. How her wide blue eyes had lit up with joy at the sight of a dusty old book. How her succulent curves had been emphasized by her pretty muslin dress.

Applause rang out for the guest of honor, and Justus joined in a moment too late, earning a black look from Gavin. Everyone made their way to the banquet hall, where tiny cakes and miniscule glasses of champagne were spread across the large table, portioned so as not to impact a vampire's digestion. Gavin nudged Justus with his elbow.

"You seem preoccupied." The words seemed like an accusation.

Avoiding his lord's gaze, Justus swigged one of the miniature champagne glasses, enjoying the tickle of the bubbles on his tongue. "My apologies, my lord. I'm still pondering a novel I finished. Kept me awake half the day. *The Monk*?" he inquired hopefully. Gavin had a large library that he constantly added to, but only read sporadically.

"I'm afraid I haven't gotten around to it yet," the Lord of Rochester said, scanning the room as if trying to spot a sign of discord. "I've been too occupied watching the Lord of London. Cecil brought back the most fascinating report."

Justus rubbed the bridge of his nose. Did no one read anymore? "I thought I was to look in on London for you."

"Burnrath is more watchful than usual. With your blazing hair, you'd stand out like a fox among hens." Gavin shook his head. "Besides, with the increased rogue activity, you're needed here."

"Yes, my lord." His logic was irrefutable. And yet, Justus was succumbing to an increasing sense of stagnation. There was something missing from his long life, but he had no notion as to what it could be. Before Gavin could catch wind of his doldrums, he bowed. "I'm off to the Medway for a bite and any morsels of news that might be of interest."

Gavin clasped his shoulder. "You're a good vampire, Justus. The best I have."

"Thank you." Justus's stomach knotted. Lately he didn't *feel* so very good.

And once he arrived at the Medway Inn, a cozy pub where gentleman of the upper classes drank, gambled, and avoided their wives, he felt even less honorable as he made his way towards Lord Wickshire, Bethany's father.

"Lord de Wynter!" Wickshire said as he spotted him. "Come, have a dram of brandy with me."

Justus inclined his head and joined him. He'd played a few card games with Lord Wickshire and spoken with him at multiple soirees, but until this summer, he'd had no idea that the man had a daughter. Of course, that wasn't unusual. Female offspring did not exist until they were out in society, and once they were married off, they returned to their previous invisible existence.

As if reading his mind, Mead launched into a tangent bemoaning what a trial it was to have a daughter.

"The expense of all her gowns and other fripperies are enough to beggar me, I tell you." Wickshire quaffed the remainder of his drink and gestured to a barmaid for another. "Not to mention the cost of her dowry. Would that I'd had a son instead."

Justus concealed his frown with a sip of the glass of brandy the barmaid placed in front of him. "I understand that Miss Mead is witty and comely. Surely you won't have too much trouble securing a respectable match."

"Yes, she is as pretty as a daisy. But I confess, my spirits are low." Mead's brows drew together in consternation. "Silly chit always has her nose in a book. Mark my words, she'll be cross eyed if she keeps it up. And she is sadly prone to fanciful notions. I sometimes worry about her mental state."

Justus's hands clenched into hard fists beneath the table. How could a man speak of his own child in such a way? "I rather appreciate a literate woman."

Wickshire chuckled. "Yes, but I'm well aware of what sort of appreciation you have with women. See that you don't extend it to my daughter."

"Rest assured, despoiling maidens is not to my taste." Justus rose from the table, suddenly not so proud of the reputation he'd carefully cultivated. "If you'll excuse me, I have an important matter to discuss with Sir Henry over there." He loathed Henry, for the chap was a pompous ass. However, that did not mean that the man didn't have his uses.

To cheer himself up, he lured Sir Henry Swinton outside. As his fangs sank into Sir Henry's neck, Justus gleaned a memory of him speaking with Bethany's parents about a supper at Fosborough Manor tomorrow evening. A twinge of pity for the poor girl pierced his heart. The Fosborough's entertainments were notoriously somber. Bethany would be bored out of her skull.

Releasing Sir Henry, he led the man back inside before circling the great room of the inn, listening to snatches of conversation. Unable to help himself, he paid extra close attention to every engagement the Meads would be attending.

Sure enough, there were several that he'd also received an invitation for. Well, he was invited to the Fosborough supper, but he had no intention of going to such a dismal affair.

***

The following evening, Justus found himself handing his coat and hat to the Fosborough's butler, still wondering why he'd bothered to come. But the Medway Inn had been deserted, Gavin was occupied meeting with vampires who had private concerns, and no other parties or card games were occurring this night.

When he joined the guests in the drawing room, his gaze lit on Miss Mead. She looked especially fetching tonight, with a lavender gown and silk ribbons threaded through her upswept hair. She gave him an inappropriately broad smile that he couldn't help returning. Her mother looked down her nose at him and ushered her off to speak with another gentleman.

Justus turned and greeted Lord Bromley, dutifully listening to his talk of a wager on a horse.

"You should attend the race, de Wynter." Bromley clapped him on the shoulder. "You could win a tidy sum and, at the least, imbibe a spot of sunlight."

A spot of sunlight would sear him like a side of beef. Justus flinched and quickly forced his grimace into a smile. "As diverting as that sounds, I'm sorry to say that I'll be hunting boar in Maidstone that day." The lie rolled smoothly off his tongue.

Once more, his attention shifted to Miss Mead, the sight of her crown of curls and the sway of her hips making his mouth water. Had she started reading *The Faerie Queene* yet? Closing his eyes, he pictured her lying in bed, propped up on her elbows reading. That golden hair of hers gleaming in the candlelight and hanging free to frame her face. A faraway look in those bright blue eyes, those lips curving in a soft smile at the flowing prose.

Or maybe she leaned on her pillow, one little hand curled under her chin. The lace of her nightgown…

Before he could dwell too much on what Miss Mead wore to bed, the hostess announced that it was time to sup. Justus found himself all at once relieved and disappointed that he was seated at the opposite end of the table from the beautiful, bookish woman who'd captured his attention.

Desolation won the inner battle as he was subjected to tepid conversation and bland food. Although vampires were unable to eat more than a few nibbles of solid food, he appreciated delicious courses and was depressed that there were none to be had.

Responding to his seatmate's chatter with equally banal remarks, Justus watched Miss Mead from the corner of his eye. She appeared to be just as bored as he was. He wagered that just like him, she'd rather be discussing books, or perhaps Medieval history. Once more he remembered their conversation the first night they met. How did she develop an interest in Chaucer? Furthermore, how did she learn to read Old English?

"Will you be at the Willoughbys' garden party on Friday?" Lady Vance interrupted his musings. "There is to be a glorious fireworks display at nightfall."

The Willoughbys. Justus remembered that was one of the parties that the Meads were attending. Fireworks were a wonder that held everyone in thrall. Distracted. Easy for one to slip away from the others.

He gave Lady Vance a genuine smile. "Yes, I shall be in attendance, though I'm sorry to say that I will be late." An idea formed in his mind. "I do indeed find myself quite looking forward to the occasion."

When at last the meal came to an end, Justus rose with the other men while the ladies retired to the drawing room.

As Miss Mead passed him, Justus dropped his napkin in her path. They both bent to retrieve it.

"Look for me at the Willoughbys' affair," he whispered. "We can discuss the book I loaned you while everyone watches the fireworks. In private."

Her gloved fingers touched his briefly as she handed him the napkin. Her little chin dipped in a subtle nod as she curtsied.

"Thank you, Miss Mead," he said for the benefit of those watching. "I apologize for my clumsiness."

He drank in the sight of her pink cheeks and licked his lips. This was a dangerous game he was playing.

And yet he could not stop.

Chapter Six

Bethany searched the Willoughbys' drawing room, clutching her reticule so tightly her knuckles went white. Lord de Wynter said he would be here and tonight they would discuss the book… in private. She couldn't help but tremble at the thought of being alone with him, perhaps anticipating that more than the prospect of literary discourse.

The setting sun shone through the glass of the French doors, casting a tinge of gold to everything, reminding Bethany of her imaginings of the faerie kingdom of Gloriana… though she knew who that character was truly supposed to represent. Still, Spenser's epic held so much whimsy that she couldn't help but imagine a truly fey monarch. She kept both the book and that sentiment hidden from her father.

Oh, she could not wait to talk to Lord de Wynter about the book. *He'd* understand.

As darkness fell and people around her chattered in anticipation of the fireworks, Bethany's mother dragged her hither and thither through the assemblage, introducing her to every affluent gentleman in attendance.

None of them were interested in spending longer than necessary in her company, and that was quite agreeable with Bethany. There was only one man she whose company she wished to share this evening. Yet the bustling room palpably lacked his presence.

Was it possible that he'd found some other diversion? She'd heard that he spent a lot of time at the Medway Inn, playing cards and dice, as well as attending certain more raucous parties hosted by less reputable members of Society. Why should he decline such amusing pursuits to be with her?

Yes, he'd probably changed his mind about coming. Lord Darkwood's manor was nearby and would have nearly as good a view of the fireworks. So perhaps de Wynter had—

There he was! Bethany's heart surged in response to see Lord de Wynter's lithe form stalking around the masses, pausing to exchange a polite greeting when necessary, while he was clearly making his way towards her. Every other step, he flashed her a conspiratorial glance, as if they shared a huge secret. A delicious thrill tremored through her body.

When he reached her side, Bethany withdrew the book from her reticule and handed it to him. Pleasure curled her toes as once more their fingers grazed each other. "Thank you for loaning me the book, my lord."

"It was my pleasure." His eyes swept over her face and form, seeming to caress her with an invisible tongue of flame.

Just then, Lady Willoughby announced that it was time to gather on the front lawn to view the illuminations. Those who were elderly or infirm watched from the balconies, where comfortable chairs had been set out for them.

"Follow my lead," de Wynter whispered with an impish smile.

With that, he wove through the masses with unobtrusive slowness, excusing himself with a quiet mutter that made people let him pass without truly noticing him. Bethany did her best to imitate him, though for her, avoiding attention was much easier, being a wallflower ever since her first ball.

She caught a glimpse of Rebecca and her friends with their beaux. The group had ignored her ever since she'd told them about her dance with Lord de Wynter. At first, Bethany thought they were merely preoccupied, now she was beginning to suspect that they didn't like her.

But as she followed de Wynter, casting a shamefully pleasing glance at his backside, snugly encased in buff trousers, Bethany decided she didn't care what they thought of her.

While everyone else made their way to the front lawn, de Wynter strode off into the azalea garden. After a quick glance over her shoulder to make certain no one was watching, Bethany ducked under a leafy bower behind him. Anticipation flooded her being, making even the air feel alive on her skin.

He sat on a stone bench and patted the marble surface beside him. Bethany joined him, legs suddenly turned to custard. It was so dark in here that they were veritably blanketed in shadows, the intimacy palpable and warm. Even in the darkness, his hair glinted like banked coals. Her fingers twisted in her lap in effort to resist touching those fiery tresses.

To break up the heavy silence, Bethany shakily began the conversation. "I am grateful that you arranged for us to discuss the book, my lord. I finished it only yesterday."

His arched lips curved with a pleased smile that warmed her to her toes. "Please, call me Justus."

"Oh, I couldn't." Heat flooded her face at the sound of his name. There was something so beautiful, so noble about it. "My mother would have the vapors if she heard me call a man by his Christian name."

He nodded in understanding. "At least when we are alone then."

"Very well, Justus." Her belly tilted at the sound of his name. "Then in such cases, you may call me Bethany." The words tumbled out, improper as they were.

"Good. Now that we have that settled, Bethany," he said, "what did you think of the book?"

"At first, I thought I wouldn't care for it," she admitted, shivering slightly at that masculine voice uttering her name. "The incessant and undisguised praise for Queen Elizabeth grew tiresome."

Justus quirked a brow. "Caught that, did you?" Impatient shouts echoed from the lawn outside their bower as Lord Willoughby's servants prepared the fireworks.

"Who could miss such sycophantic symbolism? Queen Gloriana?" She chuckled. "I understand that her patronage was needed, but at least Shakespeare managed better subtlety."

Lord de Wynter nodded. "As well as the love of the commons." He leaned forward, so close that she could almost make out the vivid green of his eyes. Inwardly, she cursed the darkness even as she knew the shadows kept them hidden. "But you said you *thought* you wouldn't care for it."

Bethany nodded, praying he couldn't see how his proximity was making her blush. "I greatly enjoyed the magic and the fact that there was always something happening. And the romance…" Heat rose to her cheeks and she quickly changed the subject before he thought she sounded like a silly girl. "Although I confess I felt bad for that blind girl and her mother living alone. I understand why they could not afford to shelter Una and her companions. I was even sad that the church robber was killed by the lion. Although stealing is wrong, that was their only source of support. What?" she broke off as Justus's shoulders shook with laughter.

"That scene, the whole book in fact, was an allegory. In those days, the Catholic church was the biggest thief of all. Of course, I wasn't around back then, but my— He broke off suddenly with a frown, then recovered his thoughts with a quick shake of his head. "I've read much about the time period."

"Of course!" Bethany breathed, feeling like the biggest hen-wit. "After what Elizabeth's sister, Mary, put the people through with her persecution of Anglicans, no wonder Catholics would be painted as villains. You must think me a fool."

"Not at all," Justus placed his hand over hers, impossibly warm in the cool of the garden. "I confess that it is a joy to speak with someone who can read a story as a story, not picking it apart for every little symbol and entrenched bias." He leaned forward on the bench and reached up to cup her cheek. "You are a remarkable person, Bethany."

"So are you," she whispered, captivated by his fey beauty and husky voice. The first explosion made her jump and gasp as the sky above them erupted with a halo of red light. Justus pulled her closer and she laughed in embarrassment as cheers echoed from the lawn.

Her heart pounded in her throat as his head dipped lower and his lips brushed across hers.

Heat exploded in her belly at the chaste kiss, every nerve ending singing with pleasure. Head swimming with dizziness, Bethany grasped his shoulders to keep from toppling off of the bench. Justus's arms wrapped around her, pulling her against his firm chest, his lips caressing hers with intoxicating fervor.

When he drew back, Bethany felt as if something vital had been snatched away from her. Another firework lit up the sky with a boom and Justus's eyes glowed like green embers as he suddenly leaned towards her once more. Her breath caught in her throat, a shiver of primal alarm crawling up her spine. But instead of kissing her again, his mouth lightly touched her neck.

She gasped at the sparking sensation and Justus drew back as if burned. His long red hair hung unfashionably loose, hiding his face. His broad shoulders moved up and down with his deep breathing as if he were struggling to tame something savage within.

"I'm sorry," he rasped. "That was extremely ungentlemanly of me. Can you forgive me?"

When he raised his imploring eyes to hers, she saw that they weren't glowing at all. They must have been reflecting the fireworks. What a ninny she was for momentarily thinking otherwise.

"Of course I forgive you," she whispered. "It is not as if I have been behaving in the most ladylike manner. Besides, I have always wondered what it is like to be kissed." She snapped her mouth closed at such an outrageous confession, but it was too late.

"And?" he whispered back.

She frowned. "And what?"

His lips arched in a wicked smile. "How was the experience?"

"Incredible," she couldn't stop herself from answering. "So much more than what the novels depict."

His grin broadened, tempting beyond reason. "That tempts me to do it again."

She leaned toward him and he chuckled low.

"No, I must remain honorable." He rose from the bench. "I will go out that way, you go the way we came in and immerse yourself with the crowd. With luck, no one will have discovered you missing." Taking her hand, he brushed his lips across her knuckles. The feel of his mouth through the satin of her gloves a poor substitute to his previous kiss. "I will see you again soon."

Before she could reply, he vanished deeper into the garden with nary a rustle.

Heaving a sigh, Bethany closed her eyes and relived the kiss in her mind. Never before had she imagined it would be so potent, so magical.

Her practical side tried to remind her that Lord de Wynter was a rake, and thus kisses meant nothing to one such as him, but her whimsical side refused to listen.

After all, did he speak with other women about his love of books? Somehow, she doubted it. Because if he already had literate lady loves, he would never have bothered to speak with a debutante like her. Not that the thought of him having lady loves didn't make her stomach churn with discomfort.

No. Her chin lifted. They'd shared something special. She was certain of it.

He'd even told her that he'd see her again soon.

Perhaps that meant that he'd call upon her tomorrow!

Bethany had to clap a hand over her mouth to suppress a giddy sigh. Although she would have preferred to linger here in the shadowed garden, basking in the bliss of Justus's kiss, her mother was bound to be looking for her.

With utmost reluctance, she rose from the bench and left the garden, pausing only to pluck a rose to mark the memory of this night.

The fireworks continued to erupt in the sky, the loud booms and bright flashes of color echoing the brilliant light and pounding in her heart.

Bethany found her mother easily. Lady Wickshire's garish puce hat adorned with green feathers bobbed up and down as she spoke with Lady Bentley, the mother of a young heir to an Earldom. The boy had shown no interest in Bethany when they'd been introduced, instead making eyes at Rebecca.

Boy. Bethany smirked at the word. The heir had to be two or three years her elder, but nearly all gentlemen she'd met appeared to be boys compared to Justus.

"There you are!" Lady Wickshire interrupted Bethany's reverie. "Where have you been?"

"I was circulating amongst the guests, making small talk so as not to look a wallflower." The lie flowed through easily. "Just as you advised me."

Cecily nodded in satisfaction. "Such an obedient girl. You'll make a wonderful wife to some fortunate gentleman." She then hammered the point home. "I was just talking with Lady Bentley and she has invited us to watch the annual cricket game at Newton Hall next Saturday. Won't that be splendid?"

"Yes, indeed." *Only if Justus will be there.*

Bethany struggled to pay attention to her mother's chatter, but her mind refused to cease incessantly wandering to the subject of a certain red-haired rake. A rake who possessed an incredible talent in kissing and impeccable taste in literature. How kind he was to have loaned her a book. She must endeavor to return the favor.

She'd read *The Italian* by Ann Radcliffe on the carriage ride to Rochester and quite enjoyed it. Gothic stories were nearly as engrossing as medieval tales. Perhaps Justus would like it. Unless he was the sort who refused to read novels written by women. No, those men never deigned to discuss novels with women, much less debutantes such as herself.

Yet Justus was different. He expressed concern and interest in her literary opinions.

As the guests watched the illuminations, Bethany searched the throng for Justus, but she didn't spot him until she and her parents were departing for the evening. Tamping down regret that she didn't have the opportunity to speak with him before leaving, she basked in the secret smile he cast her way.

The remainder of the night and next day, Bethany searched her book collection for a novel to loan him, and then spent hours sifting through her wardrobe for something to wear when he came to call on her.

By the time morning visiting hours were officially underway, Bethany had to invoke every ounce of her fortitude to avoid dashing to the window every time she heard a carriage roll up the drive.

A few matrons called upon her mother, and even a few gentleman. One that looked too young to shave, the other older than her father. Their elderly neighbor, Lord Tench even stopped by for a visit.

Justus never came.

A lump rose to her throat. She'd been so certain that there was something special between them. Apparently, she was wrong. Their kiss had been nothing but a diversion to him.

Pleading a headache, Bethany remained in her room for the rest of the evening, vowing to give Lord de Wynter the cut direct next time she saw him.

Chapter Seven

Justus winced as Bethany looked pointedly away from him at the Haverly musicale. For two nights he'd been seeking her out, and now that he found her, she cut him.

He'd done something to hurt her, but it took him a moment to discern what. Interactions with debutantes was not his strong suit. *Bloody hell…* He nearly clapped his palm over his face at his stupidity. She was a debutante.

Likely after having time to reflect, she now thought him ungentlemanly for kissing her in the Willoughbys' garden.

He rubbed the bridge of his nose. Luring her anywhere private was improper of him. One misstep, or even a spark of suspicion from another, and Bethany could be ruined. No wonder she was now avoiding him.

Guilt pervaded his being. He needed to apologize, to promise that he'd never do anything that could tarnish her reputation again.

Just as he started forward, a hand grasped his shoulder. Justus swiveled around to see the Lord Vampire of Rochester glaring at him.

"What do you think you are doing?" Gavin demanded, eyes narrowed.

"I... ah." Justus cleared his throat and tried to think of a satisfactory response.

"Don't bother prevaricating, or worse, lying to me." The Baron of Darkwood spoke through clenched teeth fixed in a false smile to detract from suspicious eyes. "You've been sniffing around the Mead chit like a stag in the rut."

Justus cringed at such crude phrasing applying to Bethany. "I'm not sniffing. She has an interest in Medieval literature. I merely loaned her a novel and we've been discussing the tale."

"See to it that discussion is all you engage in," Gavin bit out. "Or better yet, find someone less conspicuous to prattle with about your hobby. Although I've lectured countless younglings about the hazards of associating with mortal maidens, I never imagined that I'd have to warn my own second in command."

"Yes, my lord." Justus bowed before hastening away from his master. It wouldn't do to linger around Gavin when he was in a foul mood. Especially when Justus had to bite his tongue to refrain from objecting to such a high-handed scolding. And he wondered what sort of creature had crawled up Gavin's trousers to make him more disagreeable than usual.

He wasn't a youngling. He knew very well that one must maintain discretion when interacting with mortals. And it wasn't as if he were courting Bethany, or showing her his fangs.

His memory flew back to that night in the Willoughbys' garden, the feel of her warm and yielding body in his arms, the taste of her kiss, the way she'd gasped when he'd pressed his lips to the tender flesh of her neck. The temptation to sink his fangs into her pulsing vein for a taste.

He bit back a groan as his body responded with arousal.

Perhaps Gavin did have cause for concern. Justus couldn't deny that he was maddeningly attracted to the young woman. Yet even deeper than a physical response was a feeling of kinship with her.

Although Justus could restrain his lust, he could not bear to sever their friendship. A friendship that would die if he did not do the decent thing and apologize for his ungentlemanly behavior the other day. Gavin may prefer that Bethany maintain her icy distance from him, but Justus did not. Only after only two nights of not seeing her, he felt bereft without her presence. And the thought of any contention between them was intolerable.

After weaving through the manor for over a quarter hour searching for her, Justus finally spied her in the library. His lips curved in delight. He should have looked there first.

"It's unfortunate the Haverlys have such a poor collection," he said aloud.

She gasped and whirled around so fast that her skirts swept up to give him a teasing glimpse of her slim ankles, encased in cream-colored silk stockings.

"Lord de Wynter," she said coolly, bobbing him the slightest of curtsies. Yet the blush on her cheeks belied her chilly demeanor.

He bowed low. "I want to apologize for my ungentlemanly actions at the Willoughby crush the other night."

A line formed between her golden brows. "And what actions were those?"

"You are a maiden," Justus said, trying not to dwell on the implications of that fact. "I never should have been alone with you. And I certainly never should have kissed you. It was unconscionable of me to put your reputation at risk."

Something resembling pain slashed across her delicate features before the corner of her mouth curved up in a crooked smile. "You are apologizing for being alone with me the other day, even as you are alone with me now."

The tightness in his chest eased at her teasing tone. Gathering every ounce of his innate charm, he grinned. "I cannot very well do so in front of a chaperone, lest our secret be out."

This time, she smiled at him in earnest. "I suppose you have a valid point, my lord."

"Justus," he implored.

Bethany raised a brow. "How can you speak of propriety and ask me to address you in such an intimate matter?"

Because I love to hear my name on your lips, he longed to say, but that certainly wouldn't do. Only contrition could repair things between them.

"I'm sorry." He bowed so low his long hair nearly grazed the Persian rug beneath his boots. "Now do I have your forgiveness for my indiscretion? I would very much like for us to remain friends."

Bethany sighed. "Of course I forgive you. I was not even vexed at you flouting propriety with me, for I confess I enjoyed it. I know I shouldn't have, but I did."

An invisible hand squeezed his heart. Dear God, why did she have to say that? "Then what was amiss?"

The rosy flush imbued her face with a glow as she fidgeted with the sleeve of her pale green gown. "It was a silly, trifling fancy. Nothing to trouble you with."

"Bethany," he said softly, crossing the room to stand inches from her. His gloved hand touched her cheek. "Friends are honest with one another."

For a moment she leaned into his touch, before drawing back against the bookcase. "I'd forgotten that you were a rake," she whispered, her blush deepening.

"I beg your pardon?" Indeed, Justus strove to maintain that reputation, but her referring to him as such stung a bit.

"From what I was led to understand, something as, ah, affectionate as a kiss would indicate that a *gentleman*," she stressed the word, "would have interest in paying a call to a lady the next day." Her eyes widened and she shook her head quickly as if to placate him. "I don't mean for a proposal, I never presumed that. Merely that I was taught that a kiss signified interest to further acquaintance."

Justus sucked in a breath as her meaning became clear. She'd thought that he would court her. Pity at her naivety warred with a terrifying realization: the idea of courting her was immensely appealing. For the first time in almost two centuries, he wished he was a mortal man so that he would be able to ride with her in the mornings, enjoy an outdoor luncheon with her in a dappled meadow, and see the sunlight glint on her golden hair.

That longing, along with the tremulous hope in Bethany's blue eyes made Justus toss aside all the caution he'd retained ever since he first became a vampire.

"Bethany," he whispered. "Please believe me when I say that if it were possible for me to pay you daytime calls, I swear would do so. I would love to ride with you in the mornings and discuss novels over afternoon tea, but I cannot."

"Why?" she asked, disappointment and confusion flitting across her face.

"I cannot answer that. As it is, I've said too much." Far too much. Gavin would kill him if he ever learned that Justus had plainly told a mortal that he could not be out during the day. Yet his fool mouth continued its dangerous course. "But I will endeavor to see you during the evenings whenever possible."

Bethany opened her mouth to reply, but Justus heard footsteps approaching the library. Quickly, he hid in a far corner of the room, lest she be discovered in the company of a man without a chaperone.

"Bethany!" Lady Wickshire's shrill voice rang out. "I should have known I would find you in here. Why must you persist in burying your nose in these mouldering books when there are eligible gentlemen to be caught? You know how your father disapproves of your obsession."

Justus bit back a growl, whether at Bethany's mother's derisive words to treasured books, or the thought of Bethany being used as a lure for titled men, he did not know. The latter was illogical as it had always been thus with gently born females, yet he was quickly developing a distaste for the custom.

"I apologize, Mother." Bethany's sullen tone made Justus want to pull her into his arms and soothe her. "I was feeling overheated and thought it wise to remain out of sight so as not to put off the gentlemen with my appearance. Besides," a hint of mirth laced her voice, "This is a poor collection, though I'd never dare tell the Haverlys."

"Oh dear," Lady Mead sounded immediately contrite. "That is quick thinking of you after all." Justus peeked to see Bethany's mother press a gloved hand to her cheek. "You do appear to be flushed. I do hope you are not falling ill. But you had that headache yesterday evening and…" Lady Mead wrung her gloved hands. "Perhaps we should depart early and send for the doctor. Your father is growing worried of your health of late."

"No!" Bethany said sharply. "That is, I am feeling much better. The headache is gone. I only overexerted myself taking turns around the room."

Justus raised a brow. He didn't smell any illness on Bethany. Had she feigned her malady to avoid seeing him last night, or was it because his failure to pay her a call had made her that distraught? Remorse cascaded over his heart. He never wanted to cause her pain.

Lady Wickshire's voice made him draw back before he was seen. "Very well. Let us return to the gathering. Lord Willoughby's heir was looking quite alone last I saw him."

As their footsteps faded away, Justus gnashed his fangs. The Willoughby lad could stuff it. He hadn't restored Bethany's esteem only for her to waste the evening discussing the weather with milksop boys and lecherous widowers.

Withdrawing from the library, he worked to contrive a way to spend some time at her side without drawing censure from society, or his Lord Vampire.

***

The next twelve nights were a juxtaposition of euphoria and despair for Justus. He saw Bethany as often as possible, but between his day rest, his duties as second in command to the Lord Vampire, and of course, avoiding scrutiny from both the *ton* and the Rochester vampires, his time with Bethany was dismally meager.

Yet he treasured every moment he had with her all the more, participating in the contradances and quadrilles just to spend a few moments dancing with her before she was passed to the next partner. He longed to waltz with her, but that would draw too much attention. As it was, too often did they get caught up in their latest literary discussion, causing a few raised eyebrows unless others were included. Others that were definitely not desired. He'd seen Lord and Lady Wickshire casting glares at him frequently.

Still, the books they exchanged somewhat eased Justus's loneliness. Every morning when he retired for the day, Justus would light a candle and read the latest volume that Bethany thought he'd enjoy. Her scent clung to each page, often distracting him from the story. He wondered if she could detect his scent on the books he loaned her. Likely not, as she was a human.

Not for the first time, he wondered what sort of vampire Bethany would make. She was certainly brave and intelligent enough to be able to navigate through Society undetected, and her beauty would be an asset when she hunted. Yet would the prospect of drinking blood and sacrificing the sun for immortality appeal to her?

There was no way to know without breaking one of the cardinal rules of their kind: never reveal oneself to a mortal unless they were to be Changed. The quandary was enough to make him want to scream. He longed to explain why he couldn't call upon her or even court her, and why they had to be so discreet with their interactions. The sadness in her eyes when he told he was unable to see her some evenings speared him, for he could not tell her of his duties.

And, of course, there were other vexing matters. As he observed a few men giving Bethany lustful looks, Justus longed to tear their throats out and announce to the world that she was his. Almost as unnerving was the thought of the other Rochester vampires feeding on her. True, only Gavin and Benson, the third in command, were the only vampires aside from Justus who circulated among Society, but they all regularly fed upon the ton.

Justus ground his teeth in impotent frustration. It sickened him to imagine Gavin sinking his fangs into Bethany's throat, yet how could Justus presume to tell his lord who to bite?

If only he could Mark her. That would prevent any other vampire from touching her. Yet if he did that, he'd be alerting Gavin to the fact that he'd disobeyed his order to lessen his involvement with Bethany.

Justus's fury came to a head one night when he was abruptly ordered to leave a soiree to help Benson chase down a rogue who'd been encroaching on Rochester's territory. Infuriated that he'd been pulled from a deep discussion with Bethany, Justus had lost his temper and killed the rogue by driving a tree branch through his heart. Normally Gavin preferred for rogues to be brought in for a trial, but the bleeding sod had vexed him by fighting.

The Lord of Rochester would be annoyed, but Justus had hope that he'd be able to pass off self-defense as an excuse. Still self-loathing filled him at his loss of self-control and he hoped the rogue had at least been of the evil sort, rather than one who'd been exiled for a stupid mistake.

When Justus made it back to the party, he looked so disheveled that Bethany's eyes had filled with worry. Hopefully she didn't think he'd been dallying with another woman. Something in his expression must have put her at ease, for with an impish smile, she lured him away to the conservatory.

"I thought I would return the favor and loan you a book," she said shyly, pulling a thick volume from her reticule.

Justus couldn't help himself.

He pulled her small, warm body against his and claimed her lips in a fiery kiss that warmed him all the way down to the soles of his feet. She kissed him back eagerly, her soft mouth exploring his with innocent discovery. Just as he pressed his arousal to her soft belly, his sense returned with the realization of what he was doing.

Quickly, he released her before someone spied them. "I apologize once again. We should not do this."

"Why not?" she whispered, her delectable breasts heaving beneath her gown of azure watered silk.

"Because…" He sighed. She had a point. If he weren't a vampire, there would be nothing wrong with him paying court to her, kissing her, bedding her once she was his bride. "It's not proper," he explained lamely. "Now let us return to the crush before a gossip spies us."

Her pink lips parted as if in protest, but then she nodded. The rest of the evening, Justus barely had a chance to speak a word to her, for Bethany's mother was relentless in thrusting her before every unmarried male between the ages of fifteen and eighty. All except for Justus, as Lady Wickshire clearly disliked him.

As he watched a golden-haired Adonis partner Bethany in the waltz, envy boiled his blood.

It was then that he realized that he loved Bethany Mead, and he could not allow her to be given to another man.

Unfortunately, that meant he would have to tell her the truth about what he was and what that meant for his suit. And then he would have to confess all to Gavin.

But first he would speak to Bethany, for she deserved to learn the truth before anyone else.

Chapter Eight

Bethany searched the Tennyson's ballroom for Justus. She'd had the most ghastly day entertaining their neighbor, Lord Tench. He'd stayed for afternoon tea and then bade Bethany to escort him through the garden, walking slowly as he leaned on his cane and sometimes having her support him. The man was older than her grandfather, with liver spotted hands that managed to touch her breasts and bum when she walked with him.

Now she needed Justus to cheer her up and banish the day's ordeal from her mind. He'd said he was almost finished reading *The Song of Roland* and she greatly looked forward to his thoughts on the epic poem, almost as much as she anticipated the dance he'd promised her.

Her mother bent to her ear, advising her on the best way to secure a dance with Lord Willoughby's heir and how to engage Sir Hubert Huxtable in conversation at supper. Bethany sighed. Mother's matchmaking furor had risen to feverish heights over the past few days. Bethany could not fathom why Mother was in such a rush. She wasn't even due to make her official come out until next Spring. There was plenty of time to secure a match.

Though if Justus offered for her, she would gladly accept. Not only would that put an end to Mother's irksome way of throwing her at every unwed male in their path, but it would also guarantee Bethany a future with someone she was fond of.

More than fond. If Bethany was to be honest with herself, she must resign herself to the fact that she was head over heels in love with Justus. His kiss last night had haunted her dreams even more than the previous one.

Why hadn't Mother pushed her towards Justus? Surely Viscount de Wynter was a good match. He was titled, held land, and clearly had enough income to be able to afford his fine clothes. Unless he was on credit, common sense reminded her. But even if he was up to his ears in debt, Bethany would love him all the same. Certainly her parents would not object to his suit.

But did he have any interest in marrying her? He'd told her that he was unable to call upon her during the day, yet the way he sought her out every evening felt like a courtship. Not to mention the kisses he'd stolen, and the way he held her when they danced.

Yet he hadn't said a word about matrimony.

Before she plunged into doldrums, Bethany glimpsed Justus across the room. His eyes gleamed with naked joy to see her as he favored her with a brilliant smile.

Murmuring some excuse to her mother, she slipped away and planned the best way to weave through the crush without making it obvious that she was going to him. Not for the first time she wondered why Justus insisted on keeping their friendship a secret. Was he, as a rake, perhaps ashamed to call a debutante friend? Or was it because he had no intention of marrying her and did not want people to speculate?

Once she worked her way to Justus's side by pretending interest in Mr. Fenton's talk of a cricket match, Bethany met his gaze and the happiness she saw in his eyes made her happy to be his friend, no matter what.

Another gentleman overheard Mr. Fenton's remarks about a certain player and launched an ardent debate, freeing Bethany.

Justus bowed as if he only just noticed her standing beside him. "Miss Mead, you are a vision this evening. Would you do me the honor of partnering me in the next waltz?"

Bethany's breath fled her lungs. He *never* waltzed with her, except for the night they'd first met. Such a dance implied romance. Justus raised a brow at her silence and she curtsied. "I would enjoy that above all things."

He stepped closer to her, taking her gloved hands in his. She blinked. Aside from dancing, he also never touched her in front of anyone. Could he have changed his mind about courting her? "I shall count the minutes," he said before pressing a kiss to her knuckles.

The musicians struck up a tune for the first quadrille and Bethany reluctantly left him as a gentleman she'd promised the first dance to came to collect her. She too found herself counting the minutes to their waltz, sighing in disappointment that Justus didn't deign to join this dance so she could spend a few moments in his arms.

When the dance ended, she bit back a groan of despair as her dancing partner escorted her back to her mother.

Lady Wickshire favored her with a stern frown. "I saw you speaking with Lord de Wynter again. I do not approve."

"Why not?" Bethany said. "He's unmarried and a viscount."

Cecily's nostrils looked pinched. "And a notorious rake. If you'd heard half the gossip, you'd faint."

"I already promised him a waltz," Bethany said. "He's never asked me before. Perhaps his intentions are honorable."

Her mother's lips pressed together in a thin line. "Lord Tench was going to ask for the waltz."

Bethany snorted indelicately. "He can barely walk. How is he supposed to dance?" Before Lady Mead could begin a lecture, she fabricated an excuse. "I must retreat to the retiring room."

She spent the next hour hiding from her mother before it was time for the waltz. Justus met her the moment the first sweet note trilled on the violins, and when he took her into his arms, the rest of the world fell away.

They twirled and swayed together as if they were one, and Bethany's heart pounded with excitement at the feel of his firm shoulder beneath her hand and the solid heat of his grip on her waist. Their faces were so close she could see the light smattering of freckles on his cheeks and across the bridge of his nose. His deep, green eyes remained locked on hers, seeming to communicate with her in a new and magical language.

When he bent down and a silken lock of his hair caressed her cheek, Bethany gasped, at first thinking he would kiss her again right there in front of everyone.

Instead, Justus whispered, "Are you able to escape your room without detection tonight?"

A tremor of fear and excitement shivered up her spine, along with a pang of disappointment. "Are you suggesting a tryst?" Perhaps he was as much of a rake as people said.

"No. I would never dishonor you that way." His hand stroked her back beneath her hair soothing motion. "But I must speak to you in absolute secrecy, for the matter is of utmost importance."

The intensity of his gaze made her heart leap in her throat. He looked afraid, yet somehow elated all at once, as if he was on the verge of unloading a great burden. Bethany decided to trust him. Or perhaps she really did not find the prospect of a tryst to be a bad thing. If his kisses were so potent, what would it be like to experience more?

Rising up on tiptoes, she spoke softly. "There's a tree by my window. I can shimmy down it. I used to do it all the time when I was a girl."

He nodded. "Meet me in your orchard at midnight."

The music faded and he bowed before walking away from the dance floor as if indifferent to their waltz. Bethany struggled to breathe as her stays seemed suddenly tight. Did she truly agree to meet Justus alone in the dark tonight? All the gothic novels she'd read implied that such a thing was a very unwise notion. What if he planned to abduct her?

She shook her head. No. Justus was her friend. He'd never do anything to harm her.

Despite that firm truth, her mind still raced to devise his motives for such a covert liaison. Had he contracted a fatal illness and only trusted her with the tragic news? Heavens, she hoped not.

Another thought made her knees go weak. What if he wished to elope?

Although the notion was incredibly romantic, she could not fathom why he wouldn't simply court her and ask her father for her hand like a normal gentleman.

A humorous smile tugged her lips. Justus de Wynter was anything but normal. His hair was red as autumn leaves, he was more well-read than anyone she'd ever met, he did not go anywhere during the day, and no one of her acquaintance had ever been inside his manor house by the river. All that aside, there was an aura of power and mystery about him that set her imagination to flight.

As she reached the punch bowl, Bethany searched the room for him, hoping to glimpse a hint of his intentions in his eyes, but he was nowhere to be seen. Reluctantly, she sat next to a group of wallflowers and made polite conversation until Lord Tench asked her to dance.

After enduring his wandering hands and clinging to her person all for the excuse of maintaining his balance— which she suspected wasn't nearly as impaired as he wanted her to believe— Bethany sought out her mother and pleaded exhaustion.

"Oh, but it is not even ten o'clock," Lady Wickshire protested.

"I know, but I did not sleep well last night and I do not wish to have circles under my eyes." Bethany appealed to her mother's obsession with her appearance. If she could be home by eleven, that would give her enough time to bathe and ready herself for her assignation with Justus.

Lady Mead's countenance softened. "Very well, I'll ask your father to have the carriage brought 'round."

Bethany hid a smile behind her fan as she saw the relief in Father's eyes as Mother requested that they depart. He had grown progressively fatigued with the social whirlwind they'd plunged into to secure Bethany a match. Lord Wickshire was much more comfortable in his overstuffed chair in the study, reading a book by the fire. If not for their opposing preferences, Bethany and her father would have been kindred spirits. Alas, Father disdained poetry and novels. He preferred memoirs and accounts of historical battles, which made Bethany's eyes glaze over. However, if it weren't for him taking her upon his lap and having her read some of those battle stories with him when she was young, Bethany never would have learned to read Old English and thus never would have had the opportunity to fall in love with Chaucer. It was a shame Father now disdained her love of novels. Not for the first time, she wondered what made him so apprehensive of anything in the realm of fiction. He often behaved as if he feared she wouldn't be able to discern a story from fact.

When they were settled in the carriage, Bethany silently implored the horses to go faster while also praying that one did not turn an ankle or pick up a stone so they would not be delayed. Then, once they arrived at home, she fabricated a story about a popular debutante advising her of the beautifying powers of bathing with lavender in order to persuade her mother to have a bath drawn despite the late hour. There was no way Bethany would meet Justus smelling of Lord Tench's putrid odor of old sweat and fermented cologne.

Taking extra time on cleaning her hair and scrubbing her skin, Bethany breathed a sigh of relief when her mother came in to bid her goodnight and she already heard her father snoring in the next room. Mother always retired minutes after father, so she should have time to change into suitable garb and steal away in time for her rendezvous.

The moment Mother closed her bedroom door, Bethany tiptoed to her wardrobe and searched for something fetching, yet practical for climbing up and down the tree. She settled on a navy blue riding habit that had breeches instead of a skirt, along with her best riding boots.

Darting glances at the small clock on her vanity, she brushed her hair for one hundred strokes before gathering it in a loose plait so it wouldn't catch on the tree branches. Then she touched up her face with a smattering of powder and a bit of rouge that mother gave her last Christmas. Her heart fluttered like a hummingbird's wings as she reached for her jewel box to fetch her lucky necklace.

No matter what Justus had to say to her, she wanted him to know that he'd chiseled a permanent place deep in her heart and that his friendship meant the world to her. After lifting her favorite necklace, a small watch on a gold chain that had belonged to her great, great grandmother, Bethany's gaze lit upon another trinket.

Just before they'd arrived at their country manor, Bethany's mother had commissioned to have a miniature of her painted and then placed in a locket. The necklace was meant to be given to her future intended as a token of affection.

Affection… Bethany turned the word over in her mind before lifting the locket from the box. Every vestige of her heart, mind, and soul knew that she would only feel affection for Justus. It was only right that he have it. Recalling another romantic tradition, Bethany quietly slid her drawer open and pulled out a tiny pair of sewing shears. She then lifted her braid, snipped off a lock of hair at the end, and placed it inside the locket before placing the necklace in her pocket.

With that accomplished, Bethany took three deep breaths before carefully working her window open. The branch she used to leap to seemed further away than she remembered. She shook her head. That was silly. If anything, the branch would be closer, as the tree had to have grown over the years. Sure enough, once she stretched her leg out, while maintaining a tight grip on the window frame, her boot easily found the solid surface of the branch. The next step was trickier, as she had to reach out and grasp another branch to fully begin her descent. With her childhood memory guiding her, she easily found the correct branch and reflexively crouched to push the window shut.

Slowly, Bethany worked her way down the tree, not releasing her pent-up breath until her feet were safely on the ground. Checking her little watch, her heart stuttered as she saw that it was already a quarter to midnight. Looking around to make certain no one was up and about, she took off running at a very unladylike pace, only slowing when she neared the orchard.

Even as she walked, she maintained a brisk pace while smoothing tendrils of hair that escaped her plait beneath her ears. Despite her best efforts, it seemed she would look a fright when she met with Justus after all.

But the moment she spotted a vague, masculine outline leaning against a cherry tree, Bethany forgot all about her appearance as her heart threatened to beat itself out from under her ribs. She could scarcely fathom that she was actually doing this, meeting a man alone beneath the cover of darkness.

"I thought you would not come." His deep voice rumbled in the night, seeming to make the leaves around them tremble.

"You said this was important," she said, hugging her arms as a sudden chill overcame her.

"Come closer." His tone was rife with urgency and command that she'd never heard from him before.

A shiver ran up the back of her neck, as she took several shaky steps towards him, even as some primal instinct urged her to flee in the opposite direction. Though that same instinct was also certain he'd catch her anyway. A chill wind made the leaves above them whisper.

Bethany shoved aside her trepidation. Justus was her friend.

As if reaffirming that fact, he reached out and took her hands. "Before I tell you why I asked you to meet me, I want you to trust that I will never hurt you."

"I know." Though the fact that he felt he needed to make such a statement filled her with alarm.

"The next thing I wish to say is that I love you, Bethany Mead." Her name sounded sweet and velvety coming from his lips. "In all my long years of life, I have never met a woman as beautiful, as intelligent, courageous and sweet as you. You've warmed my heart that I'd long since thought barren."

"I love you as well, Justus." Bethany's heart soared to finally voice that sentiment aloud. But then something he'd said gave her pause. "What do you mean, 'in your long years?' How old are you exactly?"

"Older than I look." He chuckled drily. Then his features turned tender as he stroked her cheek with his knuckles. Her skin warmed as she realized he wasn't wearing gloves. He studied her, intent and solemn. "Do you love me truly? Enough to keep a momentous secret if I reveal it?"

She nodded and leaned closer to him. "I do."

"I wish I could pay proper courtship to you. I want you to be my wife, for us to spend the rest our nights together. But such a thing may be impossible if you find my secret repugnant." Unbelievably, he shivered and looked at his boots with an aching, morose frown.

Bethany frowned, joy at his saying words she'd longed to hear since their first kiss warring with grief at the agony in his voice. "I don't think it possible for me to find anything about you repugnant."

"Do not be so certain." His brows lowered, his mouth forming a grave line. "Do you believe in mythical creatures?"

The question was so startling, she giggled. "Do you mean like fairies? Are you a fey prince like Oberon?"

Justus shook his head, still solemn. "No. I am a vampire."

Then he opened his mouth to reveal sharp, white fangs that gleamed in the moonlight.

Chapter Nine

Bethany's breath fled her body. That was the last thing she'd expected him to say. "What?" she said dumbly even as she stared at those impossibly sharp teeth, visible proof of his words.

"I said I am a vampire." Justus repeated and stepped back, hands open and withdrawn as if to reassure her that he wouldn't pounce. "Do not worry, though. I am not a living corpse like the legends say. But I do have to drink blood to survive and I cannot go out in daylight lest the sun burn me to a cinder."

"Which is why you could not pay me a call during the day," she whispered, unsure of whether or not she should run. Awe mingled with her trepidation. Never had she imagined that such things as vampires could be real.

"Yes." Justus cocked his head to the side, his green eyes searching hers. "Are you frightened?"

The deep sorrow on his face wrenched her heart. "Only a little. But mostly I am shocked. It is not at all what I expected. Did you lure me out here to drink my blood?"

"No!" His vehement tone rang with truth. "I asked you to come so I could declare myself, but to do that, I also had to tell you the truth about what I am."

"I understand." His promise that he wouldn't hurt her emboldened her to take a few steps closer to him. "Wasn't it dangerous to do tell me?"

"Yes. It is forbidden to reveal ourselves to mortals." Justus held her gaze and took a deep breath before he continued. "Unless we offer to Change them."

The full meaning of his words slammed into her chest like a hammer. "You want to make me into a vampire?"

He nodded. "For us to wed, I would have to."

That made sense, but... "What if I do not wish to become a vampire?" And what would it mean for her if she did?

He flinched at her words before emitting a grievous sigh. "Then I would banish your memory of this night and we would have to never speak again, for your safety as well as my own."

"You wouldn't see me anymore?" A hollow ache formed in her heart at the thought. "Even though you love me?"

"*Because* I love you," he said firmly, the words warming her like a balm. "I could never place you in danger."

"And I love you." The truth remained, despite their troubling circumstances.

His eyes widened. "Even after I told you what I am?"

The vulnerability in his voice undid her. In that moment, she knew she would walk through fire to be at his side.

"Yes." Slowly she stepped even closer to him, until their bodies were only inches apart. "You've always been kind to me, and I still believe you wouldn't hurt me."

With utmost gentleness, his hands grasped her shoulders. "You are a miracle, Bethany Mead."

Remembering the dire circumstances looming over their love, Bethany searched his face and asked, "Do you kill the people whose blood you drink?"

"Never," he said fervently. "That is forbidden as well. We take no more than a pint from one or two people each evening."

That put her at ease more than anything. She didn't know if she could bear it if he was a murderer, much less having to kill anyone herself. Though the thought of drinking blood still made her queasy. "And the sun burns you. What else would I be deprived of?"

"Food, though we can take a few nibbles. Any more though, and we become ill. Same with all drink except for water." His eyes held hers as he frowned. "And we can never have children."

No children? To be honest, Bethany hadn't given any thought to children. She'd just assumed that she would have them, yet regarded the thought of offspring as inevitable rather than something she anticipated. So perhaps she didn't want them. However, the prospect of not having a choice did rankle.

"Are there any good things about being a vampire?" she asked. Though being with him was what she wanted most in the world, surely being like him wasn't all unpleasantness.

He nodded. "We never age, and we never fall ill. We can move fast as dragonflies and possess the strength of ten men. We also heal fast when wounded, so very little can kill us."

Goodness, all that did sound nice. To be young and healthy forever… She frowned. "You said you were older than you appear. How old are you?"

"Just under two hundred years." He eyed her nervously as he uttered the number.

Her head spun at his answer. And she'd thought Lord Tench was ancient. That meant that Justus had lived to see the French and American Revolutions, the Seven Years' War, and even the witch hunts in the seventeenth century. And if she were to live that long... "My parents would grow old and die before me." The notion was so strange, as was the idea of never seeing them again. Though it didn't hurt as much as she'd feared it might.

He nodded. "That is often the most painful thing about our existence. Many refuse immortality for that reason alone."

"But once I'm married off, I wouldn't see them often anyway." Her mother hadn't seen her own parents since Bethany was born. So perhaps that wouldn't affect her too much. After all, they were the ones who were trying to get rid of her. Yet there was so much more she wanted to know. "How would you make me into a vampire?"

He gave her a wary look and spoke quietly. "I would drink almost all of your blood and then feed you mine."

Struggling to hold back her revulsion at the process, Bethany raised a brow. It did not seem overly magical. "If it is that simple, why is the world not full of vampires?"

His lips curved up as if in approval of the question, the same smile he favored her with when she told him her analysis on a piece of literature. "Because it takes at least a century for a vampire to build up the strength to Change a human."

"How many have you Changed?" She pronounced the capital letter of the word, tamping down the worry that he'd fallen in love before and she could face a rival for his affections.

"None," he said so emphatically that his answer could be nothing but truthful.

Tenderness unfurled in her heart like a summer rose. After nearly two hundred years, Justus had chosen her to spend his life with. Taking a deep breath, she made her decision. "Would you Change me before or after we marry?"

"After. I first need to seek permission from the Lord Vampire of Rochester to Change you. Then I would speak to your parents and secure a special license, so that we will be permitted a nighttime ceremony." Justus bent down so his face was inches from hers. "Are you saying you'll be willing to become a vampire to be my wife?"

Many of the novels she'd read featured the protagonist enduring some great test to prove their love. Bethany couldn't think of a greater test than becoming a mythical monster. Though truly once Justus explained what being a vampire entailed, they did not sound all that monstrous. Aside from the blood drinking aspect. And she would miss the sun.

"Yes," she whispered. "But I ask two things."

"Anything," he vowed.

"First, I want you to kiss me again." She reached up and linked her hands behind his neck. "Then I want you to bite me, so I know what it feels like."

He frowned, but his eyes began to glow a bright, phosphorescent green. Just as they had that night in the Willoughbys' garden the first night he kissed her. So it had not been a reflection of the fireworks. Did they glow like that when he was hungry? Part of her longed to pull away, for he looked so deadly, yet he was also so beautiful. She had to know, to experience what was integral to his existence, to feel his bite.

Bethany tilted her chin up, silently imploring the vampire to kiss her. A low growl trickled from his throat as his lips came down on hers, teasing and caressing. Heat spiraled in her belly at the taste of him, the feel of his strong arms pulling her tight against his lean, firm body. Her limbs went weak as she kissed him back, craving more of this deep, sensuous connection.

When his mouth dragged away from hers, Bethany whimpered at being deprived, then gasped as he trailed kisses along her cheek and down her neck. He was going to do it! The feel of his lips on such a sensitive part of her body made her tingle all over. Tangling her hands in his hair, she pulled him closer, needing more of this sweet pleasure.

Justus drew back, eyes glowing bright as fiery emeralds and fangs peeking out from his lips. "Are you certain about this?"

"Yes," she gasped. "But please, be gentle." Those teeth did look awfully sharp.

His hand slid up the back of her neck, fingers slipping into her hair at the base of her scalp. Those brilliant eyes held her captive as he whispered, "No pain."

Then he tilted her head and lowered his mouth back to her neck, kissing her until she was quivering in his arms. A sharpness pierced her flesh and a sense of dizzying pressure emanated from the place.

She heard him swallowing then, once, twice, three times. It should have revolted her, or at least it should have hurt, but instead, the sensitive place between her thighs throbbed with intoxicating pleasure with every pull at her throat. Her hips arched upward of their own volition, seeking something else to ease the ache in her loins as she moaned with need.

Justus drew back, licking his lips and breathing heavily. "I hope I did not hurt you. I did not take much, for I cannot have you climbing a tree if you're dizzy."

"No, it felt... incredible. Is it like that for everyone you drink from?" Jealousy niggled at her at the thought of other women experiencing this.

He shook his head. "They feel nothing."

Bethany reached for the wound on her neck, for it had begun to sting, but Justus snatched her hand back and pierced his index finger with a fang. "What are you doing?"

"Healing you." He pressed his bleeding finger to the place where he'd bitten her. Once more, her neck tingled, albeit with muted intensity. "If we left the humans we fed from with bite marks, our kind would not be long for this world."

"Oh." She was surprised to be disappointed that there would be no evidence of the magnificent sensations he'd wrought. "That is most practical."

The glow in his eyes dimmed so he looked human once more. "I wish we could have more time together, but it is too dangerous to tarry. I will escort you home now before I go speak to my lord. Then I hope to meet with your father tomorrow evening."

"Who is your lord?" There was still so much she did not know of this world she'd agreed to join.

"That I cannot tell you until you are one of us. I've already broken the laws by telling you my secret. I will not put others at risk." He held out his arm. "Shall we go now?"

No, she did not want this night to end, but she did not want for them to be caught out. "Wait." She reached into her pocket and withdrew the locket. "This was meant for my intended, so you must have it."

He raised a brow. "Were my intentions that transparent?"

"Oh no, you maintained a maddening aura of mystery about this assignation." Bethany laughed, relief washing over her that he did indeed return her feelings. "But I decided that no matter what you had to say, I would take this opportunity to declare my love."

He opened the locket and stroked the lock of her hair as he gazed at her portrait. "I will wear it next to my heart and treasure it always."

Without warning, he pulled her into his arms and embraced her so tightly that she could hear his heartbeat where her ear pressed against his chest. When she raised her head, he kissed her again, so deep and thoroughly that her knees turned to custard.

As if sensing her tentative balance, Justus scooped her up in his arms like she weighed less than goose down. "Let us get you home now."

"Will you run faster than a dragonfly?" she asked, lacing her arms around his neck.

His low chuckle reverberated through her body. "As you wish."

In a shot, he was off. The orchard blurred in her vision and the wind from their passing whipped against her cheeks, making her eyes water. Bethany's stomach seemed to rise all the way up to her ribs at the rapid rate, so she closed her eyes tight and buried her face in his shoulder, trusting him not to crash into a tree.

Seconds later, he stopped and she opened her eyes to see that he'd already brought her to her front drive. Gently he set her back on her feet, grasping her shoulders as she regained her balance on wobbling legs.

"Until tomorrow," he said and gave her one last kiss before he vanished into the night.

Tomorrow… The word echoed in her mind. Tomorrow night her life would change irrevocably.

Chapter Ten

Justus placed a finger to his lips. They still tingled from the heat of Bethany's kiss. The taste of her blood sang on his tongue. For a moment, he paused to look up at the stars and thanked the heavens for the outcome of this night.

He'd been all but certain that Bethany would have laughed at him and accused him of being a madman at best, or fled from him in terror at worst.

Instead, she'd accepted what he was, and even made thoughtful inquiries. Most of all, she still loved him, despite the fact that he was not human. She even loved him enough to forsake her own humanity and give up her family and the possibility of having children.

She *loved* him.

Heart rejoicing with that monumental fact, Justus raced to Darkwood Manor to submit his request to Gavin to grant him permission to Change her.

Benson, Rochester's third in command, stopped him at the edge of the manicured path to Lord of Rochester's manor house. "Justus! I haven't seen you in a spell. What have you been about?"

"The same as usual," Justus said, impatient to be on. He sensed two other vampires approaching with rampant curiosity when they should have remained at their posts. "Now I must see His Lordship."

Undeterred, Benson pointed at the locket Bethany gave him. "What have you got there?"

Justus grasped the necklace in his fist, hiding it from view as if the eyes of another would taint the gold. "It is none of your concern, now let me pass. I have urgent business."

Thumb stroking the locket, he made his way up the steps to Darkwood Manor.

Gavin opened the door before Justus knocked. His elderly butler had doubtless long since gone to bed. "I'd wondered when you'd bother to come round for a report." The Lord Vampire of Rochester studied him intently, his black eyes seeming to bore into his soul. His nostrils flared and he frowned. "You've fed on that girl. Is that what you are here to confess?"

"She's a woman," Justus argued even as a shiver of unease coursed down his spine. Gavin recognized Bethany's scent.

"She hasn't yet reached her age of majority, so she is indeed yet a girl," Gavin said firmly before opening the door wider. "But let's not argue semantics. Come in."

Justus's trepidation rose as he followed his lord through the manor with mismatched décor from Gavin's past few wives. When they entered the study, Gavin poured two small glasses of Maderia and bade him to sit. "From the scent of Miss Mead emanating from you like a miasma and that new bauble around your neck, I gather you are not here to report on any rogue sightings."

"I wish to wed Miss Mead and Change her." Justus said, ignoring the wine. "I've come to seek your permission to do so."

Gavin's brows rose to his hairline. "Well then, your encounters with her have been more intimate than I'd thought. And does she return your affections?"

Justus nodded and opened the locket to reveal Bethany's miniature and lock of hair. "She gave me this and told me it was intended for the man she would marry. I will be that man."

"And when did you plan on doing that?" Gavin inquired mildly. Something in his tone made his question seem like a trick.

"As soon as possible. I'd speak to her parents and secure a special license." Justus spoke faster as his excitement built. "I love her, my lord, and I'm certain she will make a fine vampire. She is intelligent, prudent, and—"

"And a minor," Gavin cut him off. "It is forbidden to Change mortals under the age of twenty-one."

"But Julia was only eighteen when she was Changed," Justus argued.

"She was Changed before the law was made." Gavin sipped his wine. "Do you not remember when I announced the decree from the Elders back in 1750?"

Justus shook his head. "That was over sixty years ago."

Gavin snorted. "You have the memory of a mortal, I swear."

"But surely exceptions can be made." A pleading cadence imbued his voice, to his shame. "She's of marriageable age."

His Lordship shrugged. "That means nothing. Sometimes the nobility has married off infants."

"But her parents are trying to marry her off now." Justus's heart clenched with urgency. "May I wed Bethany now and Change her when she comes of age?"

"I'm afraid not." A flicker of pity flashed in Gavin's normally implacable eyes. "We cannot afford the risk of her discovering what you are and telling the world. Besides, we are already discouraged from Changing members of prominent families in the first place. The Meads have been a fixture in Rochester for centuries. Her father has a high position in the House of Lords and is being considered for governor here. One of her ancestors was the Bishop when I was training for the priesthood."

Dread pooled in Justus's belly. The Lord of Rochester could never learn that he'd already revealed himself to Bethany. Gavin wasn't called "Ruthless Rochester" for nothing. His heart sank. "Is there no hope at all?"

Gavin sighed, his stern veneer cracking slightly. "As she is a girl, her prominence is diminished at least. But you must wait until she reaches the age of majority to wed her. I cannot bend that rule."

"But surely someone has," Justus grasped at any straw that could provide a precedent.

"Very likely," Gavin agreed mildly. "But what some can get away with and what you and I can are different things altogether. I do not kowtow to the Elders, so I may miss some of their indulgences, but I am also not indebted to them for any favors and they leave me alone." Gavin sneered, his irritation with the world's most powerful vampires apparent.

Justus closed his eyes as hopelessness threatened to drown him. "I love her." Why could that not be enough?

A warm, solid hand grasped his shoulder. Justus opened his eyes to see Gavin looking at him with pity. "I may have a solution," he said quietly.

Hope flared within Justus's chest. "What?"

"A long engagement." Gavin released him and leaned back in his chair, steepling his fingers. "Secure a betrothal contract with her father, and then leave Rochester until Miss Mead's twenty-first birthday. We can fabricate a story of you having business in India and arrange for you to stay with another Lord Vampire."

The thought of being away from Bethany for four long years filled Justus with agony. But the thought of never being able to make her his was even more unbearable. Gripping the arms of his chair with painful force, he bowed his head in assent. "Thank you, my lord." He tried to conceal his bitterness in his words.

"Cheer up, old friend," Gavin said with a smirk. "You've lived in this world for over two centuries. What is a handful of years?"

The Lord of Rochester spoke truly, but it wasn't so much the span of time that would be the most difficult to endure. "What if something happens to her while I'm away? What if her parents decide to break the betrothal, or she falls from her horse, or another plague strikes the village?"

Gavin shook his head and laughed. "What if lightning strikes us in the next five minutes? What if corn stalks sprout from your ears? Honestly, if this is what love does to a man, I pray I never succumb to such a ludicrous malady. You sound like an old woman." His mirth faded as Justus glared at him. "Do not worry. Medicine is advancing faster every day, and the nobility are always the safest from plagues. Furthermore, I'll keep an eye on the girl and make sure her father does not presume to change his mind." He paused and cocked his head to the side. "But what if Miss Mead decides she wants another?"

Justus flinched at the thought of losing Bethany's love. But her happiness was the most important thing to him. "If she does, send word to me and I will release her from the betrothal contract."

The Lord of Rochester regarded him with an unexpectedly gentle smile. "You have a good heart, Justus. Guard it well, for mortals can be fickle, especially young ones." He slid Justus's wineglass closer before lifting his own. "In the meantime, let us toast your future bride."

"Thank you, my lord." Justus drank deeply, joy swelling his being that he was granted his heart's desire.

Chapter Eleven

Bethany awoke with a blissful sigh. Justus had been kissing her in her dreams, just as fervently as he had last night.

Last night… the memories struck her with such force that she sat up so fast her head spun with a wave of dizziness.

Justus was a vampire. With daylight streaming through her window, the concept should have been laughable, but last night, with the moonlight gleaming on his fangs, his eyes glowing in the darkness, and the mind-bending sensation of his bite, the truth had been all too real.

And Bethany had agreed to become one as well, to live forever, to bite people and drink their blood. She'd also agreed to become his wife. Warmth suffused her heart as she remembered his ardent declaration of love.

Tonight he'd ask her father for her hand in marriage. Breath hitching in excitement, Bethany threw off her covers and rang for the maid to bring her breakfast and select a fetching ensemble.

It was difficult to eat with her belly fluttering, but Bethany managed to eat half a scone and a bit of egg before she had her maid help her into her riding habit. A ride would help pass the time and calm her flitting nerves.

For the evening, she chose her white satin gown, for it was what she was wearing the night of the Ellingsworth ball the night she and Justus shared their first dance.

Humming a soft tune, Bethany barely heard her mother's chattering as she left for the stables. Once saddled on Canterbury, her russet gelding, she pondered what her life would be like as a vampire. No more morning rides, that was certain, so she had best enjoy them while she still had time.

She was also insatiably curious as to what her future home was like. Bethany had heard that Lord de Wynter's estate was a half mile from her own, adjacent to the Ellingsworths' lands. Digging her heel in Canterbury's flanks, she urged the gelding into a run in that direction. The wind whipped through her hair, though not as fiercely as it had last night in Justus's arms. That meant that a vampire was faster than a horse.

Bethany remained in awe over that fact until she reached a ramshackle manor house that was indeed between the Ellingsworths' and the Chattertons' properties. The de Wynter crest was cast in the rusted iron gate, though it was so pitted that it was nearly unrecognizable. Grass grew at least waist high in the lawn and the gravel drive was choked with weeds.

A shutter hinge creaked in the wind as it hung from one pitiful nail. The red bricks were faded and crumbling on the Jacobean façade of the house. Bethany's heart sank slightly to see the place in such disrepair, but vowed to restore it to its former glory once she was Lady de Wynter.

"Lady de Wynter..." she murmured, heat pooling in her belly at those words.

Was Justus in there now, hiding from the sun and dreaming of her?

Her thoughts broke as she heard a shout.

"Miss Mead!" Rebecca rode a shining silver bay up to her. "What brings you to this dismal place?"

Observing my future estate, Bethany longed to say, but it would be best to hold her tongue until her engagement was announced. "My horse was startled by a large dog," she lied. "I only now got control of her."

Rebecca smirked as if detecting her fib. "Well, you had best find your groom before you are seen in front of a rake's home without a chaperone." She sneered at the ramshackle house. "For a man who dresses so fine, his estate is in a ghastly state. He must be up to his ears in debt."

"I could not say," Bethany said thinly. "Anyway, I must be going."

With a press of her knee, she guided Canterbury away, wondering if she could bite Rebecca once she became a vampire. The thought filled her with more glee than was proper.

She wondered how Justus's conversation with the Lord Vampire of Rochester went. What if he refused to allow Justus to Change her? Would they then be unable to wed? Refusing to let such a dark prospect cloud her heart, Bethany once more urged her horse to a run once the edges of her father's lands came into view.

Who was the Lord Vampire of Rochester anyway? Could he be a member of the nobility? She thought back to all the men she'd been introduced to since they came to the country, but her mother had thrust her before so many that they blurred in her memory. Or perhaps he was a commoner, hiding from the public view. No matter, she supposed she would find out soon enough.

Suddenly, Canterbury stumbled into a gopher hole and shrieked a high-pitched neigh. Bethany jolted from the saddle, the world flying before her eyes as fast as it had when Justus carried her home.

She slammed into the ground so hard her breath was forced from her lungs. Stars exploded in her vision before blackness engulfed her.

Pain, throbbing and sharp, awakened her after what felt like an age of slumber. Bethany opened her eyes to see a balding man with white bushy eyebrows standing over her. "Ah, our patient's awake."

Patient? Bethany blinked in confusion. Somehow she'd ended up back in her own bed, and now a doctor was in her room. She must have moved, for her knee exploded in agony.

The doctor gently held her down on her bed. "Easy now. Though you haven't broken anything, you have a few sprains and bruises. Best not to agitate them." He then poured some liquid into a large spoon and forced her to drink a bitter concoction. "That should make you feel better." He placed the spoon and bottle into his large leather bag and donned his hat. "I'll look in on you tomorrow."

Bethany grimaced at the taste of the medicine. Sprains and bruises... She then remembered falling from her horse. "Canterbury," she whispered. If he'd broken a leg and had to be shot, she couldn't bear it.

"The horse is all right," Bethany's mother said from behind the doctor. She set her embroidery hoop on the end table and crossed the room. "The stable master wrapped his sprained front leg. It is you I am concerned for. You could have broken your neck!"

Bethany's brows rose at such melodrama coming from her normally staid mother. "I'm certain I'll be quite well." A thought made her freeze. "Lord de Wynter is supposed to pay a call tonight."

Lady Wickshire frowned. "What sort of man pays calls at night?"

Bethany ground her teeth, not able to answer. The medicine flowed through her, making her feel muzzy-headed, though thankfully abating the pain in her knee.

Her mother continued. "Besides, you have a caller now." She wrung her hands, looking unusually anxious. "Of course I told him he could not come up here with you in such a state, but he will be staying for supper."

"Who?" Bethany asked, curious as to what sort of caller would unnerve her mother so.

"Lord Tench." The answer came out sounding like a confession and Cecily's shoulders slumped.

Bethany sighed in annoyance. "Is that all? Can't he sup with us tomorrow? Tonight is important, and Tench smells like old beets and his hands wander where they shouldn't."

"Bethany!" Mother gasped at her words.

Bethany gave her a lopsided smile. The medicine seemed to have loosened her tongue, but she did not regret speaking the truth. "I'm sorry, Mother. I do not like him."

"Well, you had best learn to," Mother said with a frown. "Your father has accepted his offer for your hand."

At first, Bethany did not comprehend her words. "But he is far too old. He's older than father! He's even older than Grandfather!"

Mother's shoulders slumped. "All the same, his land borders ours, and he has guaranteed your father the necessary votes to become Governor. I tried to put a stop to it, to find you a better match, but your father was insistent and I ran out of time."

The terrifying reality of the situation sank in. "No!" she gasped and threw off her covers. Hauling herself out of bed, Bethany ignored the shriek of pain from her knee as well as her mother's protest. She spied a wooden cane leaning on the wall by her door that the doctor must have left behind, and hobbled to it.

"Bethany!" her mother shouted. "Get back into bed this instant!"

"No," Bethany repeated as she grasped the cane with fumbling hands and shambled down the hall with aid of the cane. She *had* to stop her father from doing something so terrible.

The stairs were a trial to navigate, between managing the cane, keeping the weight off of her bad knee, and shrugging off her mother's attempts to drag her back to her room. And once she made it to the bottom, her head was even more addled than before from the laudanum. Leaning heavily on the cane, Bethany made her way to her father's study, where she heard male voices chatting jovially.

When she opened the door, Lord Tench's face wrinkled further as he smiled. "Ah, here is my bride."

Ignoring him, Bethany fixed her father with a glare. "I will *not* wed him." Lady Wickshire gasped behind her and Tench blanched as if slapped.

Lord Wickshire's eyes narrowed. "You will do as I say, daughter."

"No," she hissed through clenched teeth. "I will marry Lord de Wynter. He is coming tonight to ask you for my hand."

Both men laughed. "de Wynter?" Tench said with a mocking grin, though she could see a glimmer of hurt in his eyes for her rejection of his suit. "That wastrel could never provide for you. Unlike me, who will see to your every comfort."

Her father, however, had sobered. "Our dear neighbor speaks truly. From the state of de Wynter's holdings, he must be light in the pocket."

Her mother nodded. "Furthermore, by all accounts, he is a rake. He cannot have any real interest in you. He's never paid you a single call, unlike Lord Tench, who has been nothing but doting."

Bethany heaved a sigh, exasperated with their lack of understanding. "He is calling upon me tonight! He would have called on me sooner, except that he's a vampire." She clapped her hand over her mouth. She had not meant to say that part aloud.

Both her father and Lord Tench looked at her with eyes the size of saucers. Tench was the first to recover. "She's mad!"

"No," Lady Wickshire said, putting her arm over Bethany's shoulders. "She's simply addled from the laudanum the doctor gave her for her fall. She does not know what she's saying."

"She's been reading too many novels," her father huffed, though beneath the veneer of bluster, Bethany detected sheer terror in his quivering jowls. "Which has given her a fanciful nature. Best keep your library under lock and key."

Tench shook his head. "No drug makes a person say such things. And I know your family secret." He rounded on Bethany's father with a glare. "She's mad, just like your mother was. I will not marry a lunatic. Let de Wynter have her."

With that, the old man stormed out of the study with a surprising spryness for a man of his years, his withered features contorted with injured pride.

Lord Wickshire rose from his desk, face red with fury. "What have you done?" he roared. "Your foolish outburst cost me acres of land and the votes I needed to be the new governor!"

"I love Justus, not Tench," Bethany stammered. "How could you sell me for votes?"

"All daughters are sold." He sneered. "It's all your good for. If I'd had a son…"

"And what about my grandmother?" she persisted. "What did Lord Tench mean about her being mad? You told me she'd died when you were a boy."

"She was dead to me, once she was committed to bedlam," Father said coldly. "Just as you'll be if your so-called vampire doesn't take your ungrateful, over imaginative hide off of my hands."

Bethany gasped at his nonchalant words. All these years she'd thought her grandmother was dead and now she learned that instead, she'd suffered a worse fate. And had Father truly threatened to have her committed as well?

She closed her eyes as another wave of dizziness engulfed her from the effects of the laudanum. Perhaps this was a dream. Maybe she'd wake up in her bed, uninjured and ready to prepare for Justus's proposal.

Her knee gave another throb of pain, refuting that hope.

At least her father had offered her one good thing. He wished to be rid of her enough to allow her to marry Justus. "Lord de Wynter *will* come for me," she said coldly. "And then you shall never be burdened with my presence again."

Her mother gently pulled her away. "Enough, darling. Let's get you back in bed. You need to rest."

Her father glared at her, jowls quivering with rage, but he didn't say a word.

Once back in bed, Bethany was unable to sleep for her racing mind and spinning dizziness from the laudanum. Though her father had treated her with indifference ever since she left the schoolroom, she never imagined that she'd come to mean so little to him.

At least her parents seemed to ignore her blurting out that Justus was a vampire, aside from her father's mocking remark. Fear and shame coiled in her belly. Justus had said it was forbidden for vampires to reveal themselves to mortals, yet under the influence of this dratted drug, Bethany had told his secret. Thankfully, no one seemed to believe her, but what if they told Justus what she'd said?

Although he'd said it was forbidden to kill people, surely Justus would have to do something to protect himself. And what if her mistake made him hate her? Her soul ached at the thought. She prayed her father would be too embarrassed to mention her outburst.

The minutes crawled like hours until at last the sun began to set. Bethany rang for her maid to help her dress. She still insisted on wearing the white satin gown, even though her right stocking would not fit over her bandaged knee. She then chose to have her hair arranged in an upswept crown of curls atop her head and threaded with white roses from the garden.

When she made her way downstairs with the aid of the cane, grimacing in pain as her knee protested with every step, her mother gaped at her.

"Are you certain that is what you are wearing this evening?" Cecily asked with lips pursed in disapproval. "I daresay, it is much too formal for a night at home. Your father is already worried about your mental state."

"I wish to look pleasing for my future husband," she said plainly.

Her mother sighed. "Are you certain he is coming? It is nearly eight o'clock."

It is not yet dark, she longed to say, but held her tongue. "Yes. He will come." As they made their way to the drawing room, she changed the subject. "Did *you* know the truth about my grandmother?"

Gnawing on her lower lip, Mother nodded. "I thought it best to conceal such a scandalous truth from you. I know very little about the circumstances of her madness, but your father told me that she saw ghosts and believed people to be possessed by demons." She gave Bethany a nervous, sideways glance, and shook her head. "Let's speak no more of it and wait for your caller. I do hope you know what you are doing, accepting that man's suit."

"I do," she said firmly.

When they entered the drawing room, Bethany's father regarded her with a thunderous frown. "You've ruined me, you know. The moment he left our home, Tench called upon every notable family in Rochester and told everyone that you are stark raving mad. The laughter could be heard across the county." His face reddened further. "Now I'll never be governor and it will take years to salvage my reputation. You had best hope for a fast engagement with de Wynter because we will have to return to London as soon as possible. Furthermore, you look like a fool, wearing a ball gown for supper at home."

A fast engagement. Bethany nodded, feeling a twinge of pity at her father's humiliation. She looked at the clock and then out the dark window, praying that Justus would arrive soon, that her father would treat him well. That maybe they could escape all of this ugliness and run to Gretna Green to elope.

That is, if the Lord Vampire of Gretna Green would allow it.

The minutes ticked by faster, yet still Justus had yet to arrive. The servants bustled in and out of the room, refilling tea and reporting on supper. Bethany tried to tell herself that Justus was seeking his own meal as her father declared that they had waited long enough and ordered them to the dining room.

Bethany picked at her overcooked roast chicken and darted glances at the doorway, waiting for the butler to announce Justus's arrival.

"I do not think your suitor is coming." Her father vocalized her deepest fear. "In fact, I do not think he is a suitor at all, much less a mythical creature. I think you fabricated all of this nonsense in your head." He heaved a long-suffering sigh. "I'd been long concerned that you were descending into madness, but refused to see the truth."

"No." She shook her head.

Bethany's mother patted her hand and addressed her husband. "Now, dear, she did suffer from quite a fall. Perhaps she struck her head. She'll come to her senses soon enough."

"I injured my knee, not my head," Bethany retorted, looking at the clock again. It was already a quarter past ten.

"All the same, I think I will have the doctor examine you again." Cecily gave her a pitying look. "Your father is right. You did not mention anything about Lord de Wynter until after your fall. Are you certain this wasn't a dream, brought on by the laudanum?"

"It was no dream!" Bethany rose from the table, crying out as her knee flared in agony.

Mother took her elbow. "Darling, perhaps you should go to bed and have another dram of laudanum. Your injuries are clearly paining you."

"No laudanum." Bethany did not trust herself under the influence of that vile substance.

When the footman handed her the cane, she bobbed a crooked curtsy, biting back a scream of pain. "I will wait in the library."

"She is mad." Her father shook his head. "It runs in the female line in my family. If only you'd given me a son, Cecily."

"Charles…" her mother pleaded.

Bethany refused to hear any more and made her way out of the dining room. With every painful step, Bethany prayed with growing desperation.

Please let him come. Please let him come.

Chapter Twelve

Justus awoke for the night with his heart pounding with excitement. Tonight he would ask Lord Wickshire for Bethany's hand in marriage. Eager to be on his way, he rose from his bed beneath the house and selected his finest garb from his antique wardrobe.

Once dressed, he left the house, stopping only to pick a bouquet of flowers from his overgrown garden. He hurried to the village to seek his meal, not wanting his hunger to interfere with the night. As it was, finding a suitable victim, a drunk wandering down Market Lane alone, took far longer than Justus would have preferred. He looked at his watch and cursed as he saw that it was a quarter of nine.

He had to hurry if he hoped for Lord Wickshire to admit him. He did not dare acknowledge his worst fear, that Lord Wickshire would refuse his suit in the first place. For the first time, he regretted purposefully leaving his estate in disrepair to dissuade people from paying calls. He would convince Bethany's father that despite outward appearances, he was more than capable of supporting Bethany financially.

As he neared Bethany's home, sadness weighted his steps as he recalled that he would have to leave shortly after the betrothal contract was signed. He hoped that Gavin would at least let him remain long enough to host an engagement party. That way, everyone in Rochester would know that Bethany was his.

Either way, he vowed to make the most of every moment he and Bethany had together.

Just as he approached the manicured drive to Wickshire Hall, a heavy weight slammed into him, knocking him from his feet.

Justus growled in rage. How dare a rogue presume to attack him? To be lurking here by his love's home? He would kill the bleeding sod!

A powerful knee dug into his back as the figure of another vampire seized his arms, pinning him. Justus roared and bucked, but it was no use as his wrists were shackled behind him. When he was hauled to his feet, Justus gasped as he recognized the vampires who'd captured him.

"Cecil? Benson?" His mind swam with confusion. "What in God's name do you think you're doing?"

Benson surveyed him coldly. "You are under arrest, by command of the Lord of Rochester."

"What the hell for?" Justus demanded, wondering how this could be happening.

Benson's frown deepened. "For telling a mortal what you are."

Dread churned his gut. "The secret is safe with her, I swear. Rochester permitted me to Change her after we are wed. She will never tell anyone."

Cecil spoke at last, eyes ominous. "I'm afraid she already has."

"No," Justus whispered, arms going slack in his restraints. "She would never."

Benson shook his head. "She has. Their neighbor, Lord Tench told everyone. Apparently she was already betrothed to him. So I'm afraid the chit played you for an utter fool. God, how could you lose your head like that?"

All the fight went out of Justus at hearing that Bethany was betrothed. Why had she never told him?

"We're fortunate that Tench thought nothing of the girl's talk of vampires. He's declared her to be a raving lunatic," Cecil said as they led him into the woods, away from view. "Well, all of us are fortunate, but for you."

Justus didn't need Cecil to clarify his meaning any more than he needed to ask where they were taking him. There was only one penalty for revealing oneself to a mortal: Death.

But without Bethany, he wasn't so certain he wanted to live anymore anyway.

When they reached Darkwood manor, Justus saw the Lord of Rochester pacing back and forth on his great front terrace.

Gavin turned and met his gaze. The mingled anger, sadness and pity in the vampire's eyes struck Justus like a fist in the gut. "How could you do such a foolish thing? How could you betray us like that?"

"There has to have been some sort of mistake," Justus said. "She wouldn't have willingly revealed that information."

"I do not give a tinker's damn what drove the girl to open her mouth," Gavin growled as he gestured for Cecil and Benson to drag him into the house. "The fact is that it was done."

Darkwood Manor was empty and silent as a tomb. Rochester must have sent his elderly mortal servants to bed, so they wouldn't intrude on this night's business.

The Lord Vampire crossed the hall, and opened a concealed door within the wall. "Lock him in the dungeon until his trial. We have to do all we can to minimize the damage he's caused."

"Wait," Justus shouted. "Gavin, we've been best friends for centuries. Please, listen to me!"

His former friend's face was cold and implacable as he turned his back without a word.

Justus's mind reeled with disbelief as Cecil and Benson dragged him down the stairs, past the cellar, and down to the dungeons that had been designed to hold the strongest vampire. Justus had thrown many a rogue into these cells. He never imagined that he'd be occupying one himself.

For a moment, he considered breaking free of Cecil and Benson's hold, but even if he managed to, running with shackles would slow him down and Gavin was likely waiting at the top of the stairs with his sword in case of just that.

After shoving him into the corner of the cell, Cecil secured the shackles to a thick steel chain that would only be long enough for Justus to sink to the floor.

Benson met his gaze, eyes full of pity. "I wish things did not have to be this way. Maybe His Lordship will grant you mercy."

Cecil nodded. "Of all the vampires I know, you were the last I expected to break this particular law." His lips curved in a humorless smile. "I'd expected you to break our other rules, but never that one."

Justus managed a half-hearted chuckle that came out more like a sob. "I understand. And know this. I bear neither of you ill will for doing your duty."

Both vampires bowed their heads, whether in mourning or respect, he did not know. They then turned their backs and left the cell, locking the steel cage door behind them. And Justus was left alone in the darkness.

He slumped against the cold, damp stone wall and closed his eyes. Bethany couldn't have betrayed him. He'd tasted the truth and purity of her love when he'd drank from her. Something must have happened, some sort of coercion.

Another thought came to him that somewhat lightened his heart despite his dire situation. He'd also seen nothing of a betrothal in her memories when he'd fed from her last night. She must not have known about it until today. Had the shock of her parents telling her that she'd be handed off to an old lecher stunned her so much that she'd declared she would marry a vampire instead?

No, that was still too illogical of a leap. There had to be something else that prompted such an outburst. Yet no matter how much he wracked his brain, Justus could not discern what had prompted her to reveal such a dangerous secret.

No matter, this was all his fault. He should have banished Bethany's memory that night and not revealed the truth of his kind until they were wed. But in his foolish arrogance, he'd reveled in the joyous revelation that she loved him despite learning that he was a vampire.

Now he would die for that arrogance and Bethany would never be his after all.

Was she even now wondering where he was? Would she be heartbroken when he never arrived and miss him terribly? Or would she curse him for a faithless cad?

To further salt the wound, would she be married off to Lord Tench after all? With the man declaring her to be insane, he did not sound too keen, yet Bethany was a beauty, so he may well change his mind. Justus's heart burned in agony at the thought of her with another man, yet he did not wish her to spend the rest of her life as a heartbroken spinster, pining away for him.

As he closed his eyes, imagining the possibilitics for Bethany's future, a horrifying realization made him jerk upright in his chains.

Gavin's words to Cecil and Benson echoed in his memory. *"We have to do all we can to minimize the damage."*

"Oh God," Justus croaked through numb lips. What if he meant to harm Bethany?

Chapter Thirteen

Bethany awoke with a burning cramp in her neck. Daylight streamed through the library windows, testifying the worst. The breath in her lungs froze as if full of January air. Last night hadn't been a nightmare. Justus hadn't come. She'd given the butler fervent instructions to notify her immediately of his arrival and had waited, facing the clock with a book on her lap that she'd never even attempted to read. Had he changed his mind? She didn't think so. Father said that Lord Tench had spread the word far and wide that she'd said Lord de Wynter was a vampire. Either Justus was now angry with her for betraying him, or worse. He'd told her that revealing his secret to a human was forbidden. Had his Lord Vampire punished him?

She shook her head, refusing to entertain the worst. Surely Justus's Lord would understand when Justus explained that he would Change Bethany. But the morning light cast a pall over her heart, refusing to abate her terror.

She must have fallen asleep after two in the morning. Rubbing her neck, she reached for her cane and rose to her feet, hissing as her swollen knee protested. If the pain continued with such severity, she may have to relent and take some laudanum.

Thumps and grating sounds along with rapid footsteps reached her ears then. It sounded like her house was occupied with an army.

Hobbling out of the library, Bethany saw a pair of footmen hauling a trunk down the hall. Then another passed her, carrying her mother's traveling valise.

She stared in stunned disbelief. Her father had meant his words when he'd said they'd be leaving the county. Panic hammered her lungs, making her stays impossibly tight as her mother's voice reached her ears.

"My lord husband, must we go through with this?" The rife pleading in Cecily's tone made Bethany pause.

"We have no choice." Her father responded coldly. "We are ruined here. If I am to have any hope in recovering my reputation and political position, we must leave and erase all traces of scandal immediately. I will not allow softness to destroy me, like it did my father."

Bethany leaned against the door frame, feeling ill. Father truly thought her mad and was ready to uproot the whole family back to London today, with nary a chance for her to explain herself or send word to Justus.

Panic fluttered in her stomach. How would Justus be able to find her then? Or would he even want to find her after she'd blurted out his secret and endangered him and his people?

Tears prickled the back of her eyes and she blinked them away. He had to forgive her. He had to still love her.

Again, fear seized her heart in an icy grip. What if Lord Tench sent men to kill him? Or had the Lord Vampire of Rochester denied his request and ordered him to stay away from her? And how was she supposed to find out if they were leaving?

Her mother swept into the hall, taking Bethany's elbow. Her face was pale and her eyes darted away from Bethany's face. "Let us have breakfast before we depart."

"Must we return to London so soon?" Bethany was unable to hide the desperation in her voice.

Lady Wickshire's face flushed, and for a moment it looked as if she would say something, but then her gaze returned to the floor. "We must leave the area to save your father's reputation. Out of sight, out of mind." Her lips thinned grimly at the last.

Father was not in the dining room, and for that Bethany breathed a sigh of relief. She did not know how she would hold her temper and refrain from castigating him for ruining everything.

Her stomach revolted at the plate of scones and sausage set before her, but her mother would not stop harping until she managed a few bites. A maid set a cup of tea in front of her with a nervous look as if expecting Bethany to erupt into hysterics as she had last night.

Mother smiled tightly. "It's extra honeyed, just how you like it."

Bethany took a sip and grimaced. Beneath the almost cloying overpowering taste of honey was bitterness. She set the cup down. "I think this was steeped for far too long."

Instead of apologizing and taking the cup away, the maid looked at her mother as if in mute inquiry.

Mother's frown deepened. "The servants are overburdened with preparations for our journey. They do not have the time to make another cup. Now drink it."

Guilt drowned her at the thought of inconveniencing the overworked servants further. They must be terribly burdened for Cecily to take notice of their plight. Bethany lifted the cup and forced the bittersweet liquid down as fast as she could, trying not to show her distaste.

When the cup was empty, Mother nodded to a footman, who passed Bethany her cane.

"Your trunks have already been loaded," Cecily said. "Let's get you into the carriage. Your father wishes to depart on the hour."

The footman remained at her side as they walked from the house. Bethany was grateful for that fact as a sudden wave of dizziness nearly made her stumble on her way into the carriage. If not for his steadying hand, she doubtless would have toppled onto the cobblestones.

Mother had not been exaggerating when she spoke of Father's urgency. He already waited in the bench across from her and Mother and signaled the driver to be off the moment they were seated.

Bethany reached under her seat for a novel she'd stashed there and gasped as her father snatched it out of her hand. "No more reading. That is likely what put you in such a hysterical state. I knew I should have forbidden you that nonsensical tripe in the first place."

She frowned in wounded disbelief. No more reading? Did he mean for the journey, or ever again? How would she survive without books? Without Justus?

Before she could protest, a sensation of hazy heaviness settled over her like a wool blanket. Bethany recognized the feeling. No wonder her mother had insisted that she finish the tea that had tasted so bitter.

She whipped her head around to face her mother. "You *drugged* me?" Even as she spoke, her words slurred like a drunkard's and a heavy drowsiness engulfed her like a shroud.

Cecily nodded. "It was for your own good. Your knee was clearly paining you and we have a long trip."

Outrage made her quiver in her seat even as lethargy weighted her limbs like lead. "You… had no… right," she murmured, sleepy from the swaying carriage.

"I'm your mother," Cecily said, though her cheeks flushed with guilt. "I had every right."

No longer able to hold up her head, Bethany leaned against the carriage window. Her eyes widened, despite the drowsiness from the drugs. "This isn't the road we take home. I thought we were returning to London."

"*We* are," her father said gruffly. "You are not."

Chapter Fourteen

Justus awoke cold and cramped, his stomach roiling with hunger. His bloodthirst hadn't been this intense since he was a youngling. And why has he so damned cold and uncomfortable? Foreboding filled him, urging him to keep his eyes shut, but he opened them anyway— and immediately regretted doing so.

The sight of the damp stone walls and thick steel bars of Rochester's prison cells was like a blow to the stomach, assaulting him with memories of every tragic catastrophic event that transpired last night. Being intercepted on his way to Bethany, when he'd been so close he could smell her. Cecil and Benson arresting him, saying she'd done the unthinkable. And that she was betrothed to another.

Gavin's sorrowful, but stern face as he ordered him locked away to await his trial. Right before he told Cecil and Benson to minimize the damage.

"Bethany," Justus croaked past dry lips. For all he knew, Gavin could have had her killed by now.

He roared and struggled against his shackles. Chunks of stone chipped off the wall from where the chains struck. But the shackles held as they'd been crafted to do. If only he'd fed last night before going to Bethany's home. If only he could feed now! After missing only three meals, he'd already begun to weaken. At full strength, he may have been able to at least pry the shackles from the wall. Even then, such would take time.

Time he did not have. He needed to get to Bethany!

Scanning the cell, Justus wracked his brain to come up with a means of escape. He'd imprisoned so many rogue vampires over the years, he should know these cells inside and out. Alas, that was the problem. He was the one who selected the special steel for the shackles. He was the one who'd urged Gavin to wall the cells up with granite instead of basalt. He was the one who made escape impossible.

The creak of the hidden door upstairs, followed by footsteps, announced the approach of other vampires. Justus smelled Gavin and Benson.

He swallowed. Gavin coming down here did not bode well. Then again, Justus hadn't really expected to survive this debacle.

The dark forms of his lord and the third in command appeared before the barred doorway of the cell, their shadows engulfing Justus like a shroud of an ominous omen.

Benson unlocked the cell and Gavin strode in, standing over Justus with that same despondent frown. "It breaks my heart to see you here."

"Then let me go." Justus growled.

Gavin sighed. "You of all vampires are aware of what happens when one violates our laws. Especially the law you flagrantly broke."

"Why can you not show me mercy, just this once?"

"Because most of the Elders detest me." Gavin threw up his hands in impotent frustration as he blurted out the confession. "I had a disagreement with the Lord of Edinburgh and he tried to block my appointment as Lord of Rochester. The only reason they do not strip me of my rank during my reinstatement hearings is because I hold to the letter of the law. The second I am caught bending a rule, they'll oust me to allow the self-titled Lord of Kent to take more territory."

"Why did you never tell me?" Justus demanded. Then he slumped in his chains, knowing that even if he'd known, it probably wouldn't have made a difference.

Gavin sighed. "Because I didn't think it mattered. I am the ruler here, not the Elders, but you see why I cannot pardon you for your crime. Yet you've placed me in a quandary. I should try you before all the vampires of Rochester. Make an example of you so they all know that no one will be spared from my wrath. Not even my best friend." His voice broke at the last. "Yet at the same time, not only was your crime embarrassing, but your reasons for it are humiliating beyond the pale. If you related that before our people, I'd be a laughingstock, and someone would send word to Edinburgh before my next evaluation."

Justus did not like where this was going. The Rochester vampires generally viewed him in a much more amicable light than their lord, who was called "Ruthless Rochester" behind his back. He'd been hoping that enough of that goodwill could be retained through a trial by his peers, something Gavin did only with vampires he respected. Justus had assumed himself to be on that list. Yet it seemed he no longer held sway with his lord's regard.

"So you will try me privately?" Justus said softly, trying to conceal his fear. Every vampire that Gavin judged on his own was sentenced to a quick death. Although he'd expected as much, the confirmation still filled his blood with ice.

Gavin nodded curtly. "I must. For this situation must be handled as discreetly as possible, for me to save face and protect my position. Also, it is the safest course, as the last thing I want to do is incite a panic from what you've done."

The severity in his eyes filled Justus with guilt. "I am sorry, my lord. You must believe that I never intended for this to happen." He realized he wasn't only worried about Bethany, but for his people as well. "Have I unleashed mobs and hunters upon us all?"

Gavin shook his head. "The humans think the chit is hysterical. The Meads have defected from the country amongst the laughter of their peers, and you had better thank whatever deity you believe in for that."

Hope tinged his soul like golden light. "So you didn't do anything to her?"

"There was no need. I heard that just this day, she was packed off to Derbyshire to stay with a relative." Gavin's thin lips curved in a humorless smile. "Her talk of vampires will not be repeated as Lord Wickshire will already have to work hard to restore his reputation and political career."

"Then no harm was done!" Justus couldn't conceal his relief. "Please, my lord, I beg you for a pardon. I'll resign as second in command and perhaps you may petition the Lord of Derbyshire for me to join his ranks, because—"

Gavin struck him so fast that Justus didn't see the blow coming. His head rocked back and slammed against the granite wall and pain exploded in his mouth where his lip split open.

"What in God's name is the matter with you?" Gavin roared. "You fool! Have you forgotten that you committed the most serious crime among our kind? Just because we were fortunate that no one believed does not negate the severity of the situation. Bloody hell, I hope I never fall in love." He paced in front of Justus with a furious scowl. "I cannot believe you are seriously considering the idea that I'd forget all this and ask the Lord of Derbyshire to take you."

"She is my intended," Justus argued. "Once I Change her, all the damage will be undone."

Gavin sneered as he went on in a mocking voice. "Oh yes, Lord Derbyshire, please allow my former second to join you. Never mind that he told a mortal that he's a vampire and wishes to continue pursuing that very loose-lipped girl and bring her into our ranks so she can know more of our secrets."

When presented like that, it did sound rather impossible. Justus's spirits plummeted. "What's to be done with me then, my lord?"

Gavin turned to Benson and nodded. Justus's heart thudded against his ribs as Benson handed their lord his sword. The sword that had cleaved the hearts and severed the heads of countless other vampires.

"The sentence for revealing oneself to a mortal is death," Gavin said, slapping the flat of the blade against his palm as he continued to pace. Suddenly he stopped and lunged the blade forward.

Justus gasped as he felt the cold, sharp point against his throat. He stared into his lord's eyes, silently pleading for mercy.

Gavin held the sword immobile. "Justus de Wynter, you are stripped of your rank. Benson will now serve as my second in command. And now, I hereby sentence you to…"

Justus closed his eyes, ready to feel the thrust of polished steel into his neck.

"Exile," Gavin finished.

"My lord?" Surely he didn't hear him correctly. Gavin *never* exiled vampires. He despised rogue vampires so much he wouldn't dream of creating another.

"From this moment on, you are no longer a vampire of Rochester. Benson and I will escort you from my territory. If you ever return, I'll have no choice but to kill you." The blade was withdrawn from Justus's skin as Gavin handed it back to Benson. Then the Lord Vampire of Rochester set to personally unlocking Justus's shackles. "I'm well aware of what the others call me. 'Ruthless Rochester.' Aye, such a moniker is more useful than not. Still, I suppose I must show my people that I am capable of mercy."

When he was free, Justus rubbed his raw wrists and blinked at Gavin in disbelief. Life as a rogue would not be easy, but at least he could find Bethany.

Gavin and Benson then seized Justus's arms and led him out of the cell, up the stairs, and out of Darkwood Manor. Justus turned his head to give one last look to the place where he'd spent so many hours of his nights. Memories of countless chess games, hours of conversations about the goings on of the territory and the meanings of their long lives, and yes, moments of laughter flashed through his mind.

All of that was now gone from his reach. All because he'd fallen in love, he'd lost his home, his position, and his best friend.

Yet it would all be worth it once Bethany was back in his arms. It was the only glint of hope that he could cling to.

They walked in silence, Justus sensing other vampires hidden in the shadows, keeping their distance, but still following to witness his fall from grace. He didn't care what they thought.

But once Gavin and Benson led him to the edge of Rochester's territory, a lump formed in Justus's throat. He'd never see Gavin again.

Gavin grasped his shoulders, giving them a slight squeeze that may have been affectionate. "Goodbye, my friend. Please, don't make me have to kill you."

Justus nodded. "Thank you for sparing me."

"Do not thank me," Gavin said through clenched teeth. "Most likely I handed you an extended death sentence. You'll have to utilize every speck of your cleverness to survive."

"I know," Justus said. But survive he would. For Bethany. He'd heard that the Americas had countless cities and villages without vampires. They could build a new life there. Maybe Justus could even become Lord of his own city. He sighed and bowed before his lord one last time. "Goodbye, Gavin."

Then he was off as fast as his depleted body could carry him.

His journey to Derbyshire was worse than expected. Had every Lord Vampire of every village and borough on the way doubled their patrols? It seemed he could not find a meal or a place to rest without being chased by snarling vampires.

The places he slept were shoddy and dangerous. On the first day, the sunlight had crept into the abandoned cellar he'd hidden in and burned his arm. Starving from not having fed last night, and nerves rattled from constantly looking over his shoulder for pursuit, Justus hardly slept. Instead, the reality of his new existence beat on him like a hammer. He'd thought rogues were amoral parasites, invading territories and hunting grounds out of pure malice and greed. Instead, it seemed like they were chased from land to land because they had no choice if they wanted to live. God, he prayed he could get himself and Bethany safe passage to the Americas within the next two nights, for he did not know if he could fend off the vampires who would try to arrest him with a human in tow.

As the sun sank from the sky, Justus nearly wept with relief to smell a human passing his hiding place. With predatory stealth, he emerged from the cellar and seized the farmer. Drinking deep, strength once more returned to Justus's body. Releasing the farmer from his trance, a pang of guilt pierced him as the mortal swayed from losing too much blood. Though he longed to flee from the area, his conscience forced him to escort the man to his home. At least no vampire would dare attack him in front of a human.

Once he saw the farmer home safe, Justus utilized the strength from his feeding to run to Derbyshire in a burst of speed.

Although he longed to seek out Bethany at once, he knew if he strolled openly into the territory that he'd be set upon at once by the local vampires. Keeping to the shadows, he carefully made his way through the area, opening his senses to detect the Derbyshire vampires and remain downwind from them.

After making his way into the township, he came across a pub where there were no vampires around. In his experience, these sorts of establishments to be the best places to gather information. The barkeep and patrons ceased their chatter and stared as he approached the carved mahogany bar. Justus was used to such stares because of his dark red hair. However, due to his disheveled appearance and his being a stranger, people looked longer than was polite.

Yet once the barkeep saw his coin and a small glass of port was placed before him, people returned to their conversations. Justus cursed under his breath as he realized that his money would soon run out. All of his investments and money were banked with Gavin, who had likely seized everything as was his right as Lord Vampire.

He'd worry about that later. His first priority was locating Bethany. God, he was a fool not to have Marked her when he'd had the chance. He'd intended on doing so as soon as their betrothal contract was signed.

As he sipped his port and listened to the conversations around him, Justus's heart sank as he heard no talk of Lord Wickshire, or even of a family receiving a lengthy visit from a relation. One would think that the appearance of a member of the Quality who was prominent in politics would set tongues to wagging. And visitors to noble families always merited speculations and gossip.

Even after he eased himself into a few conversations, he found that no one had heard anything of Lord Wickshire coming to Derbyshire. And the one person who was acquainted with him swore that he had no relatives in the area.

With a sinking heart, Justus finished his port and left the pub. He spent the next week dodging vampires and searching out information, but found nothing. Bethany was not in Derbyshire. She had no relatives here.

Justus bit back a roar as his fingers dug into the marble crypt in which he sought refuge for the day. Gavin had lied to him, most likely to get Justus to complacently leave Rochester while he either used his power to persuade the Meads to leave the country, or worse, that he arranged an "accident" to befall them, the one loophole in the law forbidding vampires to kill mortals. You could not drain them to death, but you could push one off a cliff if you were so inclined.

Pulling the locket from beneath his shirt, Justus opened it and gazed at the picture of his love. "Bethany," he whispered. "I'll find you, I swear. And if you are indeed lost to me, I vow I will avenge you."

Chapter Fifteen

Bethany's eyes drifted open just as the carriage came to a halt. Where were they stopping this time? Her head swam as she struggled to sit up. Her parents had kept her in a drugged haze for this journey which was so long that she had no idea how many days had passed. She wished she knew where they were taking her, but every time she presumed to ask, her father would order a footman to hold her down while he would force more of that vile medicine down her throat.

Peering out the carriage window, Bethany gasped as she saw that they'd stopped in front of a massive red brick structure, redolent with gothic arches topped with gargoyles, and surrounded by wrought iron fencing.

The sun was so bright it hurt her eyes, which had grown sensitive from her long hours of sleeping in the carriage. Usually they'd stopped at night to rest the horses and sleep at an inn. This was no inn.

Her mother tapped her shoulder. "Come along," she said in a faraway voice.

A footman handed Bethany out and she noticed that her knee no longer pained her. Not that it mattered anymore. This place did not look like there would be much dancing.

Her father had already marched up to the entrance where three men met him. One man spoke with her father in hushed, yet animated tones, darting Bethany lingering glances which made her increasingly uncomfortable. The other two stood in stony silence with their arms folded like dour sentries.

As her mother led her up the walk, one man adjusted his spectacles, smoothed his brown tweed overcoat and gave her a look that was nothing short of patronizing.

"Miss Mead," he said with a sharp-toothed smile. "I'm Doctor Keene. Your father tells me that you believe in vampires."

She shook her head. "I do not. There was a mistake."

"Now, now." His smile grew more sickly sweet. "I can always tell when someone lies. It's a gift of mine. But no matter, we'll have plenty of time to get to the bottom of this delusion. Come, let me show you your room."

Doctor... room... delusion. Bethany gasped as she realized where they were. She whirled to face her parents in stunned outrage. "You've had me committed to an asylum?"

Her father nodded curtly. "I cannot have a madwoman about while I salvage my reputation and political career."

Her mother squeezed her hand. "You're ill, my dear. Here you can get well."

"No!" Bethany wrenched away from her grip. "I am *not* mad!"

Cecily shook her head. "Darling, you imagined a courtship and marriage proposal that never happened."

"It *did* happen!" Bethany would hold her tongue about Justus being a vampire, but she refused to deny their love. Her breath came in sharp pants as she fought to hold back tears of despair. "Something must have happened to Lord de Wynter. Maybe Lord Tench did something to keep him away!"

Her father heaved a theatrical sigh and turned to Doctor Keene. "You see what I have been subjected to."

"Oh yes." The doctor nodded solemnly. "A classic case of hysteria combined with a desire so consuming that it has become a fantasy. And you say your mother suffered from a similar condition?"

"Yes," Lord Wiltshire said. "Ever since her infant daughter died only two weeks after she was born. Mother then claimed she could speak to angels, and Father had to send her here. I assume it is a hereditary condition."

"As a matter of fact, it is indeed. Usually passed through the female line." Doctor Keene smoothed his overcoat once more. "I wish we had time to discuss it in further detail. Do you truly have to leave so soon?"

"We must. I have a meeting with my solicitor in London." Father turned and walked back to the carriage. "Goodbye, daughter," he said over his shoulder.

Bethany flinched at such a cold parting, wondering what had happened to the man who used to dandle her on his knee and read to her.

Her mother was slightly warmer, studying Bethany's face as if committing her visage to memory. "This is best for you now. Goodbye for now, my dearest. I promise I will write to you."

Bethany hardly felt her mother's stiff embrace as her body went numb with shock. "No!" she cried again as Lady Wiltshire made her way to the carriage. "You cannot leave me here!"

She lunged to follow, but her arms were seized and wrenched back by the men who'd come out with Doctor Keene.

The doctor tsked behind her. "You mustn't become overwrought. You will be comfortable here. Morningside is the best asylum in all of England. Your parents must love you very much to bring you here."

"Love me?" she repeated incredulously. "They just abandoned me here!"

"For your own good." The doctor opened the carved oak door with an alarmingly large lock and gestured for the men to bring her inside. "You'll come to like it. In fact, I'm certain you will make new friends by week's end."

Tears pricked the back of Bethany's eyes as the guards hauled her up a flight of stairs and down a long hallway full of doors. The doctor opened one near the end and the men delivered her into a room that was cozy enough, yet the unadorned walls covered with yellow damask wallpaper gave her a chill for some inexplicable reason. The men deposited her onto a narrow tester bed and thankfully released her.

"This will be your room for your stay," Doctor Keene said. "Your trunk will be brought in shortly and I will have tea sent up. Then you and I will have a nice little chat about this beau of yours." With that, he and his assistants left the room.

The click of the lock echoed in her heart.

Bethany lay back on the bed and stared at the lemon colored ceiling, her mind racing with horror at what was happening. Was this all a terrible dream? She prayed to awaken in her own bed. For Justus to come calling as planned and ask for her hand.

Closing her eyes, she relived his kiss. How soft his lips felt upon hers. How tenderly he held her in his arms.

Too soon, the door of her new room opened and the men who'd dragged her up here brought in her trunk. The doctor followed, a maid at his side carrying a tea tray.

After the tea was poured, Doctor Keene regarded her over the rim of his cup as if she were an interesting species of insect. "Tell me about this vampire you thought you'd marry."

"His name is Viscount de Wynter and of course I do not believe he is a vampire," Bethany said, regretting more than ever voicing Justus's secret. "I'd fallen from my horse that day and the laudanum made me say odd things."

"I've never in my years encountered a patient who reacted quite that way from laudanum," Doctor Keene eyed her through his spectacles. "But what of this marriage proposal you were to receive?"

"That *was* real," she insisted, fingers playing about the edges of her tea cup.

"Your father said the man never paid you a single call."

Frustration twisted her insides. She clearly couldn't tell him why. "We danced and conversed at balls, suppers, and musicales," she explained. "And he *was* going to call on me to ask my father for my hand, but something must have happened to delay him." What had happened to Justus that night? The constant worry gnawed at her like a dog with a piece of rawhide. Had some sort of danger befallen him? Or had he simply changed his mind and decided not to shackle himself to a silly human girl?

Doctor Keene regarded her with a pitying stare. "Many a young lady such as yourself have fallen for the charms of unscrupulous men and believed them to have noble intentions. Perhaps your calling him a vampire was a metaphor of sorts for his predatory nature." Suddenly he frowned. "You haven't tasted your tea."

She raised a brow. "The last time I had tea, it was drugged by my own mother."

"You think I'd drug you? Fascinating." The doctor adjusted his spectacles. "Although I will indeed administer medicine for when you need it, I assure you I will not use deceptive means to do so. I have a soothing tonic that you will have after supper, but it will not be hidden in your food or drink. I run an honest establishment."

Bethany took a cautious sip, and found that it tasted satisfactory, with no bitter aftertaste of laudanum.

Keene leaned forward, continuing to dissect her with his eyes. "Now tell me, Miss Mead, do you ever see or hear things that are not there?"

Her father's words echoed in her memory. "*Mother claimed to see and speak to angels.*" She shivered. "I cannot say that I have. I am weary from my journey, Doctor. Would you mind if I follow your advice and rest?" If she had to endure his silly interrogations for a moment longer, she vowed she would scream.

"Of course, Miss Mead." He rose from the chair. "And when you're feeling refreshed, I will introduce you to the other ladies in the wing before supper." He then paused at the door. "My advice is to forget about the man who led you astray and do your best to find comfort here."

Bethany nodded as she handed the maid her cup, but only because that was the expected response. She lay back on her bed, staring at that hideous wallpaper.

She would never forget Justus. Even now, her heart ached for him, a gaping hole that only he could fill.

"He will find me," she whispered, closing her eyes against the garish yellow surrounding her. "Justus *will* come for me."

But after four long years of waiting, she eventually accepted the fact that she'd imagined it all. Vampires weren't real, and Justus was only a rake, taking advantage of her. Her parents' abandonment was only further salt on the gaping wound of her heart.

And after four *more* years in a gray cell in the pauper's wing, Bethany even missed her ugly yellow room. At least then there was color.

Chapter Sixteen

Manchester, 1825

Justus stood on the edge of an outcropping beside a gargoyle and stared through the bars of the dank cell of the asylum. His heart ached with agony at seeing his love crumpled on the cold stone floor from fainting at the sight of him.

His breath remained frozen in his lungs until she stirred with a whimper.

"Bethany!" he whispered as loud as he dared. "Are you alright?" If she'd injured herself in her fall, he didn't know if he could bear it.

Groaning, she slowly shuffled to her feet, eyeing him fearfully.

What kind of malicious world was this to reduce her to such a weak and subdued state? Yes, Justus had suffered from his years as a rogue, but he had deserved it. Bethany did not deserve this.

She was so thin and frail in her rough-spun frock. Her eyes were dilated and glazed like an opium addict's, and she shook like a willow in a storm. Her once lush, waist-length golden hair was chopped to shoulder length and hung dull and listless around her thinned face.

Eight years since he'd last laid eyes on the love of his life, and he hardly recognized her. But it was her, of that he had no doubt. Under the reek of terror and old sweat, he detected her unique scent that haunted his dreams since their first dance. But it was her words that chilled him the most.

"You're not real," she whispered once more, slowly backing away to her shoddy cot.

He reached through the bars, longing to feel her touch once more, but she was already too far from his grasp. "I *am* real," he insisted. "Bethany, please, believe me. I've been searching for you all these years, never giving up, even when for some time I had reason the believe you were dead."

She shook her head, eyes wide and fearful. "Vampires aren't real. Doctor Keene says so."

He sighed. "Doctors are among the foremost people who are not supposed to believe in us, but I assure you, I am quite real." Another spear of pain stabbed his chest. "Don't you remember the night I told you what I am? Don't you remember my bite? The way we ran together?"

"It was a dream," she protested stubbornly. But a flash of her old spirit glinted in her blue eyes.

"*Not* a dream," he said, fixing her with a firm stare. Reaching into his shirt, he withdrew the locket she'd given him. "Look." He opened the locket, revealing her miniature. "Since the night you gave this to me, I've never taken it off." Well, except for the time the chain broke and Gavin had taken it, but he'd confess that folly later.

Bethany studied the locket, a measure of the feral light in her eyes dimmed as her brows creased in speculation.

"Come here." He struggled to maintain a note of command, rather than a desperate plea. "Take my hand once more, only, please do not faint again. Feel that I am real."

Still shivering, Bethany crossed her arms over her breasts as she took a deep, shuddering breath and slowly walked towards him. "Are you going to bite me again?" she asked with a touch of her inquisitiveness that he'd fallen in love with.

"Good God, no!" He couldn't hide his horror at the idea. "You are far too weak and malnourished for that." Attempting some semblance of humor, he added, "Besides, I cannot fit my head through the bars. Now, please, take my hand." Reaching out once more, he was gratified to see her lips twitch with a hint of a smile.

He sighed in pleasure as her warm fingers intertwined with his. Her other hand grasped the locket around his neck, her thumb rubbing the well worn gold filigree.

"Justus," she said softly. "I cannot believe you are here. For years I waited for you. I'd given up." Her gaze held his, with wonder echoing his own. "I was finally convinced that you weren't real, that the night we met in the orchard was nothing but a delusional fantasy. That I was truly mad. But here you are. Very real." Her eyes filled with tears, then narrowed. She jerked her hand from his grasp and shuffled backward. "Why didn't you come for me sooner? I've been trapped in this horrid place for eight years!"

"I was arrested the night I was to come ask for your hand. My lord had heard that you'd told your betrothed that I was a vampire." The old pain rose to the surface. "Why didn't you tell me you were betrothed? And why did you reveal my secret when you'd made a solemn vow not to do so?"

"I didn't know I was betrothed until that day!" she protested, lower lip quivering as if she were on the verge of tears. "And I did not mean to breathe a word about your secret. It's just that I'd fallen from my horse and injured my knee. The laudanum made me voice my thoughts aloud."

"You fell?" His heart slammed against his ribs. She could have broken her neck. "Are you alright?"

She chuckled. "Physically, yes. It was only a sprain. But the medicine I was given due to said injury has done untold damage. I was declared a lunatic, rejected by my own mother and father, and you were arrested, you say? For what I said in my drugged haze?" Aching sympathy pooled in her large blue eyes. "What became of you then? Did you escape?"

He shook his head. "The penalty of revealing oneself to a mortal is death." Her sharp intake of breath made him long to pull her into his arms. "But my lord had mercy on me and sentenced me to exile instead. I'd heard word that you'd been taken to Derbyshire to stay with a relative…"

Bethany snorted. "That's what mother and father told everyone. To avoid gossip for where they really took me."

Justus cursed his own stupidity. Of course Lord Wickshire would be averse to making it public knowledge that he'd packed his daughter off to an asylum. "I'd thought that the Lord Vampire of Rochester had you killed and had lied to get me away before he did the deed." He attempted a pathetic justification for his reasoning. "Although it is forbidden to kill mortals, there are loopholes. So I temporarily abandoned my search and embarked on a foolish quest for vengeance that got other vampires killed. One deservedly so, but that's not the point. Their blood is on my hands, and all for naught."

Her soft warm hands covered his. "What happened?"

"My first years as a rogue vampire were miserable. To be honest, it is still not an easy life. I am constantly on the run, hiding from patrols of vampires who specifically hunt rogues. Securing meals and shelter are endless challenges. I blamed my lord for inflicting this suffering upon me, for without you, all I had left to hold onto was hatred." The confession came tumbling out, like leaching an infection from an inflamed wound. "I gathered together a band of rogues, intent on making the Lord of Rochester suffer as I've suffered. Opportunity struck when at last, he fell in love." And Justus knew all too well how foolish and desperate love could make a man. "I tried to cast suspicion on his bride so the Elders would strip him from his rank and exile him. Instead, my actions lured a Hunter to Rochester, which resulted in the deaths of two vampires. One of mine and one of his. Still, I was determined on vengeance. I kidnapped Rochester's bride and held her hostage in exchange for a full pardon and for him to step down as Lord Vampire. And I was going to take his love away from him, to deprive him of her as he'd deprived you of me." A bitter smile contorted his lips at the memory of the debacle he'd wrought. "Rochester offered a compromise. If I'd return his bride, I'd receive my pardon and your location, for his spies had determined that you were brought to Manchester, but not that you'd been committed. Lord knows how he managed to come by that information, but he's always been a master of knowing everything about everyone." And once upon a time, Justus had been the best of Gavin's spies. Yet it seemed that the vampire who'd been his best of friends was doing just fine without him. Justus sighed and continued. "He should have killed me for the havoc and danger I brought to his land. Instead, he offered me a pardon, which I declined the moment he told me where you were, for if I'd accepted his offer

I would have had to remain in Rochester under probation and would have been forbidden to go after you."

Bethany stroked his knuckles with excruciating gentleness. "You gave up a chance to end your misery for me?"

He nodded. "I never stopped loving you. And my guilt will never abate for giving up my search for you in favor of vengeance." His shoulders slumped. "I cannot fathom how to ask you to forgive me."

She looked down at her feet covered in worn stockings. "After all you've told me, I do not know when I shall be able to contemplate forgiving you. But you said you would take me from this place. Right now, that is all I wish."

"Oh, I will get you out of this horrid cell," he growled. "But alas, I cannot do so tonight."

Her chin jerked up so fast that her hair flew up around her shoulders like a cloud. "Why not?"

"If I tear these bars from the stone, people will hear." His fists clenched on the iron bars with impotent fury. He could easily wrest them free from the red brick, but it would make a dreadful racket. "Furthermore, the Manchester vampires will know I'm in their lands. I am still a rogue, so if they find me, they will capture or kill me."

"Heavens! You are still in danger," she gasped. For a moment she looked as if she would object to his assistance, then a mixture of resolution and fear hardened her features. "When will you secure my release then?"

"As soon as possible," he vowed. "I will find something to pry these bars free, then we will climb down and flee the area."

"Where will we go?" she asked.

He paused as the magnitude and potential danger of such a trek impressed upon his consciousness. "Cornwall."

Bethany gasped. "Cornwall? Why so far away?"

"I've heard word that the Lord of Cornwall often allows rogues and miscreants to take shelter with him, even become citizens." Hope infused his words. To be able to stop running and hiding. To have a shelter to take refuge in for the day. A place to call home, a purpose. And best of all, to have Bethany in his arms. Yet there was no guarantee that the Earl of Deveril would grant him mercy. "And if we cannot settle in Cornwall, then we will find a ship bound for the Americas."

"So far away," she breathed. Then she squeezed his hand so tightly that he could feel a shiver wrack her body. "But we must leave soon!"

The urgency in her voice filled him with unease. "Why the rush? I understand that you are miserable here, yet you sound as if there is some pressing matter."

"Greeves," she said with such terror that he longed to tear through the window and pull her into his arms. "He guards the female ward at night and does atrocious things to the patients. So far, Doctor Keene has kept me safe from his attentions, even though he refuses to believe me, but the doctor is going on holiday at week's end. And Greeves has promised to take advantage of that fact."

Justus bared his fangs and growled. "He means to violate you?" He jerked on the bars of her window so hard that the iron shrieked. "I'll kill him!"

Bethany nodded. "Though I do indeed wish him dead, and I do not care if that makes me a deplorable person, won't you attract suspicion if you do him in?"

His growl deepened. "Bloody hell, you're right. I apologize for cursing in front of you."

She laughed. "Aside from the scandalous reading material you've loaned me, I've heard my fill of impolite language during my stay. The woman next to me often has outbursts where the most clever obscenities pour from her like a volcanic eruption."

Her words did not amuse him. Instead, he'd been reminded that she'd spent the last eight years locked up with real lunatics. She could have been hurt.

Suddenly, a scent reached his nostrils, one that made dread pool in his belly. Manchester vampires. The lord's second among them. Justus had spied upon them and studied their movements ever since he came here to search for Bethany.

"I have to go," he whispered. "I will return tomorrow after sunset."

"But Justus..." she protested.

Time ran out. Just as the Manchester vampires neared the grounds of the asylum, Justus leapt across the parapet to another gargoyle downwind from them and scrambled behind it before he was in eyeshot.

Their voices reached his sensitive ears, even though they were still quite some distance away.

"I swear, Chester, I smelled a rogue nearby," one said.

"And I'm telling you, I didn't smell anything, Carl," the vampire who must be Chester replied. "I'm forty years older than you, so my senses are sharper." Their footsteps drew closer until Justus heard one of them tap the wrought iron gate. "Besides, what would one be doing around here? The only prey around is locked in the madhouse, where one can't sink their fangs into them. And why would anyone want to? I don't want to be infected by their madness."

Carl laughed. "Our kind cannot catch any illness. And I don't believe insanity is contagious anyway. But I insist that I smelled something. And Emily told me she saw a strange vampire two nights ago. A male, with hair as red as blood."

"Two nights ago?" Chester's voice went thick with mockery. "He'd be long gone by now. Frank or Rodney would have chased him away if he didn't have the sense to take off on his own. And I still say no vampire would have any business hanging about a place like this."

Justus nodded. *Yes, let them avoid this place.*

"But what if it's a mad vampire? I hear many rogues are cracked." Their voices faded as their argument continued.

Justus waited several minutes before climbing down the building. If the Manchester vampires caught him breaking Bethany out of the asylum, who knew what they would do? Keeping his senses open for others, he made his way to a set of hovels on the outskirts of the village. He'd never seen any of the Manchester vampires around this area, either because it was just past their borders, or they didn't care about the poverty stricken mortals who eked a living out of the barely sustainable soil.

Normally, Justus despised feeding on the poor. They were already malnourished as it was, and to weaken them further rattled his conscience. But the vicar of this impoverished area was a corrupt, greedy sod who leeched off the labors of the beleaguered folk. Justus had been preying on him almost every night and if the man succumbed to death from blood loss, he wouldn't feel so much as a twinge of remorse.

He found the vicar still awake, drinking a jug of ale and flipping through a dog-eared book of erotic illustrations. The lecherous wastrel did that often. Justus only hoped he'd arrived before the vicar became fully engrossed in the drawings. That was a sight he never wanted to see again.

Tapping on the window, he captured the vicar's gaze the moment the man looked up. In his trance, the vicar rose from the table and approached the window like an obedient pup. The moment he opened the shutters, Justus seized him and sank his fangs into his neck. He drank deeply this time, needing all the strength he could muster for Bethany's rescue.

Once the vicar was released and sent to his bed, Justus wove through the pitiful cluster of farms, looking for something that could help him break into Bethany's cell. A hammer and chisel would be ideal, but it would make more sustained noise than if he simply tore the bars free with his bare hands. Though, to be truthful, for all of his brash talk, he wasn't certain he was capable of such a feat. The bars were thick and deeply embedded in the red brick.

After hours of searching various barns and sheds, he at last found something that might suffice. And just in time, for the sky was turning gray with the coming dawn. Justus made his way back to the crypt in family plot behind a dilapidated manor house that belonged to the lord of the poor village. He knew better than to seek refuge in the public cemeteries. In all territories, such areas were reserved for the county's poorest vampires.

Bethany was right. He needed to secure her freedom and take them away from here as quickly as possible. Saints above, it had been agony to leave her after finally setting eyes upon her at last. Especially because the last time he parted from her, she was lost to him for eight years. Most vampires his age or older scoffed at such a short amount of time, thinking eight years was nothing but a blink of the eye, yet for Justus, those years had dragged on like decades of torture.

If he lost Bethany again after so many years of searching, he'd go mad. Heart pulsing with mingled hope and worry, Justus lay down on the stone slab amidst ancient crumbling skulls and bone dust, counting the endless minutes before the sun would relieve him from this dismal tomb and he'd be with his Bethany at last.

Chapter Seventeen

The minutes passed like eons for Bethany. And at least once an hour, she had to pinch herself to be sure she wasn't dreaming. She wasn't mad after all. Vampires *were* real, and Justus had come for her at last. She would be free from this horrid place.

Knowing that her time imprisoned in Morningside was coming to an end made the wait excruciatingly painful. It seemed her anxiousness was infectious, for her fellow patients seemed especially unruly this day. Carol, who lived in the cell beside hers, erupted into a stream of curses at the breakfast table, which in turn had made Bess scream until both had to be taken away. Susan, a woman who alternated between episodes of violence and periods of catatonia suddenly flung her bowl of porridge into Bethany's face.

Normally, this would have been quite vexing, but today Bethany was almost pleased, for that meant she could have a bath and be clean for when Justus came. She didn't even mind when the nurse scrubbed her skin raw with caustic soap and a rough bristled brush.

The nurse frowned as she rinsed Bethany's hair. "We'll have to shave you lot again soon before the lice come. I'll recommend that we do so before the good doctor departs for his holiday."

Bethany bit back a triumphant smirk. When Justus freed her, she'd never be shaved again. As it was, her once waist-length mass of golden curls that he'd so loved was reduced to a dulled mess that coiled about her shoulders. Had he been disappointed to see her hair thus?

It didn't matter. It would grow back and they'd finally be together.

When her bath was finished, Bethany was led back downstairs to walk the garden with Doctor Keene and the more well-behaved women.

Usually, Bethany savored her brief periods outdoors, feeling the sun on her face and breathing the fresh country air, but today she lamented that reflection time in the garden meant that it was only mid-afternoon. Even worse, it was May, which meant the days were growing ever longer.

Eleanor touched her arm as Bethany stared at the thorns on a rose bush, thinking of Justus's fangs. "You've been quiet today. Are you well?"

"Oh yes," Bethany nodded quickly. The last thing she needed was to be sent to the infirmary. Eleanor was notorious for being convinced that every person she spoke to was on the verge of being stricken with the plague. "I am only wondering when these will be in full bloom."

"I dread the day," Eleanor said with pinched expression. "Flowers make me sneeze dreadfully."

Doctor Keene droned on about rest and reflection, gazing at each of his patients in turn. Whenever his eyes landed on Bethany, she fought to maintain composure. Surely she was imagining that his attention remained fixed on her longer than the others.

But once they filed back inside the asylum, the doctor pulled her aside. "I can't help but notice that you appear flushed, Miss Mead. Are you feeling overstimulated?"

"Oh, no, Doctor." Bethany fought to keep her voice level. "I am very calm." If he thought otherwise, he would drug her with his tonic, or worse, put her in the quiet room, where Justus couldn't get to her.

He eyed her with a skeptical frown, then thankfully moved on to scrutinize another woman before he escorted them back inside for a prescribed nap. Bethany knew she should sleep now to rest for the night's escape, but her mind swirled with memories of her encounter with Justus, and thoughts of the future.

He'd looked exactly as he had when she'd last seen him, with his pale chiseled features, faint freckles, and beautiful mane of hair. Though he'd told her that vampires did not age, seeing the evidence was another thing entirely. But she'd certainly aged. What had Justus thought to see her now, no longer a young debutante of seventeen, but a spinster of five and twenty?

How could he even want her now?

Yet tenderness had shone from his eyes beneath the sorrow to see her imprisoned, and his touch on her hands had been affectionate. The sight of the locket she'd given him with the fervent declaration that he'd never taken it off implied devotion. Did he still wish to wed her? *Could* they even marry with her being an escaped madwoman, and he an exiled vampire?

As the light streaming in from the window dimmed, Bethany stared out into the dusk, waiting with heart-pounding urgency. Footsteps echoed in the corridor, so she quickly darted back to her bed, scrambled under the covers, and feigned sleep.

She heard someone pause in front of her cell, but did not dare move or open her eyes to see whether it was Greeves or the doctor. After countless interminable moments, whoever was watching her walked away. She remained still, eyes squeezed shut moments after the footsteps faded.

Worry crawled up her spine. What if she'd imagined Justus last night? She had been drugged with the awful tonic.

No. She shook her head. The rough fabric of her thin pillow scratched her cheek. She'd been subjected to Keene's tonic many times over the years, and never imagined something so real, not even under the influence of a large dose, much less the teaspoon she'd been given last night. Still, memories of her endless wait for him that fateful night eight years ago relentlessly haunted her. What if he decided not to come? What if he'd been toying with her all this time?

What if...

"Bethany." Justus's whisper flowed over her like a caress.

Her eyes snapped open. "Justus?" She bolted up from the bed and there he was.

Now, on her second time setting eyes upon him, Bethany noticed a few alarming details that hadn't caught her attention the night before. Firstly, Justus was much paler than she remembered. In fact, he appeared somewhat sickly. Secondly, his clothes were ragged and patched, the complete antithesis of his former elegant garb. The chain of the locket he wore was tarnished.

She remembered his talk last night of being constantly on the run, being hunted by other vampires with no place to call home. Her heart clenched with sympathy. He'd suffered as much as she had. The difference was that while her suffering would abate when she was freed from the asylum, his situation would remain unchanged. In fact, it may become more complicated, with her in tow. What if she slowed him down?

For a moment she considered asking Justus to leave her here so he could be safer. But three things stopped her from doing so. First, his talk of Cornwall and the Americas implied that he had a plan. Second, she knew if she denied this chance at freedom, she'd regret it.

Third: the potent longing in his eyes as he looked at her tugged at her heart even more intently than before.

God help her, for all of her talk of reluctance to forgive him, her love for him refused to die.

"Will you break me loose tonight?" she asked, struggling to maintain sensibility.

He shook his head and held up an object that resembled an oversized corkscrew. "This will take some time to drill through the brick to free the bars." At her indrawn breath, his brows lowered. "But I will get you out before week's end. This I promise you."

She breathed out in relief and walked to the window. Reaching through the bars, she placed her hand over his. "Thank you, for coming for me at last."

His features softened for a moment before hardening once more. "You never should have been in this place." He stroked her hand, feather light, making heat swirl in her belly. "You were supposed to be my betrothed, waiting safely until you came of age and I would return to wed you."

"When you returned?" Bethany repeated with a frown. "What do you mean?"

"According to vampire law, it is forbidden to Change minors," Justus said as he dug the tip of his tool in the mortar of a stone beneath one of the window bars. "I did not know that until I asked my lord for permission to make you my bride. He nearly denied me, but then decided that I could secure our engagement and leave Rochester until your twenty-first birthday, when I would return to claim you." His lips turned down in a frown. "That is, until he'd discovered that I'd told you my secret."

She'd just passed her twenty-fifth birthday. Agony roared through her soul as Bethany closed her eyes and imagined what it would have been like to have waited for him for four years instead of eight. To have done that waiting in the comfort of her home, with her mother and father. To wake up on her twenty-first birthday preparing for her wedding day, rather than a breakfast of gray porridge and a day of captivity.

The sound of metal chipping away stone brought her back to the present. It did no good to dwell on what couldn't be changed. But oh, how different things could have been if she hadn't fallen from her horse. Or if the laudanum had not affected her so. "Who is the Lord Vampire of Rochester?" she asked to deflect from her grief.

Justus shook his head, locks of crimson hair sweeping his cheeks. "That I cannot tell you until you are one of us. I've endangered him enough."

Bethany froze. When she was a young girl, full of dreams and fantasies, she'd been willing to do anything to be with the man she loved, even if it meant becoming a creature who had to drink blood to survive and could never see the sun.

Now that she was older, her dreams dashed to pieces, cold practicality reared its head. Did she want to live as Justus did, outcast and having to hide from both humans and vampires more powerful than she?

Closing her eyes, she took a deep breath. She could ponder that later. Right now, her primary concern was escaping Morningside.

"Very well," she said. "No talk of vampires. How will you get me down once the bars are free?" He was making good progress, several inches gouged away from the base of the first bar.

"I'll carry you," he replied as casually as if he spoke of helping her down from a horse.

"Carry me?" She peered over his shoulder and her stomach lurched at the sight of what must be at least a fifty meter drop.

Justus nodded. "Yes. I have the strength." His eyes searched hers, full of concern. "Don't be frightened. I would never drop you." He reached through the bars and cupped her cheek, stroking his thumb over her skin. She shivered once more, though not from the cold. His lips curved in that rakish smile she'd fallen in love with so long ago. "Now, let's talk of something other than taking a tumble. Have you read any good books over the years?"

Bethany couldn't hold back her laughter. "Despite the doctor's fervent efforts to stop me, yes. A few of the women in the ward smuggle novels to me." She sighed. "No Chaucer, unfortunately, but I absolutely adore Allan Winthrop's gothic novels."

This time, it was Justus who laughed. "You've been reading Alan Winthrop?"

She raised a brow. "Why is that so amusing? Is it because of the rumors that the author is really a duchess?"

"Oh, she is indeed, but that's not why…" He shook his head and chiseled away more stone. "I shall have to explain later. At any rate, yes, I've read the duchess's novels. A very talented authoress for one so young. Reading has been difficult for me as well. One cannot have a library when constantly traveling."

They talked as he worked, exchanging stories of their various struggles to secure worthwhile reading material. When the conversation drifted to books they'd particularly enjoyed, the years fell away, and it felt like they'd never been parted.

As if voicing her thoughts aloud, Justus halted with his telling her of Voltaire and smiled. "This is what I've been searching for all these years. Your taste and wit remain sharp." He reached through the bars and brushed a lock of her hair behind her ear. "And impossibly, you've grown even more beautiful."

He bent his head and Bethany rose up on her toes and leaned forward, her heart pounding with excitement. He was going to kiss her again!

But the moment their lips touched, Justus broke away. Bethany opened her mouth to ask what was wrong just as the privacy panel of her cell door slid open.

She turned to dart back to her bed, but Doctor Keene strode in and held up a hand. "Miss Mead, I have heard the most troubling things about you."

Bethany took a shaky step backward, not daring to look at the window. Had Keene seen Justus? "What do you mean, Doctor?" she asked, a tremor creeping into her voice.

"Greeves said he heard you laughing and talking to yourself in strange voices," Keene replied as Greeves entered behind him, grinning at her like a malicious jester.

The doctor withdrew his stethoscope from his bag and placed it below her collarbone. As he listened to her pounding heart, she glanced over his shoulder at the window. The tension in her shoulders eased as she saw that Justus was gone from view.

"And your heart rate is accelerated." Keene made a clucking sound in the back of his throat. "This is most alarming. Were you imagining a voice speaking with you?"

She shook her head rapidly. "I was only lonely."

"But that laughter was abnormal, I'm told. Deep, as if you were pretending to be a man."

Bethany glared at the doctor and the guard. Damn them for intruding when she was on the verge of freedom. "Perhaps it is Greeves who is imagining things."

Greeves spat. "I am not the loony here, you are."

A low growl sounded from the window, but the men in her cell didn't hear as they were too occupied voicing assumptions on her mental state. Keene with his usual pedantic lectures, Greeves with more crude sentiments.

"Either way, it is clear that you are overwrought," the doctor finished. "I'm afraid I have no choice but to take you to the quiet room for a spell. That way all that is stimulating you will be suppressed."

"No!" she shouted. If she went to the quiet room, Justus couldn't get to her. "Please, no! I only need some rest."

Doctor Keene looked at Greeves as emitted a tragic sigh. "It is as you say. She is in complete hysterics. Now if you'll assist me?"

Bethany tried to lunge away, but Greeves and Keene seized her by the arms and hauled her out of the cell. For the first time in years, she kicked, struggled, and screamed at the top of her lungs. Perhaps Justus could then hear the direction she was going. Or perhaps her heart was merely breaking at being so close to her dreams being fulfilled only to have them cruelly torn from her grasp.

When Doctor Keene released her to unlock the door of the quiet room, Bethany broke free and ran down the corridor. If she could only make it down the stairs and out the front door, Justus could meet her in the lawn and carry her off with his preternatural speed.

"Justus!" she shouted, hoping he could still hear her. "Justus!"

As she rounded the corner, she crashed headlong into Nurse Bronson. The nurse emitted a garbled cry as they tumbled to the floor.

Before Bethany could utter an apology, her arms were seized and she was roughly yanked to her feet and dragged back down the corridor to the quiet room. Nurse Bronson followed behind with the enormous ring of clanking keys, her lips clamped in a severe frown.

Bethany struggled and called out Justus's name, but it was all in vain. As the nurse unlocked the door, a sharp needle pierced the tender flesh of the crook of her arm.

"No," she whispered, horrified. Some of the patients received injections to subdue them when they grew unruly, but Bethany had never been subjected to one. She was only given Keene's tonic.

A wave of dizziness buckled her knees and her jaw went slack as she tried to call out. Only a feeble moan emerged, and to her humiliation, a stream of spittle trickled down her chin. Greeves squeezed her bosom painfully before shoving her into the dark, padded cell.

Keene looked down at her with quizzical, pitying eyes. "I'll look in on you before I depart for my holiday. In the meantime, you must strive to calm yourself."

As the door slid shut, She heard Greeves ask the doctor, "What do you suppose she meant when she was screaming for justice? Does she imagine she's been subjected to some criminal mistreatment? This lot is pampered like spoilt children, I say."

Keene sighed. "Who can fathom what goes on in the minds of the insane? We can only do our best to keep them calm and protect them from themselves and others." His voice faded as the door latched and the lock clicked. "Now, let's see to the poor patients that Miss Mead disturbed with her episode."

Darkness pressed around Bethany like a leaden blanket, ominous and suffocating. She shifted only slightly and her back met the wall. Only the size of a closet, the quiet room was the most hated thing in this asylum. Its purpose may be to calm people, but the cramped cell made Bethany feel like a trapped animal. Her heart pounded in terror and she always felt like she couldn't breathe.

Under the sway of the drug Keene injected her with, it was even worse. Her muscles felt like jelly and she couldn't control even the most basic movements of her body. And Justus was out there.

Another grievous wail escaped her lips. If she was going to be locked in here until Keene's departure, there was no way Justus could free her before Greeves fulfilled his dastardly promise.

Bethany closed her eyes as an unnerving spinning sensation engulfed her. But that only intensified the topsy-turvy feeling and made her stomach lurch. Her eyes sapped open, but the darkness pressed on her eyelids like lead weights, making her feel sleepy. Shaking her head, she willed herself to stay awake, just in case Justus would be able to get inside the asylum and find her.

But it was no use. The drug pulled her down into a pool of black unconsciousness.

Chapter Eighteen

Justus clenched his teeth so hard his jaw made a cracking sound as Bethany was hauled away screaming. He wanted to rip the bars out of this accursed window and slaughter everyone who'd made her cry out like that. But this rescue demanded a degree of discretion. If he burst through an eighth story window with his eyes glowing and fangs flashing, he'd have more than the Manchester vampires to be concerned with.

Suddenly, a realization struck that made his lips peel back in a savage grin. As long as he didn't present himself as a vampire, perhaps he wouldn't have to be so discreet.

Mind turning with countless plans, Justus scrambled down the side of the building and dashed back to the ramshackle village where he took his daytime refuge. First, he visited the crypt and gathered up his meager possessions, stopping to cover his hair with a dark woolen cap and hide the lower half of his face with a scarf, then he left the shelter without a backward glance. He had no affinity for the cold, barren shelter.

His next destination was the home of the unscrupulous vicar. The man was asleep, but he'd left his window open. Justus made his way through, crept through the house, and found the vicar in a drunken slumber in his bedroom. Striding across the carpeted rug to the bed, Justus seized the vicar's shoulders and captured his gaze to place him in a trance. He then sank his fangs in his throat and drank until he was full, not giving a tinker's damn whether the cretin lived or died. After healing the puncture wounds, he then left the room and grabbed an old blunderbuss hanging over the hearth and loaded it. Lord knew whether or not the antique would fire or not, but it would suit his purpose.

Keeping his senses open for the Manchester vampires, Justus returned to the asylum twice as fast, the strength from his feeding pulsing through his being. Strength he would need to break Bethany out of this horrid place and get them far away from here.

Instead of climbing up the side of the red brick monstrosity, Justus strode down the gravel drive, up the stone steps and to the thick oak front door. With a swift, hard kick, the door cracked and toppled inward from broken hinges. The ensuing thud echoed through the high vaulted ceilings. Immediately, shouts and footsteps hurtled down the long staircase towards him, but Justus did not mind. The more people who were away from Bethany, the better.

Four hulking men dashed into the foyer, two of them in their sleeping gowns. A wiry man with graying hair and wearing a tweed suit followed them, eyeing Justus with a puzzled frown. From the black satchel he carried, Justus surmised that he was the doctor. The one who'd ordered Bethany hauled away somewhere. The one who'd made her scream.

Ignoring the guards, he trained the blunderbuss at the doctor. "Halt, or the good doctor will be missing the top of his skull."

The guards looked at each other and froze. Their shoulders slumped and lips thrust out with petulant pouts. Justus wondered how many patients these brutes had tackled, and how many times that patient had been Bethany. He was beyond tempted to blast them all away.

But that wasn't his primary goal. Keeping the weapon aimed at the doctor, he growled. "Where is Miss Bethany Mead?"

"Who are you?" the doctor warbled.

"Never mind that!" Justus roared. "Where is Bethany?"

The doctor swallowed. "The quiet room. She'd had an outburst, talking to people who weren't there, suffering delusions..."

"She was talking to me, you blithering idiot," Justus snapped, striding towards the doctor. One of the guards lunged forward and Justus slammed the cur into the wall with a slight push. "And I am no delusion. Now get her out of there and bring her to me, or I will kill you and anyone else who stands in my way."

The doctor held up his hands and shook his head. "I don't have the key."

Justus shoved the barrel of his weapon under the doctor's chin. "Then take me to the one who does."

Slowly, they made their way up the stairs and Justus sniffed the air for the essence of his love. The doctor knocked rapidly on a door, darting nervous glances at Justus. "Bronson, come out here straight away!"

The door opened and a surly looking woman emerged with a cheroot clamped between her yellowed teeth. Then she caught a glimpse of Justus with his blunderbuss and her jaw dropped. The smoking cheroot fell to the floor and Justus stomped on it before the rug caught fire. "Release Miss Bethany Mead at once, or you and the good doctor will die."

The woman nodded, face pale and clutched a ring of keys at her waist. Keeping an eye over his shoulder, Justus followed Bronson and the doctor up another winding staircase. Groans, whimpers, and hair-raising screams reached his ears, sounds of illimitable suffering. The fact that Bethany had spent eight years in this literal madhouse made Justus's soul contort in agony.

Two of the four guards lurked behind about twenty paces, but Justus was fully prepared to shove them down the stairs if they drew too close. The screams and howls of the inmates grew louder, accompanied by pounding on the walls and doors.

The doctor cast Justus a glare. "You're upsetting my patients."

"I don't give a damn," he bit out.

The man's face reddened. "I do not know what you presume to accomplish from this menacing crime. If you think Miss Mead's parents will pay a ransom, you will be deeply disappointed. They haven't written so much as a letter to her in three years."

"I don't want any bloody money," Justus growled, appalled that her own family had abandoned her like that. "Just her." He didn't elaborate, as the less people knew about Bethany's liberation, the better. He did not doubt that this incident would spread to the London papers. But as long as nothing preternatural was assumed, he could manage.

At last, Bronson and the doctor turned down a shadowy corridor and stopped in front of a narrow oak door secured with a massive iron lock.

The keys clanked and rattled as Bronson unlocked the door with shaking hands. Justus kept the blunderbuss fixed on her and the doctor as the door slid open to reveal a dark, closet-sized room lined floor to ceiling with yellowing padding. Bethany lay on the floor in a crumpled heap.

"Bethany!" Justus called out, praying she was unhurt.

"Justus?" she groaned, voice slurred.

"Come to me," he said. "Let us leave this place. Hurry."

She lifted herself on her elbows and blinked at him hazily, eyes dilated and confused.

Justus rounded on the doctor. "You drugged her."

"She was hysterical," he protested.

"I should kill you," Justus growled before turning back to Bethany. "Come to me," he repeated. If he put down the blunderbuss, he had no doubt that the louts behind him would tackle him. Not that it wouldn't be easy to dispense with them, but it was imperative that these idiot humans believed him to be a mortal.

Bethany grasped the padded wall and tried to pull herself to her feet, but fell back to her knees. "I'm so dizzy and my limbs won't obey me."

"You must try," he said, willing her to have strength.

Inch by painful inch, she crawled towards him as Justus backed into the doorway of the cell so he could keep an eye on the doctor and his cohorts while she reached him. When he felt her delicate fingers grasp his leg, he knelt and scooped her up with one arm. The angle was awkward, but he cursed under his breath at how light and frail Bethany felt in his grip. Had they starved her here as well?

Another set of footsteps clattered down the hall.

"Doctor," an irritated voice called from around the corner. "What in the bloody hell is going on? This place sounds like a, well... madhouse." A wiry, rat-faced man came into view. His eyes bulged out of his sockets at the sight of Justus holding Bethany, armed with the blunderbuss.

But it was Bethany's reaction that made him take note of the newcomer. "Greeves," she whimpered with a cringe and clung tighter to Justus.

"He's the one who was going to assault you when the doctor left town?" Justus snarled. He pointed the weapon at Greeves. "I'll kill him!"

"No!" Bethany cried out the same time as the doctor gasped.

"What do you mean assault?" The doctor narrowed his gaze at Greeves.

Justus looked between the doctor, Greeves, and Bethany.

"I'd kill him myself," she whispered, "but then we'd be wanted for murder."

Justus sighed. She was right. However, there was a way to at least ensure this worm never harmed another patient again. Capturing Greeves's gaze, he commanded, "Tell the doctor what you do to his patients when he is not around."

Greeves flinched like a whipped cur and launched into a sordid confession, his chin wobbling like a jelly mold. The things he said he'd done to defenseless people made the doctor suck in a breath and inflamed Justus's urge to kill him even more.

The doctor recovered first. "You will leave this place at once! You're relieved from your position here and you will not receive a reference."

"But Doctor Keene," Greeves protested. "Don't you need my assistance with this man holding you at gunpoint?"

"Never mind that." Keene actually sounded bored. "Since he is not willing to kill *you*, I assume I am quite safe. The authorities will be searching for him at once at any rate."

While that was true, Justus planned on leaving the area so fast that they'd be long gone before the constable made it to the asylum to hear Keene's tale. And with any luck, they'd be safe in Cornwall before the story was printed in the papers.

Still, nervousness churned in his gut and he resisted the urge to reach up and make certain that no stray red hairs had escaped his woolen cap.

Just then, a sharp point dug into his neck. Justus seized Keene's hand before the doctor could depress the plunger of the syringe. Bones crunched beneath his grasp, making Keene cry out like an injured rabbit.

"You shouldn't have done that," Justus snarled.

"H-how did you move so quickly?" Keene cried, clutching his broken hand.

Damn! Justus cursed inwardly and lied. "I'm an accomplished fencer."

The woman called Bronson glared at Justus before turning to the doctor to examine his hand. "You foolish man. Now we'll have to summon a bonesetter along with the constable."

Justus decided that was their prompt to leave. "We'll be going now." He adjusted his grip on Bethany and slowly headed down the corridor. The guards shrank back, and Greeves suddenly remembered that he'd been sacked and scurried off in the opposite direction.

Keeping hold of the blunderbuss, he carried Bethany down the endless flights of stairs as fast as possible while still trying to appear human. One of the guards and a few servants lurked in the corners of the main floor, but they did not try to stop him as he took his precious love out the broken front door.

The gate squealed open after a swift kick to the rusting iron and as he crossed the threshold, Bethany looked up at the moon and laughed. "I'm free. I cannot believe it. Lord in heaven, please don't let this be a dream."

He paused to press a kiss to her forehead. "No dream, I promise. You will never have to go back to that place again." He then carried her to the cluster of bushes where he'd hidden his pack. Still maintaining hold of Bethany with one arm, he slid the blunderbuss into the pack and then switched her to his other arm to get the straps over his shoulders. Then, cradling her with both arms at last, he sighed at the feel of her. "Hold onto me tightly. We're going to run faster than we did the first time."

She complied, clinging to his shoulders and wrapping her legs around his waist, making him bite back a groan of desire at her softness pressing against his groin.

When he took off, her breath hitched near his ear. They covered the ground in a blur of motion, dodging trees and boulders. Bethany trembled at the furious speed, but there was nothing to be done for it. They had to get as far away from Manchester as possible.

As if conjured by the thought, a shout echoed behind him, followed by the sound of pursuit at the same pace he ran. The Manchester vampires had spotted him.

But the border was only a few kilometers away. If he could elude them a little longer, they'd be in Cheshire and out of their reach. And hopefully there were no Cheshire vampires about. Silently praying to whatever deity favored damned souls like his, Justus mustered every ounce of strength his last feeding had given him, and quickened his stride.

The Manchester vampires drew closer, until Justus swore he could feel their breath on the back of his neck.

"He's got a human!" one of them shouted.

"Hurry up then, before he gets away!"

Lungs heaving, Justus kept running, willing his body to move even faster. A tree branch whipped his cheek, slicing a burning gash, but still he pressed on. The road turning to Cheshire came into view and he focused on it like it was a beacon in the darkness.

Just as he sensed that one of the vampires was about to lunge for him, he crossed the border. The Manchester vampires cursed. According to Rochester's spies, the Lord of Cheshire despised the Lord of Manchester and forbade any of his vampires from entering. Justus prayed that would continue to work to his advantage, but there was likely no hope that the Cheshire vampires would be any kinder to him. Thankfully, he didn't sense any of them around.

Though his chest burned, Justus did not dare slow down. Eyes darting around for shelter, he continued his punishing dash even though the Manchester vampires had given up their chase. After four more miles, he saw piles of old stone ruins.

"Thank you, God," he breathed. It was an old church razed in one of England's countless wars. Which meant there would be a cellar, maybe a crypt.

Ducking under the crumbling arch, he searched until he found a stairwell at the far end of what used to be the south transept, almost completely buried in rubble.

"Bethany," he whispered. "Can you stand a moment? I need to clear the way."

She murmured, but didn't stir. The drugs still held sway over her.

As gently as possible, Justus laid her on the floor and set to moving chunks of charred wood and broken marble out of the stairwell. When the path was clear, he lifted her and carried her down.

Even with his preternatural vision, the chamber below was almost too dark to see. Hopefully, that meant the sunlight would not penetrate. And to his further optimism, he did not detect the slightest scent of another vampire, or any living being, for that matter.

"Justus?" Bethany's teeth chattered in his ear as she spoke. "It's so dark in here. And so cold."

Concern squeezed his heart. It had to be pitch black to her. Focusing his vision, he looked around until he saw the vague outline of a slab and what looked like catacombs. It was a crypt, thank heavens. He carried her to the slab and brushed off the dust, grateful that there weren't any bones on the marble surface.

After he set her down, he rummaged through his pack and pulled out a blanket.

"Thank you," Bethany whispered as he wrapped it around her shoulders.

"I'll build a fire," he said and searched for his matches. In the darkness he could make out shapes that he hoped were wooden boards. He could fetch some from above, but he didn't want to leave her.

Matches secure, Justus gathered up all the scraps of wood in the crypt and built a fire at the base of the stone steps so the smoke would vent up and out. Others may smell it, but he'd deal with that then. Now his only concern was seeing to Bethany's comfort.

Once a little blaze was going, he cringed at the sight of the dusty, cobweb laden crypt. Eight years ago, he never would have dreamed of bringing a debutante to such a hideous place. But for their own safety, he had no choice.

He turned back to see Bethany lying on the slab, huddled in his blanket. Unease trickled down his spine as he noticed her bare feet. She'd need shoes, clothes, food.

For the first time since he set on his course to free her and take her to Cornwall, Justus experienced a wave of doubt. How could he expect to care for her when he was a rogue vampire, having to avoid both the sun and other vampires?

Chapter Nineteen

Bethany dreamed of the quiet room, cold and enclosed, screaming for help, but none came. She curled into a ball and shivered until she heard Keene's brisk footsteps coming down the hall. The knob on the quiet room door rattled and turned...

She awoke, sore and muzzy-headed. But even though the surface she lay on was cold and hard, her back felt deliciously warm. As awareness imbued her, she noticed the well-muscled arm draped around her waist, and locks of deep red hair draped around her shoulder.

Happiness swelled her heart to bursting. Justus had saved her from the prison of Morningside last night, from Dr. Keene's abominable tonics and Greeves's lechery. Not only was she finally released from that abominable asylum, she was also reunited with her love at last.

She basked in the sheer bliss of it all for several moments before taking note of her surroundings. The dusty, crumbling stone chamber, dimly illuminated by the coals of a dying fire and a meager shaft of sunlight from the top of the stairwell on the far side of the room made stark reality rear its head.

They were in here because Justus was a vampire. He couldn't go out in daylight. Furthermore, he was a rogue, hunted by others of his kind. And it was all her fault. If she hadn't blurted that he was a vampire in front of her parents, and especially in front of Lord Tench, Justus wouldn't have been exiled. Shame curdled her belly. How could he have forgiven her? Yet he had. And after eight years of misery, they were together again at last.

But now they were both fugitives. She prayed they'd be able to make it to Cornwall, and that the Lord Vampire there would indeed provide refuge. Their predicament was already far too precarious for her to be able to contemplate what would happen if he refused them. Justus had said they'd flee to the Americas in that case, but how would they secure passage on a ship, much less endure such a long voyage without him being exposed to the sun?

Taking a deep breath, she willed herself to be calm, for her relentless trembling to abate. Justus had a plan. He would know what to do. Just then, her stomach rumbled, reminding her of more pressing matters.

"We need to find food for you, but we have to wait until the sun goes down," Justus said, and stroked her shoulder, easing her shivers. "I do have a skin of water to tide you over until then. I am so sorry not to have gathered victuals for you."

The remorse in his voice tugged at her heart. She grasped his hand and snuggled against him, reveling in the warmth and security of his embrace. "It is not your fault. You did not know we would be departing last night."

He eased them to a sitting position and adjusted the blanket around her. "Let me fetch you water and build the fire, and then we can plan our next move."

Her body cried out with bereavement as he left the slab, though the promise of a warm fire and water for her parched throat were very welcome indeed. Lord, how it burned.

Justus handed her the waterskin and then walked around the chamber, gathering up scraps of rotting wood. Bethany took a deep drink of the blessedly cool water and nearly choked as she saw a human skull on the floor just below where her feet dangled.

"Where are we?" she asked, fighting a tremor in her voice.

"Beneath the ruins of an old church," Justus replied as he lit a bit of tinder to start a fire. "The crypt, to be exact. I know it's macabre, but it's the safest choice."

Orange light illuminated the dusty crypt as the blaze grew. Avoiding the skull, Bethany slipped off the slab to get closer to the fire. That's when she noticed the oversized, but thick wool knee stockings covering her feet. He'd also covered her with his worn, but sturdy blue coat.

"Are these your stockings?" she asked.

He nodded. "Your feet were bare and cold. We'll need to get some that fit you." His frown deepened. "Shoes as well, but we have to wait until dusk." He paced in the shadows, keeping far away from the patch of sunlight on the stairs, looking so forlorn and frustrated that she was compelled to cross the chamber and take his arm.

"I will be fine until then," Bethany said, marveling at the firm muscles beneath his worn linen sleeve. "I've went without food longer at Morningside. Keene believed that fasting would clear one's head of excess fancy."

His eyes narrowed in fury. "That does not make it right."

"Well, thanks to you, it is in the past." Bethany tugged on his arm, trying to ignore the almost queasy gnawing of hunger in her stomach. "Come, sit by the fire with me."

His expression relaxed slightly as he walked with her to the warm blaze. After bidding her to sit on the canvas pack, he sat beside her and took her hand. "I still cannot believe I've found you after all these years. All those days dreaming of holding you in my arms..." He sighed. "But always in much better accommodations."

She laid her head on his shoulder. "The accommodations may be less than cozy, but at least this is real."

His knuckles brushed her cheek as he looked down at her, his eyes impossibly green. "You're right. Finally, it is real." He lowered his head until his lips brushed hers.

Desire rushed through her body at his kiss, more potent and thrilling than her memories ever conjured. Bethany turned and pressed herself tighter against him, moaning as he pulled her fully into his embrace.

They kissed with all their pent up hunger from being separated for so many years. Grasping, touching, exploring each other with sustained longing. Bethany moaned in bliss as the tender place between her thighs pulsed with primal need. Of its own volition, her body moved until she was in Justus's lap, his hardness pressing against that sweet, throbbing place.

Justus's low growl sent tremors of exhilaration through her being. His tongue stroked hers, a forbidden and delicious dance. Bethany arched her hips against him, craving even more.

Abruptly, Justus pulled her off his lap and set her back down firmly, albeit gently beside him. "No," he said in a rasping voice. "You are still a maid and a lady. I cannot dishonor you."

"I'm no lady anymore," Bethany ran her fingers through his crimson hair, in thrall with its softness.

He took her hand and kissed her knuckles. "You'll always be a lady to me."

"Does that mean you will never—" She broke off as her cheeks burned too much to finish.

He shook his head. "Not until we are wed."

The seriousness of the word was like a splash of cold water on her ardor. "You still want us to be married?"

Justus frowned. "Yes. Do you no longer accept my proposal?"

"That is not what I meant," Bethany said quickly. "That is… I'm not certain. It's been so long since we've seen each other. I feel as if we should become reacquainted. Not to mention the fact that we are both fugitives until we find some sort of sanctuary."

Though he still appeared wounded by her words, he nodded. "You speak wisely." Something alarming yet unreadable flickered in his eyes and he scooted away from her.

Hurt speared her chest. "You don't want to be close to me because I wish to wait?"

Justus shook his head vigorously. "I want nothing more than to hold you, but my hunger is too strong to bear. Our long run last night took my strength. I'll need to hunt as soon as the sun sets."

Relief that he was not rejecting her bled away to concern at his plight. "Couldn't you feed from me?"

"No," he said so sharply that she flinched. "You'd be weakened even further."

Bethany sighed. He had a point. Still, she hated feeling helpless, a burden, unable to help him. And more than ever she longed to pull him into her arms and offer comfort. But his glowing eyes, forbidding expression and glimpses of white, sharp fangs indicated that wouldn't be the wisest course of action. "Well, what do you propose we do to pass the time?"

At last, his lips curved in a smile. "Your optimism is a balm on my soul. I have a few books in my pack that I've long wished to discuss."

They spent the next four hours reading passages of *Beowulf* together and having a spirited discussion. If not for the hard floor they sat upon, the chill of the crypt, and the hunger in their bellies, everything would have been exactly as it was when they first met.

As the light at the top of the stairs shrank away, Justus closed the book and shook his head. "After we feed and clothe you, we'll have to try to secure more books."

Bethany nodded emphatically. "I was hardly ever allowed to read at Morningside. And the few books permitted were so dull that they seemed more punishment than escape."

Justus's jaw dropped. "They didn't allow you to read?" he repeated, aghast.

"They thought most books would overstimulate me, make me hysterical," she replied, downcast at the memories of deprivation of anything good or interesting.

"That is cruel beyond measure!" Justus nearly shouted. "To deprive you of one of the greatest and most harmless pleasures of mankind. How in the world did you endure it?"

"I think I went mad in truth." She laughed shakily. "There was a raven that often perched by my window. I named him Percival and talked to him all the time. Until one day, a few months ago, he never returned. I was so lonely after that."

His hand covered hers. "You'll be lonely no longer. Not as long as I am with you." He rose to his feet, pulling her up with him. "Dusk has fallen. We will procure food for us both, but first there is one thing I must do."

"What?" she asked, then gasped as he punctured his index finger and held the bleeding digit towards her.

"I need to feed you a few drops of my blood."

She frowned. "But I thought you needed to drink blood." Another thought occurred. "Are you going to Change me into a vampire now?" She wasn't certain she was ready for that.

He chuckled. "No. This is so if we are separated, I will be able to find you. I'd rather Mark you completely, but that would be too dangerous at this time."

"Mark me?" she asked.

"I'll explain in a moment." He pressed his bleeding finger to her lips. "Hurry, before the wound closes."

Scrunching up her nose, Bethany opened her mouth and allowed Justus's blood to flow across her tongue. The subtle, mineral-like taste wasn't as bad as she'd feared, but the electric spark on her tongue was alarming indeed. When he withdrew his finger, she licked her lips and frowned. "What was that jolting sensation?"

Justus shrugged. "Some sort of magic, I suppose. The blood forges a connection between us, so if we are separated, I'll be able to find you. But since I didn't say the words, or give you enough blood, the effect is only temporary. Usually this method used so vampires can tell whether or not a human has been fed on, so we don't accidentally drain a person."

"Your blood has magic?" she repeated with fascination.

"Yes. It also has the ability to heal wounds, so after feeding, we use our blood to heal the puncture marks from our fangs, which also creates the temporary Mark."

"What of the permanent Mark?" she prodded.

"That Mark is used to declare a mortal to be under a vampire's protection," Justus explained. "I cannot yet give it to you, for the vampires would then know that you're Marked by a rogue and they would follow you to hunt me down."

Her eyes widened. "That would be very bad." Without Justus, Lord knew how long she'd be able to survive on the run. Not only that, but she'd have nowhere to go. And of course, the thought of losing him again filled her with terror.

Justus slung the straps of his pack over his shoulders and held out his hand. "Shall we go?"

Bethany nodded emphatically as her stomach growled. She was so hungry she could eat an entire side of beef. Furthermore, she'd be happy to never see this dismal crypt again. Justus's fingers entwined with hers as he carefully guided her up the cracked stairs. The strong, yet gentle touch made heat unfurl in her belly. Until last night, their hands had almost always been gloved, impeding contact.

The moon hung bright and full in the sky, the scent of wildflowers heady in the night air. There was even something beautiful about the ruins of the church, an echo of another time. Bethany's heart sang with joy to be out here with Justus rather than alone in her cell at Morningside. Yet she tried to keep her jubilance suppressed, as she watched Justus glancing over his shoulder and studying their surroundings with studied concentration. They were still in danger.

"We'll go east," Justus said quietly. "I don't sense anyone in that direction." They only walked a few yards before he suddenly scooped her up in his arms. "I'd forgotten. You need shoes."

Although being in Justus's arms gave her a rush of pleasure, Bethany resented feeling like a burden to be carried. She only hoped they would find some food soon, before hunger made her light-headed.

He ran with his preternatural speed, and this time she kept her eyes open, watching the world rush by in a blur and feeling the wind on her cheeks as they passed acres of wilderness, then farmland before Justus stopped at the edge of a town. The streets were fairly busy with people heading home from their workdays, or going to a pub or assembly hall for an entertaining evening.

The sight made Bethany dizzy. It had been so long since she'd seen this many people in any semblance of normal behavior. Now her mind reeled with it all. Would she ever grown accustomed to the world again?

"Shouldn't you put me down?" Bethany asked.

Justus shook his head. "I have a plan."

Bethany tried to hide her flushed face behind her hair at all the stares as Justus walked down the main street carrying her. She must look a fright with her disheveled hair, oversized stockings, no shoes, and a man's coat over her plain linen frock from the asylum.

Justus paid no attention to the scrutiny as he marched across the lane to a cobbler's shop. After he knocked on the door, a squinting man answered with an irritated frown.

"Pardon me, do you have any ladies' shoes?" Justus asked with a smile. "My dear fiancé's were thrown in the pond by a group of ruffians."

The cobbler's features softened. "Oh dear. The youths these days. Come inside and I'll see what I've got. Do you have the coin?"

"No," Justus replied while fixing the man with an intent stare. "But you will help us all the same."

Bethany expected the cobbler to slam the door in their faces, but instead his eyes glazed over and a bemused smile lifted his narrow lips. "Yes," he said dully. "I will help you."

With the same distracted air, he opened the door further and went inside. Justus followed behind, watching as the cobbler lit lanterns throughout the shop. When Bethany's gaze lit on the plethora of shoes, a bittersweet wave engulfed her heart. How long had it been since she'd seen such simple, yet crucial items on display? How many years since she'd even thought of the shops she'd visited with her mother?

The cobbler cleared his throat. "Miss? If you'll sit on the stool, I can measure your feet."

To her disappointment, the fetching pair of black leather shoes were not in her size, but perhaps it was for the best, as the brown leather half boots she donned were far sturdier. She thanked the man profusely before she and Justus left the shop.

"That was so kind of him to give me shoes," she said. "But I wonder why he decided to do so. He looked so odd when he said he'd help."

"I didn't give him a choice," Justus said tightly. "I bent him to my will."

She gasped. "You can *do* that?"

"Yes. It is how we are able to feed without people remembering," he explained, his features wavering as if confessing to a sin. "Speaking of, it is time for us to have nourishment."

They walked to a nearby inn, where Justus instead used his ability to make the proprietor believe they'd handed him money. A large plate of roast beef and potatoes was set before Bethany. The savory aroma rendered her oblivious to the rest of the world. She took her first bite and bit back a moan of pleasure. Years ago, she would have disdained inn fare, with it being so greasy and salty, but after years of bland porridge and dry toast, this meal tasted like it was served from the King's table.

Alas, her stomach was so shrunken from not eating for so long that she could only finish half the meal. Justus took her dinner rolls, sliced them in half, and made cunning little sandwiches before wrapping them in the napkin and stowing them in his pack. He then beckoned a maid and ordered a bath for Bethany.

"I have to leave you for a few minutes," he told her as the maid beckoned her up the stairs to a room.

Bethany understood. He still needed his meal. Yet that didn't stop dread from crawling up her throat throughout the entire bath as she waited for him to return. Her senses remained rattled at being back in the world, amongst strangers, and the clamorous noise of humanity drifting up from the rooms below. Though she had to admit, the steaming water felt heavenly and being clean after a night in a dusty crypt was pure bliss.

Just as she was dreading donning her filthy shift, a soft knock sounded on the door. The maid pushed her behind a privacy screen before answering. Bethany's shoulders relaxed as she heard Justus's voice. He'd returned to her safely after all.

The maid murmured something before closing the door. "His Nibs brought you clean clothing. He should have thought of that before your bath, but you know how men are."

Bethany bit back a chuckle. He couldn't have done so because she'd had no clean clothes. She wondered where he'd gotten them even as gratitude welled in her being as she beheld the soft wool stockings, linen chemise, navy cotton dress, and a rich dark green cloak. In her old life, such garments were far from elegant, but now she thought them luxurious in their usefulness.

She rejoined Justus in the hall as the maid tried to prod them to stay the night. The lush bed in the room Bethany bathed in beckoned her like a song. But she knew that Justus wouldn't be safe in such a room. Not to mention the fact that they weren't married… unless he'd told the innkeeper otherwise. From the lack of censure she'd received, he must have.

Bethany closed her eyes as she remembered Justus's declaration that he still intended to wed her… and her response of being uncertain. She imagined being his wife in truth, a warm flush suffusing her at the thought of being joined with him before cold uncertainty doused the fantasy. They had no home to build together, and he could not make her a vampire… not yet.

Furthermore, she did not know if she was ready to become a vampire when she was only now relearning how to be a normal person.

Her lips quirked upwards in a sardonic smile. She never would be normal.

But perhaps that was all right. Hand on Justus's arm, she walked with him outside of the inn and back into the unknown.

Chapter Twenty

Justus couldn't stop glancing at Bethany as they walked through the dark, sleepy village, an ache burrowing deep in his heart every time he beheld her beloved face and form. The memory of her reaction to his insistence that they wed echoed in his mind, a relentless litany of rejection. True, she hadn't outright rejected him, but after years of imagining their wedding, the night he would at last be joined to her, physically and emotionally, her blatant uncertainty and wish to wait still stung and filled him with fear. What if after they became reacquainted, as she wished, she then decided she no longer loved him?

Another thought speared his soul like an icicle. What if she already no longer loved him?

As if sensing his turmoil, Bethany looked up at him, tenderness and trust radiating in her blue eyes. He forced a smile and took a deep breath. Her reasons for delaying wedlock were indeed practical. For now, he had no way of securing a special license to permit a legal nighttime ceremony and dismiss with reading the banns, and Gretna Green was in the opposite direction of their destination. Besides, what kind of wedding could they have on the run? Surely she deserved better than a covert ceremony and a quick dash to some cellar or crypt to spend their wedding night.

His shoulders slumped. She deserved so much more than he was able to offer her.

But at least he'd freed her from that dreadful asylum. Her talk of hours in a cell, deprived of books and company, made him want to run back to Manchester and dash that mad doctor's brains into the wall. How strong she must have been, to suffer such isolation and deprivation and not have her mind broken.

His lips curled in a self-deprecating sneer. And here he was, sulking because she hadn't leaped for joy at the prospect of rushing to the altar. Of course she needed time to grow accustomed to the world around her after her long imprisonment. He was an ass of gargantuan proportions. Hell, he hadn't even thought to fetch her shoes or food before breaking her free from the asylum.

At least that catastrophe had been rectified. She wore sturdy shoes, and while she was in the bath, Justus had fed on a barmaid before dashing out back and stealing clothes from the wash line outside of what looked like a prosperous home. He'd then played a quick game of cards with a group of merchants in the back room of the inn and now had a few pounds to be able to buy more food. Stealing was easy, but it came with too much danger. Do it too often, and even the dimmest human would realize something was amiss. Not only that, but taking from others usually left a bad taste in his mouth. Who knew if a person had been reduced to their last shilling? But using his preternatural senses to best men at the gambling table? That never so much as pricked his conscience. Only fools played hazard with their coin over a silly deck of cards.

As if reading his mind, Bethany gazed up at him. "Where did these clothes come from?"

He chuckled and told her the tale.

Her eyes widened. "How did you do that so fast?"

"You've seen how fast I can be." He grinned. "Now our next goal is to find shelter before dawn, so we shall have to run once we're away from town."

She sighed. "And I was so enjoying walking on my own." Suddenly, she frowned. "Were you able to feed?"

He nodded, but didn't tell her that ideally he should feed once more before dawn. That was another challenge of being a rogue. Balancing the need to hunt with finding safe shelter. He prayed the next place he found would be better than a crypt.

Thankfully, it was. An old cave whose previous inhabitant, some sort of animal, had long since vacated. After inspecting it to make certain it went deep enough to avoid the light, Justus led Bethany inside and quickly built a fire before going back out and gathering soft grass and moss to make a bed of sorts.

"I could have done that," she told him as she laid the blanket on the nest he'd built.

"No need for you to dirty your hands," Justus said, pleased that she looked far more comfortable than the previous evening, no longer shivering. "I enjoy caring for you."

Something flashed in her eyes before she gave him a tremulous smile. "Thank you." She removed the water skin from his pack and took a drink before removing the sandwiches he'd made her, the blunderbuss, and other objects that hindered the pack's use as a pillow. "We are still heading south?"

Justus nodded and built up the fire. "We should reach Shrewsbury tomorrow. That should place us a third of the way to

Cornwall, though I wonder if it would be safer to cross into Wales for a time, despite the delay that could cause. The nights are growing shorter, so I hope for us to be settled before June."

"I hope for us to be settled at all." Bethany's gaze hardened on the fire before softening when she looked back at him. "Tell me about your time as a rogue."

He took a deep breath and answered carefully, acknowledging the dangers of pursuit, while interlacing his tale with amusing incidents and sights he'd seen on his travels, such as the time he'd come across a troupe of travelling actors stranded in the mud and spent an evening helping them free their carriage while they all took turns acting out *A Midsummer Night's Dream,* and an incident where he'd blackmailed a vampire who he'd seen visiting another territory without a writ of passage.

As he sensed the deadly approach of sunrise, Bethany patted the blanket beside her. "Lay beside me?"

Justus regarded her a moment. Her hair lay across his pack, gleaming gold in the firelight. Those large blue eyes glittered with an exquisite blend of warmth and intelligence. And her figure, he'd tried not to notice it, but now that she was garbed in that form-fitting dress, his gaze would not stop trailing over her body. Bethany's curves had rounded further in some areas and slimmed in others since she was a maid of seventeen. At twenty-five, they'd become sculpted, the epitome of womanhood. Though she was much too thin from her imprisonment.

Desire roared through him in a blazing inferno. Memories of those soft curves pressed against him last morning, her tender kisses, and the potent scent of her arousal made his cock harden with need.

It had been agony not to make love to her then. But what kind of a monster would he be to ravish a maiden in the ruins of a crypt or a dark cave? He wanted their first joining, and every joining thereafter to be perfect.

Though the temptation was excruciating, Justus was helpless in the face of her soft plea. Unable to deny the pleasure of holding her, he lay down next to her and pulled her into his arms, breathing a sigh at the warmth of her body. They spoke in hushed tones before drifting off to sleep.

Justus's rest was broken and plagued with worry. Not for the first time did he wonder if Cornwall was the best course. The Lord Vampire there was often called the "Devil Earl" by mortals, and "Mad Deveril" by vampires across the British Isles.

Had Gavin been right in recommending Justus go to such a vampire for solace? Alas, he and Bethany had no other option. At least Cornwall was a coastal region with many ships that could carry them away. That would open a whole new set of challenges, but he didn't want to think that far ahead unless he had to.

Instead, he cradled Bethany in his arms, listening to her relaxed breathing and silently vowed that he would do everything in his power to ensure her safety during their journey and ever after.

When they awoke in the late afternoon, Justus felt slightly more optimism. Perhaps it was because Bethany appeared content eating her sandwiches rather than starving until nightfall as she had previously. ...Though haunted shadows still lurked beneath her eyes and her fingers held a faint tremor.

Once more, they talked about books until nightfall, forming concrete plans to find a library or bookseller at the next town or village.

When they left the cave, Justus frowned as he realized they were further from civilization than he'd expected. He ran with

Bethany as long as he could, but aside from an isolated cluster of small farms, nothing promising lay in sight.

Thunder rumbled in the distance, chasing away his previous high spirits.

But Bethany lifted her skirts and trotted over to a vegetable garden, gathering up radishes, turnips, asparagus, and various leafy greens.

"I feel like a rabbit," she said with a giggle, loading the pack. Her hands trembled slightly and there was a feverish glaze in her eyes.

Yet she looked so cheerful that his concern abated. He felt like a fool for not considering gardens in the first place. Years ago, his tenants had harvested Spring vegetables and it hadn't even occurred to him that they would be in abundance. Some provider he was turning out to be.

His self-flagellation ceased as he scented the presence of other vampires. They burst out of a copse of trees, surrounding him. Justus counted three.

"And who might you be?" one vampire asked, eyeing Bethany warily.

"Just travelers, passing through," Justus answered, taking advantage of their reluctance to reveal what they were to a mortal.

"We know better than that," the second one snarled before turning to Bethany. "Is this man bothering you?"

Bethany took Justus's arm and lifted her chin with all her haughty aristocratic upbringing. "He is doing no such thing. Now let us pass."

The Cheshire vampire glared at her. "I'm afraid I cannot allow that. This gent needs to come with us for a spell. Now run along home, woman. This is no place for you."

"My home is with him," Bethany said, and threw a turnip.

The dirt-coated vegetable struck the vampire's forehead, making the others step back in shock. Justus wasted no time in taking advantage of the distraction she afforded. He lifted Bethany in his arms and ran as fast as his vampiric speed would allow.

Another crack of thunder sounded before rain came pouring down in sheets. Despite the discomfort, Justus thanked the heavens for it, because rain would obscure his scent. His body protested running so soon without having fed, but he urged himself forward.

He didn't know how long he pressed on, how many miles passed before the sense of his pursuers no longer lurked behind him. He carried Bethany another few paces before he slowed and set her down, panting with exhaustion. She stumbled and he reached out a hand to steady her.

She murmured thanks and sat, cupping her face with her hands, shivering. "I'm so dizzy. I thought you'd never stop. How far did we come?"

"I don't know," Justus said, shoulders still heaving. "At least three miles." He looked up and bit back a curse. They'd gone further into the wilderness instead of towards a town as he'd hoped. Many a time had he been able to lose himself in a crowd of humans and have a bite before moving on to another territory long before those chasing him found his trail.

And though he'd lost these pursuers, there were no humans nearby to provide sustenance. The pouring rain plastered his hair to his skull, soaked through his clothes, and ran in icy runnels down his spine. Bethany's discomfort had to be worse, with the encumbrance of skirts. His chest tightened with sympathy as he watched her rub her arms in vain attempt to warm herself. She shook like a leaf.

He sighed in resignation. It wouldn't be the first time he'd gone without food, and he needed to get Bethany out of the rain.

"Are you all right?" she asked softly as they walked deeper into the woods.

"I'm fine," he said. "We need to find a way out of this rain."

She nodded in agreement, shivering. "I just wish I could see where we are going."

That was right, her night vision wasn't as good as his. Another pang of worry and impotent frustration speared him at his throwing her into such a situation. "Don't worry, I'll guide you through."

The boughs of the trees provided a semblance of shelter from the pattering rain. Justus held tight to Bethany's hand, warning her when to duck, or step over a hole or large stone. He hated the sound of her teeth chattering, the panic in her eyes as they darted sightlessly in every direction. Never had he been more tempted to throw caution to the wind and Change her. Then she could see. Then she could run.

But if he did so, she would be a rogue and hunted as he was. Dejection gnawed in his belly, easing slightly when they came upon an abandoned hovel. Half the roof was missing, but at least it would provide some shelter.

"You sit in here, and I'll try to find some dry wood," he said over his shoulder.

"Let me help." She shifted as if to stand.

He shook his head. "No. You are soaked to the skin. I don't want you to fall ill. Besides, you can't see out there."

Her lower lip thrust out mutinously, but she didn't argue. Justus went back out in the rain, and between foraging for dry wood, he also found a dried out well he could burrow inside to hide from the sun's deadly rays.

That would mean leaving Bethany alone for the day, but he didn't know what else he could do. Returning to the hovel, he built a meager fire.

"You should take off that wet cloak," he told her, willing the small flames to grow.

She did so, hanging the sodden garment from a splintered beam. "And you should feed from me."

With the cloak unfastened, her throat gleamed smooth and succulent in the firelight. Hunger roiled in his belly as he licked his fangs.

"I won't." The words came out more hesitant than he'd have liked.

She crossed the room and placed her hands on his shoulders, rising up on her toes. "But you must. You're hungry and your strength is flagging."

God, she smelled so good and sweet. Memories of the last time he fed from her haunted him, mercilessly. His upper lip peeled back of its own volition, revealing his fangs. Biting back a growl, he gently pushed her back. "I said no. I can find other food. A rat, an owl, maybe a deer."

Her lips twisted in revulsion. "A rat?"

Face hot with embarrassment, he nodded stiffly. "One does what one needs to survive."

Bethany's gaze softened. "I realize that, but truly, you don't have to resort to rodents. I'm right here."

"I don't want to drain you." His hunger was so fierce that his eyes tracked her like prey, saliva filling his mouth at the thought of her taste. "Now get back near the fire and dry off. I'll see if there's a stream or pond nearby to refill the water skin."

She nodded sullenly and withdrew a radish from the pack. "Will you fill that with water as well?" She pointed to a chipped and dusty crock in the corner. "I may be able to boil the turnips."

Justus looked at the ancient thing doubtfully. Would it even hold water? But she looked so pitiful that he couldn't refuse her again. "Of course."

Before temptation overwhelmed him, Justus left the crude shelter and went out into the rainy night. Through the patter of raindrops, he did indeed detect the gurgle of a nearby stream. At last, something went right this night. Even better, he found a doe drinking from the moonlit water. No rats after all.

He set down the crock and was on the deer in a flash. Since he was unable to bespell it with his gaze, the damned creature bucked and kicked like a wild stallion, but Justus held tight and sank his fangs into its furry throat, drinking long and deep.

When Justus released the doe, she remained still and trembling before cautiously hobbling away, as if unable to believe she'd lived. Too bad he and Bethany lacked the time and resources to smoke and transport the meat, else he'd have butchered the deer. He did hope he hadn't weakened the poor creature so it would be taken down by a wolf, but he'd needed the meal. It wasn't enough to fully restore his strength. Only human blood provided all the nutrients his kind required, but he still felt ten times better than he had after fleeing from the Cheshire vampires.

Were they in Shrewsbury yet? He tried to calculate how far they'd traveled as he washed the dirty crock in the stream before filling it, surprised the vessel did not leak.

After filling the water skin and walking a quarter mile circle around Bethany's shelter, he had no answer as to their whereabouts, but he did at least see what looked like a path to civilization off in the distance. Hopefully a town or even a small village.

When he returned to Bethany, the sky was already growing lighter. He watched her lifting her feet one in turn to dry her stockings by the fire and wanted nothing more than to curl up against her warmth. Damn these shortening nights. Dawn would come in little more than an hour.

"I cannot sleep with you this day," he said as he handed her the crock of water.

Her head tilted to the side, disappointment glittering in her eyes. "You can't?"

He spread his arms helplessly. "There is no shelter from the sun in here."

"Oh." Her shoulders slumped. "Can't you find another cave?"

Justus tried to hide his equal disappointment. What he would give to "There are none nearby and it's nearly dawn. I found a dried up well. I can burrow in there." He thought of the doe he'd fed on and the possibility of wolves, those on four legs as well as two. "Don't stray far from the cabin and keep the blunderbuss close." He found a rotting chair in the corner and ripped it to pieces, providing both firewood and an outlet to his frustration. "Keep the fire well fed."

She nodded and took the blanket from the pack. His heart ached to know that she'd spend a miserable day sleeping on a hard floor in damp clothes. Worry gnawed at him at the feverish glaze in her eyes. Though the rain had chilled her, surely she couldn't have fallen ill so quickly. Then the obvious became apparent. She was likely suffering a bit of a shock from being returned to the world. After years of isolation, all this fresh air, the bustle of encountering other people and villages and enduring such a hazardous journey had to have jarred her senses.

Before he did something foolish, like carry her to the well, he bent down and kissed her. "I will see you at dusk."

He would do better tomorrow, he vowed. His Bethany would not spend another night or day in a mouldering crypt or wretched hovel. She wouldn't be raiding a garden for radishes and wanting to boil turnips either. Somehow, some way, he would secure a full hot meal and a warm bed for her.

Chapter Twenty-one

Bethany tried to hide her proud smile as she stirred the crock with a stick she'd whittled with a knife she'd found in the pack. The turnip, spinach, and wild onions made a semblance of a stew. What made it truly good were the morel mushrooms she'd found growing behind the ruined cottage. Those had been her favorite, when Cook had served them sautéed with venison. After hours of shivering on the hard floor in the gray morning in a disquieted sleep, she'd awakened fairly early in the afternoon, expecting a dull and lonely day waiting for Justus, but instead the hours had flown as she'd ventured outside to gather firewood and whatever else she could find.

The rain had quit sometime in the early morning, so she'd savored the feel of the sun on her face as she tried to forget her disturbing dreams of being back at Morningside Asylum. The dream had seemed so real, with her sitting up in her cot in the cell, awaiting Doctor Keene's approach. Only in the dream, she hadn't been frightened. Instead, she was almost… eager.

That had frightened her enough to wake up.

The shivers she'd experienced upon wakening abated. Who knew when would be the last time she'd feel the sun's warmth? Finding dry wood had been difficult, but the discovery of the morels lightened her frustration.

With muttered curses and luck, she built the fire up enough and made a sort of cooking rack for her crock. By the time her pilfered vegetables and found mushrooms were sliced and simmering in the crock and everything else was gathered in the pack for their journey, Bethany was sore from her efforts, but satisfied to have finally done *something* for herself. Just wait until Justus saw the proof that she was capable of more than being a helpless creature.

She frowned at the darkening doorway. Why did he insist on not allowing her to do anything to help their predicament? Irritation gnawed at her for him denying her offer to get wood last night along with hurt as his refusal to feed from her. She could help him. She wasn't starving and weak. She had made her own food.

The stew wasn't nearly as appetizing as she'd liked. And nearly impossible to eat without a spoon. Bethany ended up spearing the chunks of turnip and mushrooms with the stick she'd used to stir them and chewed resolutely, though the turnips could have been boiled longer. Her stomach ached, but she forced the repast down anyway.

"Well," Justus said as he strode into the hovel. "I didn't know you'd learned to cook."

She chuckled, nearly choking on a bite. "Learning would be the proper word. This needed spices and Cook's other concoctions, but at least it was filling and I managed to make it myself." She gave him a pointed look and finished chewing.

His admiring gaze warmed her all over. "I promise you'll have better fare tonight. I have an idea."

Curiosity welled within as she took one last sip of the soup and dumped the rest on the fire to douse it. "What is it?"

"I do not wish to risk disappointment." He took her now dry cloak and settled it over her shoulders before putting out the rest of the fire. "But we do need to hurry."

"Are you strong enough?" she asked, rubbing her aching back.

He nodded. "There was food in the forest for me as well. Deer, not rats."

When he lifted her in his arms, Bethany curled against his body, feeling as if that was what she'd been missing all day. Closing her eyes, she concentrated on his heartbeat as he ran through the forest with his impossible speed.

Gradually, the woods cleared out and more farmlands came into view. Justus passed those swiftly and stopped near a manor house just as the rain began falling once more.

"Halfax," he said, studying the crest.

Bethany blinked, recognizing the name. "One of my father's biggest rivals in parliament."

Justus smirked. "Do you suppose he is at home?"

She shook her head. "They always go to Bath this time of year. I remember because Mother wants to go in the Spring, but Father refuses her because he doesn't want to encounter Lord Halfax."

"Splendid." He extended his arm and led her down the drive.

"What are you doing?" she whispered as Justus knocked on the front door.

"You'll see." Justus's grin broadened as a tired-looking butler answered. "I apologize for my late arrival, but Lord Halfax said I would be welcome any time."

"His Lordship is away," the Butler droned.

"Yes, I know." Justus infused an aristocratic clip in his voice. "I spoke with him while my Lady wife was taking the waters. We're on our way to visit her family in Wales, you see, and my good man Halfax said if we passed this way, we could stay the night."

The butler's eyes narrowed. "And who might you be?"

"Viscount de Wynter." He gave the slightest of bows, which Bethany echoed with a curtsy. Her knees seemed to creak as if unaccustomed to bending like that. She watched as Justus leaned forward and captured the butler's gaze. "But you will not remember that. Now awaken your head housemaid and cook. My wife requires supper, and we both need hot baths and a room."

Bethany watched, jaw agape as the butler bowed and did exactly as told. Moments later, they were led to a sumptuous guest chamber and given hot baths before a sumptuous meal was served in the dining room. Justus also wore a fresh set of clothes, a snowy linen shirt and a bottle green tailcoat with matching trousers. He'd disdained a neckcloth and she couldn't stop peeking at the glimpse of his bare chest.

"I cannot believe you've done this." Bethany whispered as she wiped the crumbs of cobbler from her lips. "Tricked our way into a nobleman's home. Was it wise to give him your true name?"

"The Lord of Rochester apparently did not announce my exile to the Elders or the other Lords, so my identity is safe for the most part. Besides, my Lady deserves better than another night out in the rain," Justus said, sipping his wine.

"I wish you wouldn't refer to me as such," Bethany replied a little more curtly than she meant. She softened as Justus looked at her sharply. "I did not mean to take such a churlish tone. It's just that in my perspective, Ladies are delicate creatures, shielded from the realities of our world. After all I've endured, I'm certainly no longer sheltered and naive. And I'd like to think I'm not completely helpless, that I can contribute to our endeavors."

Justus stared at her with something akin to shock. "I never meant the word to imply that you're to be hidden from the world. I am so sorry if I'd given you such an impression." The sincerity in his voice warmed her all over. "When I refer to you as my Lady, I mean that I see you as the woman I value most in the world, my counterpart, my companion in literary exploration. I may never be able to truly live as Lord de Wynter again, but you will always be my first choice as Lady de Wynter, for I've never met a woman with more strength and wit than you."

"Oh," Bethany said quietly, overwhelmed by his passion. "That is a much better interpretation, and I apologize for assuming you meant something different. However, I do wish you would stop perceiving me as helpless. I am indeed grateful for all you've done for me, but I would much rather that allow me to help you. Teach me how to build a fire, to catch a fish so I may feed myself. Allow me to mend your clothes. Let me feed you when you are hungry." Maybe if she had something useful to do, her increasing sense of unrest and nightmares about Morningside would abate.

His eyes glowed with said hunger. "Bethany," he said hoarsely, "We've discussed this."

"I am no longer weakened from my captivity, Justus." She fixed him with a hard stare. "You've kept me well fed. But you are weakened if you go too long without blood. You should allow me to donate mine, so we may be stronger together."

His blazing eyes searched hers so thoroughly that she shivered. "I will think about it, though there is food aplenty for me here. Tonight, I hunger for something else."

"What?" She licked her lips, hoping it was the same thing she craved.

"To see the library." A gleeful smile curved his lips.

Only a flicker of disappointment glinted in her mind before elation chased it away. "Heavens! I didn't think of that. Of course a house such as this would have a library!" And reading would settle her jangled nerves. Pushing her chair back, she rose in tandem with him, her desire for kisses momentarily quenched by longing for books.

Like children on Christmas, they approached the library with giddy eagerness. The Halfaxes' collection surpassed their most fervent imaginings, with floor to ceiling shelves lining a cavernous room. Three fireplaces were arranged in the chamber to provide optimal warmth in the winter. Justus lit the gas lamps to further illuminate the gleaming shelves, embossed book spines, and sumptuous furnishings.

"Oh, Justus," Bethany breathed. "Look at all of those books." Tears pricked the corners of her eyes at the beautiful sight.

"We have all evening to read," he said, squeezing her hand. "Furthermore, I wager that if we borrow a few, they won't be missed. The Lord and Lady of the house will be too busy searching for missing gold and jewels when they hear of their unexpected visitors."

Bethany tried to feel guilty about what amounted to theft, but the lure of stories and verses she'd long been denied made her welcome the idea. "Besides," she added. "We can always send them back once we are settled."

That assuaged the last vestiges of remorse as they explored the library, reveling in the smell of the books nearly as much as their contents. A joyous cry escaped her lips when she found a work of Chaucer's that she'd never read before.

Together, they curled up on the largest chaise she'd ever seen and read aloud to each other, pausing once in awhile to discuss the meaning of a particular passage.

Bethany rested her head on Justus's chest, more content than she may have ever been in her life. A slight, balmy breeze blew in from the window he'd opened, bringing forth the scent of the warm spring night. His heartbeat pulsed against her ear and delicious heat spiraled in her belly at the feel of their bodies pressed together.

She lifted her chin to gaze at him, enraptured by the strong line of his jaw, his brilliant eyes, and sculpted lips. "Justus?" she whispered. "I know it is not ladylike for me to ask, but I very much would like for you to kiss me again."

Those sensuous lips of his curved in a smile that made her belly flutter. "See, you *are* my counterpart, for I was just going to do just that."

He lowered his head, those silken red locks of his hair caressed her face before his lips came down on hers, fervent and sweet. When his tongue slipped inside her mouth to slide over hers, Bethany gasped at the new sensation. Her hands tangled in his hair as her body curled to meet more of his.

Justus broke the kiss, but her whimper of disappointment changed to a moan of desire as he trailed kisses down her jaw before nibbling on the sensitive place between her shoulder and neck. The heat in her belly spread to the juncture between her thighs, making her hips arch against his. The hardness she felt pressing into her leg turned the heat into a throbbing ache and she longed to feel it at the source of her need.

"Justus," she gasped. "Please."

"We shouldn't," he whispered against her ear, but didn't pull away.

"Yes, we should." She tugged his shirt out of the waistband of his trousers and ran her nails up his bare back. "I'm in a place I love with the man I love. I don't want to experience this with any man but you."

His head snapped up to look at her, eyes suddenly vulnerable yet full of hope. "You do love me?"

She laughed and cupped her cheek. "Of course I do, you silly vampire." Her heart thudded against her ribs as the solemnity of the moment overwhelmed her. "Now please, Justus. Make me yours." When he hesitated, she frowned. "Or am I too old now?"

His shoulders shook with laughter and he seized her hand and pressed a kiss to her palm. "Not at all. I'm still nearly two hundred years your senior. When we first met, I felt guilty for my attraction to you after learning you were only seventeen. Now you are what, five and twenty?"

She nodded, relief washing over her that he did not think her to be on the shelf.

He continued, interspersing his words with kisses. "Now you are fully a woman… completely… perfect…" His hand slid down to cup her breasts. "…in all the right places."

She arched her back at his touch, never imagining that someone grasping her bosom could feel so delicious. He then reached behind her back and unfastened her gown. As he undressed her, he kissed every inch of flesh he exposed. Bethany writhed beneath him, fumbling for the buttons on his shirt.

Once they were both naked, they paused for a prolonged moment, devouring the sight of each other. Kneeling above her, Justus looked like a mythological deity descended from Olympus, with his alabaster skin, lean, chiseled muscles, and nimbus of rich red hair framing his angelic face and emerald eyes. The sprinkle of freckles across his shoulders and the fine red-gold hairs on his body rendered her rapt with fascination.

"You're so beautiful," she breathed. Even the alarming length of his shaft— much larger than the diminutive members in Greek paintings— held its own allure.

He chuckled. "I'm a scrawny ginger. It is you who are exquisite. You'd make Botticelli weep. His fingers danced over her supine body, eliciting new delightful sensations she'd never imagined.

When he cupped her mons, his thumb sliding across the most tender part of her, Bethany cried out at the electric sensation and reached up to explore him. The combination of the silken softness of his skin and the steely hardness beneath its surface captivated her almost as much as his groans of pleasure when she stroked him.

"Enough," he whispered and lay down, propping himself up on his elbows. "I'll go mad if I don't have you now."

His weight atop her was more delicious than she'd imagined, a wonder of closeness. Bethany brushed his hair from his face, meeting his gaze in silent entreaty.

His eyes searched hers with silent entreaty. "Are you ready?"

She took a deep breath and shifted her hips beneath him, gasping at the feel of the tip of him brushing against her moist, sensitive flesh. "Yes."

His hard length pressed against her entrance. Bethany held her breath, ready, but wary of the culmination of their joining.

"I love you," he whispered before sliding inside her just an inch.

Bethany twined her arms over his shoulders, feeling his heartbeat against hers. The feel of him was daunting, but not the bloody agony she'd heard of. "More," she dared to whisper, wanting all of him.

"Not yet," he whispered. "It would cause you pain." But he did slide in a bit further before withdrawing and repeating the process. Gradually he increased the depth of his thrusts until Bethany felt swollen and aching with need. When at last he was fully inside her, she breathed a sigh of contentment, feeling somehow complete.

"I love you," he repeated, remaining still yet holding her close.

"I love you too." Her hips shifted to adjust to the feeling of fullness, which only brought forth a tempest of new sensations.

Justus's breath hitched near her ear as he moved slowly within her, an intoxicating rhythm that rose to a drugging tempo. Bethany clung to him and wrapped her legs around his waist, crying out for more.

His hands slid to cup her buttocks, guiding her into an angle that made all of her sensitive points sing with pleasure. They rocked together in a rising dance that made all the new exciting sensations climb higher and higher.

The rising tide of intense sensations crested and spilled over in a flood of ecstasy. She cried out Justus's name and he held her tighter, guiding her through the storm of his lovemaking. For what felt like the juxtaposition of eternity and mere seconds, she rode the wave of pleasure, before he growled and shuddered within her.

"My God," he whispered, "I never expected it to be so intense."

She nodded and they held each other in blissful silence until the sky began to lighten. Then Justus carried her upstairs to the room they'd been given and set to covering the windows before slipping in beside her in the curtained bed.

Bethany supposed she should feel ruined, but instead she felt fulfilled. Even more importantly, she felt hope.

Chapter Twenty-two

Justus grinned as he and Bethany left Halfax Hall far more enrichened than when they'd arrived. They now carried two packs. One filled with clothes, and another with books, a cooking pot, spoon, fork and other useful items as well as enough food for Bethany to last a week. He'd even found a bedroll so Bethany would no longer have to lay on a hard surface. But more importantly, they left with the culmination of their love.

He frowned. Well, not quite. They still needed to be wed. Hell, they still needed to find sanctuary and a home to call their own. Even more pressing was the need to find shelter for the day. Justus wished they could have spent one more night at Halfax Hall, but it would be too dangerous as well as more difficult to ensure the servants only retained the vaguest of memories of their visit.

Running was slightly more difficult with the extra baggage, but Justus managed, stronger from feeding from the Halfax servants. He slowed as he glimpsed firelight in the distance and heard exotic music.

It was a Roma encampment. That took care of food for him at least.

But just as he began to head in that direction, a voice echoed from a nearby tree. “Not so fast, Rogue.”

Justus froze as a vampire with the dark hair and eyes of the Roma people dropped from the tree to stand before him.

He backed away, holding Bethany tight. “Please, let us pass. I do not wish to make trouble.”

The vampire cocked his head to the side, “And where are you going with this sweet morsel?”

Though something in the vampire's eyes compelled honesty, Justus only answered partially. “Somewhere where we can be wed and become citizens.” He did not mention his destination.

The vampire chuckled. “An ambitious journey, to reclaim legitimacy, though I can see why that is a necessity.” His gaze flicked to Bethany. “And do you know the sort of man you're eloping with?”

Bethany remained silent and Justus praised her for her courage and wisdom in refusing to answer a trick question.

The vampire chuckled. “I can see that you do.” He met Justus's eyes. “Quite illegal, but I understand that you have no choice unless you wish for her to become a rogue too.”

Justus nodded curtly. "Who are you and what do you want?"

"I'm Luca of the Roma." He bowed with mock flourish. "And a rogue as well."

Justus relaxed slightly. That meant he would not be arrested at least, though there was still danger. Many rogues were prone to attack others. "I'm Justus, of nowhere. And this is Bethany. You did not answer my second question."

"At first I wanted to ensure my tribe's safety and satisfy my curiosity, which is still not sated." Luca said. "I presume you wished to feed on one of my camp?"

"Yes, but as those people are clearly protected, I shall seek my meal elsewhere." Justus turned to take them in the opposite direction.

"Wait," Luca said. "What do you have to trade?"

Justus shook his head. "Very little, I'm afraid."

"I disagree." Luca smiled. "Aside from the two packs you carry, you must have a marvelous story, to be so far from Rochester and taking an escaped lunatic to Cornwall so you can wed her."

"How did you—"

Luca laughed. "There is only one rogue vampire with hair of that shade, and only one place someone of your sort could hope to find haven. As for the beauty? The sketch in the newspapers favors her greatly. They do love a sensational story."

Unease swirled in Justus's gut at the fact that so much of his situation had been deduced, even if Luca seemed jovial. He blinked at him in disbelief. "Are you offering me the right to feed in exchange for my story?"

The Roma vampire nodded. "I'll offer you shelter as well, but only for one day. This camp is not large enough to support more than one vampire for long."

Not knowing where the next village was, Justus could only bow his head with cautious gratitude. "I thank you for the kindness."

Luca chuckled. "And I thank you for the diversion you provide. There is one thing, though. My people will not look kindly upon an unwed couple out and about unchaperoned. We are a decent people, contrary to what the *Gadjos* say."

Justus sighed. "With me being a rogue, and her a fugitive, we can hardly secure a special license and find a vicar."

The vampire regarded them with sympathy. "I understand. However, you can be married tonight in the Roma way. It won't be recognized under English law, but it would make you more welcome among my people, and at least be something until you are settled."

Justus frowned. "Why are you helping us anyway?"

"Rogues should help each other out once in awhile." Luca clapped him on the shoulder. "Besides, I do love circumventing the law. Both human and vampire."

Heart in his throat, Justus looked down at Bethany. He'd understand if she refused, yet it would sting.

Her lips curved in a smile reminiscent of the dawn. "A gypsy wedding? My mother would faint."

Luca frowned. "We prefer to be called Roma."

She looked down, abashed. "My apologies. A Roma wedding."

"Is that a yes?" Justus asked tentatively as he set her on her feet.

She nodded. "Who knows when we shall have another opportunity? It is a pity that I do not have a gown."

Luca shrugged. "The women of the camp may be able to help. Follow me."

While still on guard, Justus and Bethany allowed the vampire to escort them to the Roma encampment, where they were greeted with a mixture of curiosity and suspicion. Luca explained to them that Justus had kidnapped Bethany to wed her, and before Justus could argue, the people broke out into smiles and cheers. He'd forgotten that bride kidnapping was a custom among these folk. Luca continued, but this time he spoke in Romani, so Justus couldn't discern what he'd said. Whatever it was seemed to put the people further at ease.

The women hauled Bethany away into one of the caravans to prepare her for the ceremony while Justus joined Luca in his.

"Do they know what you are?" he asked when they were alone, looking at the covered windows.

Luca shook his head. "They know that I am different, but that it is forbidden for me to speak about it. I never stay with one tribe long enough for them to notice that I do not age. Truly, it is a good life for a rogue vampire. The rest of our kind pay no attention to nomadic societies. But other rogues are too blinded by their prejudice to think of it. Perhaps that's a good thing, since as I'd said, these tribes really could not safely sustain more than one of us. But perhaps you could find a tribe."

Throughout Justus's centuries in England, he'd only noticed the Roma in a periphery manner. Embarrassment filled him at his longtime ignorance. When he'd been exiled from Rochester, the thought of joining the Romani never occurred to him. "If I was on my own, I'd consider it, but Bethany will have enough of a challenge learning how to be a vampire when I Change her. I'm reluctant to add learning a new culture to her trials as well. Besides, we both love books and hope to one day have a home full of them."

Luca grinned. "I understand. That is one of the things I dislike about living among the Roma. We only get new books when we encounter other tribes to trade with. Speaking of trading…" His eyes gleamed with interest. "Tell me your story."

Justus sighed and did so, trying to speak as quickly as possible. Still, he was shifting with impatience to leave the caravan and make certain Bethany was all right.

Luca shook his head in wonder. "My God, you're in quite the… what do you *Gadjos* call it? Sticky wicket."

"Indeed."

The rogue vampire patted his shoulder. "I hope you make it to Cornwall safely. I'll ask the tribal elders to bless you."

"Thank you." Doubtless, they needed it.

When they left the caravan, Bethany was already waiting, dressed in a long, ruffled lavender skirt and a white blouse. Her hair was braided, tied with matching lavender ribbons. No jewels or other adornments graced her neck or wrists, unlike the other women of the tribe, but the love in her eyes made her beauty outshine them all.

The ceremony was short, with one of the patriarchs of the tribe saying some words in Romani and swinging a brazier of incense over them while they stood with their hands joined. When the people broke out in cheers, Justus took it as confirmation that they were wed.

The men offered him congratulations in both English and Romani, as well as wishes that his bride would be fertile. Justus smiled with a touch of bitterness. She likely was fertile, but he was not. He'd never contemplated children before, but now the fact that he and Bethany never could have them stung slightly. He shook off the melancholy sentiment. He was beyond lucky to have found Bethany and be joined with her at all.

The women unbraided Bethany's hair and tied a lavender kerchief on her head. Observing the many women with similar kerchiefs and young girls with braids, Justus guessed that must be the symbol of a married woman. The sight of Bethany with one was suddenly appealing, despite his disliking of her covering her golden hair.

They were then treated to a delicious feast and music. Justus sampled all of the dishes with miniscule nibbles that his digestion would allow while Bethany ate with gusto. Justus fed on one of the people in the shadows, carefully erasing the person's memory with an apology. They then danced to the music, laughing at their clumsiness.

Luca offered them his caravan to spend their wedding night and then day sleep. "There is a cave nearby where I go to be alone." He smiled at both of them. "I wish you both luck, both in your marriage and on your journey. I will see you at dusk. You may hunt one more time before you leave."

Then they were alone in the caravan, a soft bed with fresh sheets illuminated in golden light from the lanterns.

"What was it like with the women?" Justus asked, resisting the urge to toss her onto that bed at once. Instead, they both sat upon the down-filled mattress.

Bethany sighed. "They interrogated me for an eternity on my purity, making certain that I was with no other man. Then they asked if you'd offered my parents a bride price." She chuckled. "They were so perplexed when I explained that things are done the opposite way among the *Gadjos*. And when they learned we both have no family, they softened, though they were merciless in washing me free of all impurities. I was afraid they'd scrub my skin clean off!" She rubbed her arms, clearly still experiencing discomfort.

Justus laughed. "I thought I'd choke on all the incense they wafted around me, and I was given a thorough cleaning as well. Luca said we could try to find another tribe to live with." At her horrified look, he continued. "I told him we'd rather have a house and an enormous library."

Bethany beamed, her relief apparent. "I'm pleased that we are in accord. Now enough about our Roma wedding. We do not have long before dawn." She reached for him, eyes dilated with passion.

"If I'd known we would have our wedding night so soon," Justus began with a touch of guilt, but Bethany placed her finger over his lips.

"Do not say something that will hurt me deeply," she said with an enchanting half smile. "Last night was perfect. And this night will be the same." Then she withdrew her finger and leaned forward to kiss him.

And it was indeed perfect. Like the most addicting drug, Justus couldn't get enough of her. He yanked her onto his lap, groaning as his hardness met her softness. His tongue delved between her lips, tasting the mead she'd sipped earlier.

Slowly, he untied her blouse and reached down to caress her firm breasts. Her nipples tightened to hard little peaks beneath his thumbs, and her gasp echoes his own when she leaned forward to kiss his neck, all the while undulating against him in an erotic rhythm.

Bethany was just as eager as he was, fumbling with his shirt until he pulled it over his head and tossed it on the floor. Her hands explored him with unabashed curiosity and he was electrified by her touch.

"God, you feel so good on top of me," he whispered, rucking up her skirts to feel more of her silken skin.

"No, you feel good." Her hips arched against his erection and she licked her lips. "Is it possible for us to…" she trailed off with a blush.

"Oh yes," he whispered, claiming her lips for another lingering kiss. With utmost reluctance, he lifted her off his lap to remove his trousers. When he glanced back up, his breath caught as he saw that Bethany had removed her clothing as well.

His eyes devoured her deliciously curved form, her lush breasts crowned with rosy tips, the hypnotic indent of her belly button, and the triangle of golden curls covering the treasure between her thighs.

Justus knelt before her. "First, there is one thing I must do."

Reverently, he licked and kissed her labia and clitoris, grasping her hips to steady her when she swayed. Her arousal tasted like the nectar of the gods, her gasps and moans of pleasure a symphony to his ears.

When he'd reduced her to shudders and incoherent moans, he once more sat and lifted her on his lap. Slowly, he guided himself inside her, sucking in a breath as her tight sheath closed around his cock.

The Roma music continued to play outside, lending a primal rhythm to their movements. Bethany undulated against him like an erotic dancer as the beats of the drums set fire to their blood. Their pleasure built like a gathering storm before crashing through them like thunder and lightning. Justus buried his face in the hollow of her throat as his climax reduced him to a quivering mass.

"I love you," he groaned, unable to say it enough. His adoration for her had become a never ending song in his heart and soul.

When at last they descended back to reality, Justus's lust had only been slightly slaked. He made love to her twice more, the sunrise barely noted due to the blocked windows. Then he tucked her in his arms, settling the coverlet over them in the surprisingly comfortable bed.

For the first time since they set off on their arduous journey, Justus wasn't gripped with panic as to what would happen when they made it to Cornwall. Instead, hope and joy permeated his being. Bethany was his wife at long last, and as long as they were together, all would be well.

Chapter Twenty-Three

The following evening, Bethany was stunned when the Roma people gave them gifts blankets, a little more food, salt, and other useful items for their journey. With how the women had questioned her purity and the subtle scorn in their eyes when they referred to her as a *Gadji,* she'd assumed that all but Kallia, the woman who'd provided her clothes for her wedding and given her a protective talisman, would only provide the bare minimum of hospitality. Not that she blamed them. Aside from the fact that she and Justus were strangers and not of their kind, the tribe had limited possessions as suited for their nomadic lifestyle. She was more than grateful for the wedding, feast, and accommodations. To receive more was a delightful surprise and she hoped that someday she could repay them.

Justus disappeared quickly to feed. As she waited for him, trying to listen to the women's advice on making a good marriage, that strange, twitchy sense of unrest crawled over her body, making her shiver. She fought back a frown of confusion. She hadn't felt this so severely since her day alone in the abandoned cottage, and that had been from her nightmares about Morningside. Why was she experiencing this situation now, when she was so happy?

All those unpleasant thoughts vanished when Justus returned. Bethany took a deep breath, trying to suppress those odd shivers as they said their goodbyes and walked away from the Roma with smiles plastered on their faces. Once they were out of view, he lifted her into his arms and ran with his blinding speed.

Bethany's stomach dipped, but not as often as badly as it used to. She wondered how it would behave when she would be able to run like that. As the miles to Cornwall lessened, she thought more and more about her impending transformation into a vampire. Part of her warred with asking Justus if they could find another abandoned cottage to camp in so she could enjoy the sunlight a little longer. The other part wanted to get to Cornwall as soon as possible so their future was resolved and maybe her jitters would abate. Perhaps the Lord Vampire there would allow her to enjoy a day or two walking along the famous seaside cliffs and watch the sun rise over the ocean.

After an eternity of running, Justus slowed to a stop and set her on her feet. "We've arrived in Gloucestershire." A broad smile illuminated his handsome face. "We could be in Cornwall in a matter of days."

Suddenly, two dark figures tackled Justus, knocking him to the ground. Bethany was seized from behind by a pair of mercilessly strong arms.

As she watched Justus struggle, one of the shadows spoke. "Where's your writ of passage?"

"If you thought I'd had one, you wouldn't have tackled me," Justus grumbled.

The other sniffed in derision. "You'll have to come with us, Ginger."

Bethany's stomach dropped. These must be the vampires of Gloucestershire.

The one holding Bethany turned her around to face his implacable visage. "How much do you know about your traveling companion, girl?"

Girl? She was a woman old enough to be a spinster. Still, she answered as Justus advised. "That he is a kind and honorable traveling companion who is safely escorting me to my relatives in Bath. What of it?"

"I think she's lying," one of the vampires restraining Justus said.

"What is this about?" she demanded, playing her role of ignorance to her utmost. "Are you implying that he is some sort of criminal?"

"I'm afraid so," the vampire holding her said. "You're lucky we arrived to save you from an unsavory fate."

"And just who are you?" she asked, challenging them to come up with their own untruth.

"Scotland Yard," they answered in tandem.

If the situation were not so dire, she might have laughed. With their clearly expensive overcoats and shining hessians, they clearly were thicker in the pocket than Britain's harried investigators.

"What should we do with her?" One of the Gloucestershire vampires asked. "Do you suppose his Lordship will wish to question her?"

"A delicious morsel such as this?" the one holding Bethany said, twirling a lock of her hair around his fingers as Justus snarled and tried to break free. "Undoubtedly. But I am not inclined to grant him the pleasure. Not after his cruel punishment of Phyllis."

The third vampire shook his head. "I daresay, denying a Lord his rights because you're put out with him is not a good reason. However, I have a feeling that he'll be occupied with this rogue and inconvenienced by a prisoner of her ilk. She may be dressed like a rag tag Gypsy, but her speech is clearly that of a lady."

The second one frowned. "But we can't just leave her here, alone in the dark. She could be set upon by brigands."

The first one scoffed, while the second scratched his chin. "You're right. 'Twouldn't be proper. We'll escort her to the village on our way to delivering this scoundrel to His Lordship."

Bethany couldn't hold back a sigh of relief, even if it just meant that her parting from Justus would only be slightly delayed. However, perhaps she could discern where they were going.

"And who would His Lordship be?" she asked, lacing her voice with aristocratic scorn. "Perhaps my father, Lord Wickshire, may be acquainted with him. It would be rude of me not to pay a call upon a family friend."

"His Lordship has more friends than he can keep track of, and very little time to cater to social niceties," the vampire grasping her said loftily. "Have your father post him a letter if he is so keen."

"How am I supposed to do that if you will not tell me who he is?" Bethany feigned irritation, though the vampire had unwittingly confirmed an important piece of information. The

Lord Vampire of Gloucestershire was part of the peerage. "And what does he want with this gentleman who was escorting me?"

"That is none of your concern," the vampire snapped, eyeing her with derision.

"Of course it is my concern!" Bethany cried out. "This gentleman is accompanying me to my destination and ensuring my safety. My father will have something to say about this."

"This rogue is no gentleman," the vampire laughed. "He'd have a carriage and you'd have a chaperone."

Justus spoke for the first time. "Actually, I am indeed a gentleman. I'm the Viscount de Wynter."

The vampires laughed harder, their leader elbowing Justus in the ribs. "Right, and I'm Duke of Devonshire! Enough out of you, cad. Anything you have to say isn't fitting for the Lady's ears."

Bethany understood the veiled warning. They did believe she was an ignorant mortal, and they didn't want Justus to say anything that would reveal the truth of the situation. She prayed the deception would hold, for if they knew that she was privy to their world, the Lord of Gloucestershire would likely kill Justus— if he wouldn't already. And who knew what they would do to her.

Her heart ached with misery and terror as they walked. How in the world would they get out of this disaster? Justus was outnumbered, and she was a weak human woman with no hope of fighting three vampires.

"Well, I don't like the shifty look in that one's *eyes*," Justus retorted, giving Bethany a lingering look. "How do I know you'll ensure her safety?"

Bethany caught Justus's message. *Don't look any of them in the eyes.* That way they couldn't feed on her or banish her memories. Her chin dropped to look at her boots. She'd never be able to find Justus if she didn't remember what happened. Another thought made panic grip her lungs. What if they made her forget Justus altogether?

"The woman is no concern to us," the leader said loftily, looking down his nose at Justus. "We only want her out of the way so we can deal with you."

"Out of the way does not sound promising," Bethany grumbled, trying to sound petulant rather than frightened. "Perhaps I may accompany you to your lord and he may provide me his carriage."

"Quiet, woman," the sandy-haired vampire snarled. "His Lordship wouldn't loan so much as a spoonful of sugar to a ragtag female that may or may not be a lady."

The grass they trod upon turned into a path, and gaslights gleamed off in the distance. Time was running out.

Bethany willed herself to be calm. Justus had said that the last time he'd been arrested, he'd been imprisoned before he was sentenced. Hopefully that meant the Lord of Gloucestershire wouldn't kill him outright. And she'd have time to break him free. Somehow.

When they arrived at the edge of the village, the vampire who held her turned her to face him. "Look at me, my lady."

She lifted her chin and stared at his nose.

His lips turned down in a scowl. "I said, look at me!"

"I am!" she said stubbornly.

"I mean—"

"If I may," Justus interrupted placidly. "I'm certain she'd rather look at me, if you catch my meaning. And I would very much like to tell her goodbye. I may be a rogue, but I am no scoundrel. I still need to return her money and her luggage."

The three vampires exchanged glances before the one who must be their leader nodded. "Fine. Do what *needs* to be done. And if you try any funny business, you will regret it."

They were going to allow Justus to erase her memory, only she knew he wouldn't. The vampire holding Bethany released her reluctantly. She ran to Justus and threw her arms around him. In his embrace, their enemies momentarily vanished.

Justus cupped her face and gazed into her eyes. Instead of his hypnotic power, she saw only his love for her. When he bent down and kissed her, she felt that electric spark again and tasted his blood.

When he broke the kiss, she felt like her heart had broken as well. "Goodbye, Bethany," he whispered. "Even though you won't *remember*," a touch of emphasis imbued the last word, "I'll always love you."

"That's enough of that," one of the vampires growled, breaking them apart.

Justus sighed and lifted the packs from his shoulders and set them at her feet before reaching into his pocket and handing her his purse with its meager coins. "This should be enough for a meal and a room for the night. In the morning, send a post to your uncle, telling him of your delay. Do not travel alone."

Bethany nodded, even though she had no uncle, so she wondered if he was stalling for time, or trying to send her a hint. Her eyes widened. Justus must be referring to the Lord of Cornwall. Yet how would she send him a letter when she did not know who he was? Or did he wish her to indeed keep going to Cornwall? She chewed her lower lip, struggling to discern his meaning.

The vampires pushed them further apart as she struggled to shoulder the heavy packs.

"Take her to the inn," the lead vampire said. "We'll meet you at His Lordship's home."

With that, Bethany and Justus were taken in opposite directions. She peered longingly over her shoulder and studied the direction Justus's captors were headed.

"Come along, Miss." The vampire escorting her tugged at her arm, making her almost drop one of the bags. To her surprise, he offered to carry one of them for her.

Far behind them, she heard one of the other vampires say, "So it was like that, eh? Why didn't you make her privy to your circumstances?"

"You know why," Justus said gruffly.

She saw one last flash of his dark red hair in the moonlight before he and the others faded into the shadows. She made note of the landmarks and the direction they'd gone.

"Come along, woman." Her vampire escort tugged on her elbow.

Bethany jerked her arm from his grasp and shot him a glare. "Just because you are vexed with being saddled with the duty of escorting a woman to safety does not mean you have to be so rude."

To her surprise, his features softened. "You are right. I apologize for my poor manners. What is your name?"

"Beth," she replied, knowing he'd think that was short for Elizabeth. "What of you?"

"Edward," he said stiffly, not indicating whether or not it was a real name. He glanced at her from the corners of his eyes and she shifted her gaze downward so he couldn't mesmerize her. "I do wish you'd tell us more about what you were doing with that rogue— er man."

"And I wish you would tell me who you people are and what you intend to do with Justus!" she fired back.

Edward chuckled. "It seems we are at an impasse." They walked in silence for a while before he spoke again. "You really love him, don't you?"

Too taken aback to lie, she nodded.

He regarded her with a pitying look. "Most unfortunate. I advise you to do your best to forget him. Find another beau."

Bethany refused to dignify that with a response and they walked the rest of the way in silence. Edward left her side the moment they entered the closest inn.

The innkeeper frowned at the idea of renting a room to a woman alone, but reluctantly agreed once he saw Bethany's coin. However, he insisted that she stay in her room and keep the door locked until daytime. That suited her fine. Glancing at the vampire making his way to a cluster of men crowded at the bar, she prayed he would linger awhile longer.

It took all of her effort not to run up the stairs behind the servant who escorted her. And the moment she was alone in the Spartan room, she thrust the window open and peered out. A tree sprouted near the edge of the building, but unfortunately, not by her window. Breathing a prayer, she made her way out the window and kept her feet balanced on the narrow ledge. Not daring to look down, she inched her way along the wall. If her tremors returned, she would tumble down and break her neck.

After an eternity of shuffling along, her pulse pounding as she crossed each adjacent window, Bethany at last reached the tree. Her breath escaped her lungs in a whoosh as she saw a thick limb within reach. It would be just like the times she'd climbed down the tree in her bedroom window in Rochester.

No, not quite. She uttered an unladylike curse as she remembered she still wore skirts. But there would have been no time to change into trousers, even if she'd had them. With another deep breath, she hopped carefully onto the branch, grasping the one above her as she teetered a moment.

Further grumbles ensued as she untangled her skirts from the other branches and knotted them as best as she could around her knees like awkward pantaloons. She nearly fell out of the tree on her last knot. Recovering her balance, she made her way down the tree, the skill coming back to her like second nature.

When she reached the ground, Bethany's spirits lifted when she saw that the front door of the inn was in view from her hiding place behind the trunk. She'd be able to see the vampire leave. …If he hadn't already. She shook her head, refusing to be brought down with hopeless doubt. With luck, she'd be able to follow the vampire.

She grasped the talisman that Kallia, the Roma woman had given her, saying a silent prayer to whatever deity or patron saint it appealed to.

The talisman must have answered her, for only moments later, Edward left the inn and walked unhurried down the road in what looked to be the same direction Justus's captors had headed. Bethany unknotted her skirts and followed behind trying to remain at a distance so he wouldn't spot her.

A few times she had to duck against the wall or into a nearby alley to keep him from seeing her if he glanced behind. To make matters worse, another attack of the shivers rained down upon her making her feel like a palsied old woman as she shuffled through the shadows.

A carriage rolled down the intersection, blocking her view. When it passed, the vampire was gone. Bethany's heart sank. Which way had he gone? When she reached the splitting roads, she looked in both directions, but saw no sign of him.

Panic roiled in her belly, making her queasy. If she couldn't find Justus, all was lost. Her eyes squeezed shut to stave off the threatening tears.

A strange shiver prickled the back of her neck, different from the other sort, along with a tight urgency in her chest and a wordless voice compelling her to turn left. The odd feeling was reminiscent of that electric sensation she'd felt when she tasted Justus's blood.

Her lips parted in astonishment. He'd told her that giving her his blood would help him find her if they were separated, but what if the reverse was true? Hope welling through her being, Bethany chose the left road and walked as fast as possible. Soon, the dark outline of a figure came into view. Just as it began to turn, Bethany ducked behind a large barrel. Had it been Edward? It had to be.

She peered around the barrel and crept out when the figure continued walking. As she drew closer, she confirmed that she was indeed following the correct individual. Hiding places grew more scarce as the buildings gave way to green hills and fields. Bethany's legs ached from the long walk, even as confidence filled her that she was on the right course. For now, sprawling mansions were visible off in the distance. Even better, her tremors had subsided.

Edward scurried to one of the smaller manors and Bethany drew as close as she dared. Following the vampire up the long drive would be folly, but she studied the crest on the gate until it was committed to memory. Her blood hummed in her veins the nearer she came. Justus *had* to be in here. She swore she could feel him.

Though every vestige of her being railed at her to charge into that house and find Justus, she knew that facing a Lord Vampire and his cohorts in their own domain would be hopeless.

But perhaps there was something she could do during the day while they slept.

Squaring her shoulders, Bethany walked the long way back to the inn, a plan beginning to form in her mind. She'd need her supplies and other things. More importantly, she needed to learn who that family crest belonged to.

When she made it back into the village square, a rat-faced man lurched toward her, but at her straight posture, clenched fists and blazing eyes, he rethought his approach and passed her by.

Chapter Twenty-four

Justus heaved a sigh as he was shackled to another damp stone wall in yet another underground prison. This one was more cramped and rat infested than Rochester's.

Squire Ridley, the Lord Vampire of Gloucester, peered up at him with a smug smile. "So, de Wynter, it seems your illegitimate gallivanting through the country has come to an end." His hands shifted to smooth his neckcloth, putting to mind a preening bird. "You will soon learn that I don't take kindly to rogues in my territory."

"I was only passing through," Justus said blandly. "And I am seeking citizenship so that I will no longer be a rogue."

Ridley snorted. "Only so you can have your way with that golden-haired beauty my second and third found you with."

"I found her too," the vampire who'd escorted Bethany to the village said from the doorway. "Dropped her at an inn."

It took every ounce of will in Justus's being not to turn to him and ask if she was safe.

"Yes, Edward. And you." Ridley fussed with his cravat a moment longer before turning to him. "By the by, what did you learn about that human woman? Did she have an inkling as to who she was keeping company with?"

Edward shook his head. "I don't think so. She was far too calm. In any case, we made that one banish her memory. Still, I think the chit had secrets of her own. She said her father was a lord and huffed about telling the man about the rogue's arrest, but something in her eyes made me think that was bluster. Either the girl's father is no lord, or she is not in contact with him. No decent man would permit his daughter to travel alone at night with a man."

Ridley nodded and his gaze flicked to Justus. "I wager you know her entire story."

Justus remained silent, facing him calm and stoic in his chains.

The Lord of Gloucestershire laughed, a high-pitched titter. "We'll get it out of you one way or another when I try you. Still, it is no great feat to deduce that you've lost your heart to the chit. Her scent is all over you." He reached out and grasped Justus's treasured locket and opened it. "And then here's this keepsake she gave you. Yes, she is a beauty. Is that why you've embarked on this foolish attempt to regain legitimacy?"

There was no reason to lie, so Justus nodded curtly. His love for Bethany was something he'd never be able to deny.

Laughter greeted his response, brittle and mocking. "Only something so foolish as love would inspire such a preposterous idea." The humor vanished from Ridley's face, his countenance turning sour and twisted with obsessive rage. "Do you truly believe that any Lord Vampire with a half a mind would make you a citizen again? Rogues are evil cretins and will *always* be evil cretins." The declaration came out in a roar, spittle running down Ridley's chin. "A rogue like you killed the woman I loved."

And there it was. Confirmation that he would not be leaving this place alive. If Ridley held such a grudge, he'd be blind to reason.

"Then I suppose there is nothing more to say," Justus said tiredly.

Ridley's face reddened. "I decide when this interrogation is over, you filthy ginger cur!" The back of his hand struck Justus's cheek in a resounding slap. Justus's head rocked back to slam against the wall. He tasted blood from where his teeth collided with his cheek, but refrained from making a sound.

"Where were you taking the woman on your foolhardy venture?" Ridley demanded.

Justus licked his blood from his lips and did not answer.

Ridley smiled, revealing narrow fangs, looking out of place in the midst of his crooked teeth. "Jacob, heat a poker. We'll see if that will prod him into being more conversational."

Bloody hell... Justus closed his eyes against the tidal wave of dread. He'd heard that some Lord Vampire utilized torture for their prisoners, that a few even reveled in it. However, it gave him no surprise that Ridley was of that persuasion. Many squires he'd encountered had a mean streak, perhaps to make up for their lower social status. Of course, after everything had been going so well, he had to fall into the clutches of a bully.

The vampire named Jacob, who Justus gathered to be Ridley's second in command, approached with a glowing red poker. From scenting his power, it seemed he was younger than Justus, but that didn't matter so long as Justus was restrained.

Ridley took the poker with a smile like an eager child receiving a sweet from the cook. "I'm going to give you one more chance to do this the easy way. "Where were you taking the woman?"

"It is not of your concern," Justus said as mildly as if they were discussing the weather over tea. He doubted Ridley even cared what he was doing with Bethany in the first place. Likely he just wanted an excuse to torture him. But he wouldn't tell in case Ridley decided to go after Bethany.

Blazing pain exploded in his side, the smell of burnt fabric and charred flesh making his gorge rise. If he'd had a substantial breakfast, he would have cast up his accounts. Justus gritted his teeth against the agony, refusing to give Ridley the satisfaction of a scream.

Ridley frowned, as if his metaphorical sweet lacked sugar. "Did you not understand the question, rogue? Where were you taking her?"

Again, Justus remained silent and again, Ridley seared him like a side of beef.

"Maybe next I'll have to burn your pretty face," Ridley snarled, though his eyes shone with delight at the notion. "Let's try another question, shall we? Is the woman truly the daughter of the Baron of Wickshire?"

Having no reason to lie, he nodded. "Yes, but they have been estranged. However, fathers always have a soft spot for their daughters, so I'm quite sure he would be very vexed if any harm came to her.

Ridley pursed his narrow lips, as if considering arguing and deciding on another course. "And neither father nor daughter know what you are?"

"No." It was only a half lie.

"I don't believe you." Ridley pressed the poker to Justus's cheek, but it was only warm. Still, Justus flinched reflexively. The squire grinned. "We'll have to continue this discussion tomorrow. It is past my meal time and I have more important affairs to attend to." Once more, he grasped the locket.

"Please," Justus croaked. "Let me keep it."

Ridley's lips twisted in a mocking smirk and for a moment he looked as if he would yank the locket from Justus's neck, but then he let it drop back beneath Justus's shirt. "Very well. I suppose I can wait to collect it from your corpse later."

When Justus was left alone in the dark cell, he slumped in his chains with mingled relief and despair. Though his torment had ended, the reprieve was only temporary. Tomorrow, Ridley would begin torturing him in earnest. And since the vampire was seeking information on Bethany that Justus would die before revealing, he would endure pain greater than he could possibly imagine.

Drowning in desperation, Justus tugged and twisted in his shackles, looking for the slightest increment of yield. His heart sank the longer the shackles held. Ridley may not have put forth much effort in upkeep for his dungeon as Gavin did, but he clearly spared no expense with his restraints. A pity, because the bars of his cell appeared rusted and weak enough to snap.

Hopelessness settled over him like a leaden shroud. Torture and death awaited him tomorrow at nightfall, and he would never see Bethany again.

Chapter Twenty-Five

Bethany jerked the reins, cursing the mule who'd stopped yet again to nibble on the grass. Irritation and anger roared through her being, and it took every vestige of her will not to take it out on the animal. But if the beast kept at this rate, it would be dark before she arrived at Ridley house. Sweat poured down her back. The homespun gown she wore was too thick for the May sun, though perfect for the cool nights. Her whole body ached from her trek to find Justus and her dash back to the inn. Her eyes burned with lack of sleep, and there was an odd burning sensation in the back of her throat. But her jaw clenched with determination. She would save Justus as he'd saved her—or die trying.

She reached into the satchel beside her and withdrew a roll to nibble on. It taken all the coins in Justus's purse as well as her nicest gown to purchase the rickety cart and cantankerous mule who'd likely been put out to pasture a year or more ago. But there was no help for it. She needed this cart, along with the battered trunk inside that she'd recovered from an alley.

Eventually, Ridley House came into view, much smaller than it had seemed in the darkness last night. It sat almost hunched and aloof from its neighbors, like a child wanting to sit at the dining room table with its elders. Such was often the case with squires, to hear her father talk of them.

The lowest ranking of the peerage, squires were often either kowtowing sycophants or stuffy prigs who hid their insecurities about their status with snobbery. Looking at the hideous gilded architecture, Bethany expected the latter, especially since this particular squire was the Lord Vampire of an entire county. What power he lacked among humans, he likely wielded like a club amongst his own kind.

She urged the mule around the back to the servants' entrance, securing the cart as close to the door as possible. Her foolhardy plan depended on so many unconcluded variables, the main being that like Justus said most vampires tended to do, Ridley likely had few servants to lessen the chances of humans learning his secret.

The mule cropped at a clump of overgrown weeds, lending hope to her supposition. A decent gardener would have cleared those out. Swinging Justus's satchel over her shoulder, she dropped down from her perch on the wagon and strode to the door.

Keeping one hand on the satchel, she pounded on the door. A stooped, elderly cook answered and blinked at her myopically.

"I 'ave a delivery for Squire Ridley," Bethany said, trying to fake a Cockney accent.

"What is it?"

"Mead," she said, and gestured to the trunk. "If you or a footman can help me carry it down to the wine cellar, I'd be most obliged."

The cook pursed her lips. "I didn't receive any word that the Squire was expecting any mead."

"Ah, that is because he won it at cards the other night," Bethany recited her prepared excuse. "Do tell him that my master apologizes for the delay."

"And who is your master?"

Bethany bit back a groan of impatience. If this woman refused to get out of the way, she just might have to box her ears. "Mr. Bingley, the owner of the Duck and Barrel." If anyone was likely to play cards and gamble mead, it would be the proprietor of the inn she'd stayed at. She'd been certain to gather up all the local gossip about who was whom in the area before setting out on her mission.

For a tense moment, the cook remained silent before she finally nodded. "I'll get Ames to help you unload that thing. You'll have to take a handle, though. He has bad knees and cannot manage on his own."

Bethany blinked and suppressed a wry smile at how different women in the lower classes were treated compared to her idle, sheltered upbringing. They were expected to do actual work, be useful for more than overseeing households, hosting parties, and birthing heirs. And though her aching muscles protested the prospect of bearing more weight, a giddy delight teased her senses. She would handle Justus's rescue with her own hands and the strength of her back.

Though if the servants grew hostile… She shook away the impending dread and remorse. It was too late to go back now.

When the footman emerged and helped her unload the trunk, Bethany saw that poor old Ames had more than bad knees. His hands shook with palsy, making her writhe with guilt for what she may have to do even more unbearable.

They carried the trunk down into the wine cellar. Bethany's shoulders ached with the strain and her own hands shook. She'd filled the trunk with stones to give it weight, but it would be even heavier on her way out. Once down in the cellar, she strode toward a thick door reinforced with iron.

A trembling hand fell on her shoulder. "We're never supposed to go in there," Ames said.

Bethany sighed and pulled the blunderbuss from the satchel. "I'm very sorry, but I must. Now, please open the door. I truly do not wish to hurt you."

Ames jerked away from her like she'd burned him, his jaw gaping like a fish's. His hands shaking like windblown leaves, he fumbled with the locks and catches on the door. Once it swung open, he unbelievably scurried back to Bethany's side, as if she would protect him from what lay ahead. And perhaps she would.

"Bring the lantern," she ordered, before plunging into the dark passage.

The servant's quivering hands shook so hard the light flickered like angry lightning. Bethany hoped her own tremors wouldn't return. Still, she made out the unmistakable shape of barred cells lining the walls.

Ames's shuddering breathing echoed in the damp stone walls. "We're not supposed to be in here," he wailed in a feeble, thin voice. "I don't even know what's down here. Only that it is forbidden."

"Hush," she said, turning the blunderbuss toward him, though not having the heart to aim it. "If you're not supposed to know, you should be able to plead ignorance of this entire matter. Light these cells, please."

Ames shuffled closer, his wobbling light steadying enough for her to see an achingly familiar glint of red from the depths of one of the dank cells.

"Justus!" she whispered loudly, shuffling forward.

He hung from shackles on the wall, his head resting on his chest in what must be an uncomfortable angle.

Ames gasped behind her, clearly not expecting to find a dungeon beneath his master's forbidden door.

"Do you have the keys?" Bethany asked without much hope.

The elderly footman shook his head. "I told you, Miss, we're not permitted back here! What is this place? Is it some sort of prison? Or is the Squire like the Marquis de Sade?"

Bethany cursed under her breath. How in the devil was she supposed to unlock the cell door? Much less the shackles?

"Bethany?" Justus lifted his head and peered at her with groggy, unfocused eyes. He was often lethargic like this during their days together, but she still couldn't fight off a pang of worry that his captors had tortured him. "W-what are you doing here?"

"I've come to rescue you," she said flatly.

A bubble of laughter escaped his lips. "Maybe you *are* mad. Please, leave this place before they find you as well. Go to Cornwall… to the Earl of—"

Justus cursed as another door slammed open and one of the vampires who'd captured Justus strode out, looking cross, yet also bleary-eyed. "What in bloody hell is going on here?" His eyes lit with recognition when he saw Bethany. "I *knew* you were wise to our kind. We should have taken you as well."

Fear cascaded through her being like storm-tossed arctic waves. It was then that the full awareness of where she was doing struck her. She was under the roof of other vampires. Though she knew Justus would never hurt her, to the rest of his kind, she was food. Her basest instincts felt the vampire guard's appraisal of her. He was a predator, she was prey.

But fear would not aid her in this mission. She brought back the alien anger that had taken residence in her soul and nurtured it.

Bethany aimed the blunderbuss at his chest. "Unlock him, or I will blast a hole in your heart."

The vampire sneered. "Foolish human. Do you really believe you are fast or strong enough to stop me from wringing your neck?"

"I have people waiting for me," Bethany said coolly. "If I have not returned with my cart in one hour, they will bring the constable here. I know the squire would not appreciate that sort of scrutiny."

"The constable will find nothing here when I'm done with you." The vampire charged, a blur of speed.

Bethany pulled the trigger of the blunderbuss.

The blast roared in her ears as she jolted backwards. Her head slammed against the stone floor, making white spots flare like exploding stars in her vision. Her breath left her battered lungs in a whoosh as smoke filled the air.

Her ears rang like church bells as she struggled to sit up. When the smoke dissipated, she saw the vampire lying on the floor, his chest a gaping wound of blood and viscera. And yet he still breathed.

"You killed him!" Ames squeaked. He sounded a hundred miles away, though she saw him cowering against another cell wall.

"He'll likely live," Justus said coldly from his prison. "Now fetch his keys. They are on his belt."

Bethany crawled over to the sprawled vampire, her gorge rising in her throat at his injuries. She kept her weapon trained on him as she removed the ring of keys from his belt loop.

It took multiple tries to find the right key as Justus stared at Bethany as if she'd sprouted an extra head and Ames continued to cower in the corner, praying for salvation. No one else came charging down here, though surely someone upstairs had to have heard the shot.

Finally, the correct key slid into the lock, turning the rusty tumblers. Bethany pulled the cell door open and ran to her love. "Did they hurt you?"

"They were saving that particular pleasure for tonight," he said as she once more tested keys in the locks on his shackles. "I cannot believe you've done this mad thing."

"Why not?" she replied, sighing in relief as she found the right key. "You saved me. I am simply returning the favor."

When she unlocked the shackles, Justus yanked his wrists from the restraints and pulled her into his arms. "I thought I'd never see you again. But it's still daylight. I'm trapped here. You should leave before Ridley comes down."

"I'm not going anywhere," Bethany said, running a hand through his hair. "I've brought a trunk for you to hide in and a wagon to carry you."

"A trunk?" Justus laughed as they walked out of the cell. "Well, that will have to do, I suppose."

When they left the cell, the vampire Bethany had shot glared at them, his chest wound already healing. "You'll never make it to Cornwall," he snarled between gasps of pain. "And His Lordship will have you begging for death long before he grants your wish."

Bethany and Justus ignored him and headed to the trunk, quickly removing the stones before Justus climbed in and she secured the clasps. Ames tried to protest helping her carry Justus, but Bethany convinced him with the blunderbuss.

"I'll have to report this to the constable," he huffed.

Justus knocked on the lid of the trunk, so Bethany opened it. "Your master would not appreciate the involvement of the law in his affairs. Of this, I swear. You would do better to give notice and find a master with less dangerous proclivities. And speaking of…" He fixed the elderly footman with his gaze. "You *will* help her carry this trunk and you will not tell anyone what happened down here. In fact, you will forget this whole ordeal as soon as your task is finished."

"I will forget," Ames repeated dully.

"Very good," Justus said and closed himself back in the trunk.

With Bethany's thin arms and Ames's palsy, their progress with the trunk was slow and cumbersome. The vampire guard cursed behind them and Bethany breathed a sigh of relief as they closed the door to the hidden dungeon, silencing that vengeful voice and entering the safety of a shaft of sunlight bathing the cellar stairs. She hoped the crate was sealed tight and would not let any light in to burn Justus.

The servants gave them wide-eyed looks when they emerged, but at Ames's quick shake of his head, they went back to their duties.

Once the trunk was loaded onto the cart, Bethany turned to Ames. "I truly am sorry I had to put you through such a disagreeable ordeal, but please believe me when I tell you that the man you helped me save was innocent of any crime."

The old footman regarded her with a skeptical frown. "I do hope so, Miss, but either way, I'll be glad to see the back of you." With that he shambled back to the manor.

At first, the mule refused to move, but with some agitated coaxing, they were at last on their way.

After five long plodding miles, Bethany's neck ached from craning around to look for pursuers. A deep ache throbbed in her throat, spreading to her chest, a maddening need for something, but aside from freedom, she didn't know what.

She didn't breathe again until they arrived in the next county.

Chapter Twenty-six

Justus sucked in a gulp of air as Bethany opened the trunk. Her face, illuminated by a sliver of moonlight, was the most beautiful thing he'd ever seen. "My dashing rescuer." He took her hand. "I owe you my life. How far have we gone?"

Her brilliant smile illuminated his soul. "We made it to Somerset."

A measure of the tension in his jaw eased. They were safe from Ridley at least. "One more county to cross after this one." He climbed out of the trunk, his muscles sore and stiff from being cramped in such a tight space. Exhaustion weighted his limbs and hunger chewed at his insides. Not to mention the burning pain in his side from being burned by Ridley's poker. If he didn't feed soon, the wounds would scar. He should be grateful for the slow healing, since that was the only thing keeping burnt linen from being permanently embedded in his flesh. As it was, he had to keep pulling his shirt from his wounds. The garment would have to come off at the soonest opportunity.

"Somerset?" He couldn't hide his astonishment at the distance she'd covered with a mere cart. "You must have driven the mule all day." The beast was now unhooked from the wagon and lying in the tall grass, idly cropping at the green blades.

She nodded and he noticed her ashen face and forgot about his own aches and weariness.

He could only imagine how Bethany felt after carrying out her daring rescue and then driving this rickety mule cart all day long.

"I wish we could run now, but we should find shelter close by." Justus eyed the dark circles under Bethany's eyes with concern. "You need to rest."

"*I* need to rest?" Bethany lifted one honey-colored brow. "What about you? You haven't fed in two nights, and you cannot have slept well either during your imprisonment or your time stuffed in a trunk."

Her tone was alarmingly waspish. Yes, the woman needed sleep.

To be truthful, Justus hadn't slept more than a few minutes in the last forty-eight hours. He was dead on his feet and weak as a kitten. But he couldn't bear to admit it.

"Besides," Bethany continued, absently rubbing a knot in her shoulder. "I've already found shelter for us, so there is no sense in arguing with me."

Justus was too tired and too hungry to argue. "Where?"

"I found a way inside a book shop that has a cozy cellar." Her lips curved up in a crooked smile. "I've become quite the criminal."

"A book shop?" Justus couldn't imagine a better place to rest his weary bones. He pulled her into his arms, ignoring the twinges of pain from his wounds. "I love you."

He helped her carry the bags and they walked into the book shop right through the front door as Bethany had already unlocked it. Even though he was bone tired and weak as a mortal, the smell of old parchment, vellum, and leather bindings soothed him, like spring blooms after a winter chill.

Bethany lit a lantern and led him to a pair of massive overstuffed chairs covered in worn burgundy velvet. "We can go to the cellar before dawn. For now, you should sit down. You look pale."

Justus laughed at her commanding tone as well as her words and tried to keep his tone light. "I'm a ginger. I'm always pale." He stripped off his shirt, hissing as the fabric peeled from the charred wounds on his sides.

"My God!" Bethany cried. "What did he do to you?"

"Burnt me with a hot poker," Justus grumbled, more angry at the worry in her eyes than the pain of his wounds. "Sadistic whoreson."

She bent down to inspect the wounds, worry lines creasing her brow. "We must find a doctor."

"No!" He barked out the word more harshly than he meant to. Bethany flinched as he grasped her shoulders and he gentled his grip and tone. "A doctor would wonder why I am healing so rapidly, not to mention ask questions that neither you nor I could provide satisfactory answers to. What I need to do is hunt. Blood will help me heal."

"Feed from me." Her eyes were intent as she moved her braided hair over her shoulder, revealing her creamy white neck. "You need to heal and regain your strength before you venture out again. I cannot fight off the Somerset vampires alone."

"You should not fight them at all," Justus growled, unable to forget the sight of her in Ridley's dungeon, arms quivering with the weight of the blunderbuss as she'd aimed it at the vampire guard. "Furthermore, you need rest and nourishment as well."

"I had a satisfactory rest at the inn in Gloucestershire." Her chin lifted in implacable determination, affording him a view of her vein pulsing in her throat. "And I have eaten while I drove the wagon. I also have provisions for at least three days."

Justus licked his lips, hunger roiling through him at the sight of her delectable neck. To avoid lunging for her, he sat and clenched his hands on his lap. Which turned out to be a mistake of epic proportions, for she cornered him then, placing her hands on the arms of the chair, and leaning forward so her braids caressed his cheeks. The scent of her, sweet and feminine, teased his nostrils, making his upper lip peel back to reveal his fangs.

"Please, Justus." Her lips caressed his ear. "Let me give you what you need."

His control was as tenuous as that of a newly made vampire. Every fiber of his being screamed for her blood. He wondered if his eyes were glowing yet and avoided her gaze in case he accidentally mesmerized her. "I can't risk hurting you or taking too much."

"Don't worry so much. I trust you." She tilted her head, her neck inches from his mouth.

Justus's resistance snapped like try kindling. With a bestial growl, he yanked her into his lap and sank his fangs into her tender flesh.

She tasted better than he'd remembered. Passion and power infused him with every swallow, an intoxicating drug, tempting him to drink more and more. Bethany's low moan was music to his ears, making him harden. Sweet torment wracked his form as her hips undulated against him. His strength returned in a mammoth surge that made his nerve endings sing.

When she sagged weakly against him, Justus's senses returned and he removed his fangs. He cursed at her pallor as he healed the puncture wounds. He'd taken too much.

"Bethany," he whispered, holding his fingers to her neck. Was it weaker than usual? "Are you all right?"

She grasped his shoulder and sat up, her weight pressing further on his groin, though he didn't mind. "I'm perfectly fine. I only had a brief faint spell. A little water and a nibble from an apple and I will be right as rain." Her eyes searched his. "Are you feeling better?"

"I feel completely restored," he admitted, guilt roiling through him at the cost.

"Are you well enough to make love to me?" she asked, shifting her hips in a suggestive manner.

His cock hardened further. "I always feel well enough to make love to you." He grasped one golden braid, reveling in its silken texture. "You're like a drug to me." And intoxicating she was, he thought as he kissed her, exploring every crevice of her lips before delving his tongue in her mouth to taste her sweetness.

He kissed her long and deep as he unbuttoned her dress, shivering in delight as she reached for his buttons. When she shifted off his lap, he groaned with disappointment until he was treated to the sight of her dress falling to the floor. Her skin looked soft and delectable as a peach, her figure exquisite in only a thin white chemise and stockings.

"You look like an angel wrought of gold and ivory." He reached forward and caressed her thigh. "And rubies."

She raised one brow in that quizzical manner he adored. "Rubies?"

"You're blushing." He stripped off his shirt and unfastened his trousers. "Let's see if I can make you do it more. Take off your chemise."

Just as he'd hoped, her skin turned the shade of peaches and cream even as she smiled and pulled the chemise over her head. His mouth went dry at the sight of her lush breasts, curved hips, and the triangle of burnished curls between her legs.

Bethany gasped suddenly. "Your burns! They're almost healed!"

He glanced down. The two charred and red wounds had faded to a pale pink and they were half the size, quickly diminishing as new skin formed. Still, it was likely there would be some scarring.

"*You* healed me," he said, and sucked in a breath as she bent to kiss his wounds. The feel of her hair brushing across his chest and belly made an ache flare in his groin. "Turn around," he said huskily.

She obeyed and he grasped her hips and pulled her back on his lap. From this angle, he was able to hold her in his arms and caress her body at the same time. His hands cupped her breasts, thumbs grazing her nipples until they grew taut.

Bethany gasped and leaned against him, her thighs parting slightly, tempting him to delve lower. A delightful moan purred from her lips as his fingers found her mons and stroked around the edges of her plump, damp flesh.

When he found her tight little bud, she cried out and wriggled her backside against his hard length, filling him with a hot surge of lust. Still, he teased her relentlessly until she was wet and musky with desire, whimpering his name.

"Justus," Bethany panted. "Please…"

Happy to oblige, he lifted her and poised himself at her entrance. Slowly, she sank down upon his length, making him bit his lip at the sheer bliss of her tightness clenching around him. Everything felt different at this angle, new, exciting, intense.

He rocked her on his lap, reveling in the new sensations. One hand reached up to toy with her breasts, the other plunged back down between her thighs, his fingers circling her clitoris. The effect was rewarding. Bethany threw her head back and gyrated her hips in an intoxicating motion that took his pleasure to more dizzying heights.

When she began to spasm around him, Justus lost control and thrust deeper and harder, his own climax surging in time with her own. The pleasure went on forever, blurring his vision in a euphoric haze.

At last she collapsed against him, leaning against his chest as they caught their breath. "Do you feel closer to me now?" she whispered.

His hand slipped up to press against her pounding heart. "I did not think such a thing was possible, but yes." Worry filled him at the sight of her pallor and the fact that she still trembled. Damn it, he'd taken too much blood.

With burning reluctance, he eased her off his lap and sought his clothing. "You should eat now to restore your strength from what I took."

Bethany laughed as she pulled on her chemise, though a shadow of unease flickered in her eyes. "I'm fine. I'm not even all that hungry. I'd much rather explore the book shop."

"Food first, books after," he said sternly, not liking the dark shadows of fatigue beneath her eyes. Who knew when she'd last slept? "And then we should rest early."

She heaved an exasperated sigh and hugged her arms. "Very well."

Justus watched Bethany withdraw a half-eaten meat pie from one of the packs and felt another trill of alarm when she nibbled on it with disinterest. Especially when he noticed the fine tremor in her hands. At first he'd thought that her bouts of shaking were because she was overwhelmed with being out in the world again, but now he was starting to worry that something else was wrong with her.

Chapter Twenty-Seven

Bethany dreamed of Morningside again. She paced inside her cell, awaiting Doctor Keene's visit. A most alarming emotion accompanied the dream: relief to be back in those stone walls and eager anticipation for the doctor's soothing tonic. When he arrived with his spoon and bottle, she opened her mouth like a baby bird.

Instead of the usual bitter flavor, the tonic tasted sweeter than honey. Happiness welled within her and she fell back on her cot, soothed at last.

Then the sweetness turned into fire.

She awoke shivering, with that odd burning in the back of her throat again. Her heart thudded in her chest and a restless sensation crawled over her skin like a thousand insects. It was much like the feeling that had overcome her yesterday afternoon when driving the wagon, only a hundred times worse.

Justus opened his eyes and stared at her quizzically as his hand shifted from her waist to her forehead. "You're sweating like you have a fever, but you do not smell as if you have one. How are you feeling?"

"Dreadful," she admitted. "I cannot stop shaking, and I feel as if I am covered in flies. My back aches terribly as well."

"Probably from driving that blasted cart," Justus said with a deepening frown. "Perhaps you're shaking from going too long between meals?"

"I'm not even hungry," she said miserably. In truth, she was a bit queasy, but she didn't want to worry Justus further. "But I'll nibble on some bread when you hunt. Is it dark yet?"

"It feels like dusk is about an hour off. I heard the shopkeeper lock up and depart two hours before that, but you were still asleep." Justus cupped her face and peered at her more closely. "Do you suppose the food you ate last was spoiled?"

Bethany shook her head. "I've eaten bad meat before. I'd be casting up my accounts if that were the case. I feel more restless than ill, to be honest. And my bones hurt and my throat burns." She frowned. That wasn't right. "I mean, it doesn't feel hot, it's a different sort of burn."

"We're leaving the wagon." Justus said firmly. "I can carry you faster than that mule can."

"But I could carry you safely in the trunk during the day," she protested, blurting out the idea.

His brows drew together. "I think not. I do not care to be stuffed in that trunk again, for one thing. For another, you've clearly overexerted yourself driving the wagon."

"I do not think it was the wagon. The soreness perhaps, but not the rest." Bethany rubbed her arms, trying to calm that prickling sensation. "I've felt this way before. The day you had to sleep in the well."

Justus's eyes narrowed. "Why didn't you tell me?"

"I didn't want to worry you." She rose from their makeshift bed and stretched. Her back popped in a satisfying manner, but her anxiety remained. "I'm probably just impatient to continue our journey."

"Impatient to leave a book shop?" Justus gaped at her. "Something is definitely wrong."

His words sank in with ominous truth. She was never eager to part from books. Her shoulders slumped as fear coiled in her belly. "I hope I haven't caught the plague."

"You honestly do not smell ill," he said, though uncertainty wavered in his eyes. "But just in case…" He bit his index finger and held it to her lips. "Drink."

Bethany obeyed, tasting his blood and feeling that electric jolt of his blood on her tongue. Whatever magic sang in his blood did seem to ease her pain and phantom panic slightly. Yet it still remained, boiling under the surface of her skin, like a monster waiting to tear her apart from the inside. She licked her lips and kissed the tip of his finger. "I'm going to go upstairs and see if there is something for us to read while we wait until dark."

His broad grin soothed her soul. "There's my Bethany. But if you feel faint or feverish, I want you to come back down at once."

She nodded, embarrassed at making such a goose of herself. The shivers and sweats were probably just a reaction to dreaming about Morningside. Revulsion filled her as she recalled her ludicrous happiness to see Keene and his horrid tonic.

Bethany made her way up the stairs, her heart sad that Justus couldn't accompany her. A measure of her melancholy ebbed when she once more laid eyes on the tall Maplewood shelves filled with leather backed books and gilded spines. She browsed each section, searching for Medieval verses and tales she'd always held so dear. When she came upon a copy of Sir Gawain and the Green Knight, she held the volume to her breast, savoring its weight. Then, to her delight, she saw a copy of Chaucer's *Book of the Duchess*. Long ago, Justus had said that was his favorite.

She wished she could take more books, but knew they couldn't carry that many. When she returned to the cellar, Justus read her regret.

"Don't worry, my love. Soon we will have our own library." The determination in his eyes refuted any doubt, despite the tenuousness of their situation.

"Which one shall we read?" she asked, handing him the books.

His face lit with delight at the copy of *Book of the Duchess*. "Let's save this one for a better time and read Sir Gawain. It has been so many years since I've read that one."

"And I as well," she replied, though for her it had only been a decade while he could have meant a whole century.

They took turns reading and Bethany fidgeted in her seat, trying to focus on the story and not the alternating bouts of pain and restlessness. Alarm creeped over her like a shadow. What was wrong with her?

Justus closed the book and cocked his head to the side, peering at her with a frown. "You haven't paid attention to the last two pages I've read."

"Yes, I have!" she argued in a shrewish tone that made her clap her hand over her mouth in shock. This wasn't her. If Doctor Keene had heard her he would have sent her straight to her room with a dram of his tonic. She salivated even as a deep ache gnawed at her bones and tore at her belly.

"You're suffering." He stood and packed the book in one of their satchels. "Whatever this malady is, my blood isn't helping. The sun has set. Let us go and we'll see if we can rouse a doctor for you."

"No doctor." She shook her head. "You said that it would be too dangerous. I'm likely just overwhelmed with yesterday's unpleasantness. I'm sure I'll be all right once we're well on our way."

"You're suffering." His implacable gaze refuted any lies.

"Oh Justus," she whimpered as another flare of pain roared through her body. "It hurts! My bones hurt, my stomach is roiling, and I feel so desperate, but I don't know why."

He sighed and held out his hand, pulling her to her feet when her fingers intertwined with his. "I will feed and then I will find help for you. Somehow."

She hated the worry in his face. She'd been so proud of herself for rescuing him and now she needed him to save her yet again. Would she ever be strong and capable again?

On shaking legs, she followed him up the stairs and out of the book shop, casting the place one last longing glance. If only she hadn't been feeling so wretched she could have enjoyed its wonders more fully.

Before she could protest, Justus lifted her in his arms and ran. The wind on her cheeks burned at his urgent speed and her stomach heaved. When at last he stopped in the next town, she bit back a sob of relief.

Justus set her down at the mouth of a crooked alley, where a drunkard was relieving himself against the crumbling brick wall. She swayed like she was drunk herself as Justus launched himself on the man, bespelling him and drinking deeply. She barely had the time to gather her bearings before he lifted her and they were off again.

He ran for another mile before Bethany dug her nails in his arm. "Stop, please."

He halted immediately in a hay field and the world tilted and dipped before her eyes. When he put her down, she cast up her accounts.

"My God," Justus whispered. "You've gotten worse."

"I know," she admitted miserably. "I hurt all over."

He reached for her. "We need to—"

"What do we have here?" a voice rang out.

Bethany froze in dread as a vampire emerged from the shadows. He was dressed all in black and a rakish slouch hat covered his head. "A rogue and a drunken wench cavorting in a hay field. Now that is a sight. Though I think she's imbibed overmuch on the spirits."

"I'm not drunk," Bethany snapped, humiliated as well as afraid.

"Please," Justus said. "She is ill. I need to find a doctor to help her. Leave us be and we will leave your lord's territory."

The vampire stepped closer. "Lucky for you, I have no lord. I'm a rogue, same as you." His nostrils flared and he frowned. "She doesn't smell of illness. Not of drink, either."

Justus sighed. "I know."

The vampire considered them in silence for a few moments before he sighed. "Well, her health won't be improved lingering out in the open where the Somerset vampires can pounce. Come with me. There's a no-man's land at the coast about a mile. I have a shelter where she can rest and we can get a better look at her."

"Thank you," Justus said gratefully. He then looked down and stared so hard into Bethany's eyes that she started to take a step back, but froze, trapped in his gaze. "Sleep," he said softly.

She fell into his arms, darkness, pain and fragmented nightmares taunting her.

When she awoke, she lay in Justus's lap in a cave that smelled of saltwater. The other rogue vampire sat beside them, next to a crackling fire, doing something with his shoulder.

"Sleeping Beauty awakens," he said and extended his hand. "I'm Rhys Berwyn, formally of Manchester until my lord exiled me. Your husband has been telling me of your escape from the lunatic asylum."

Bethany blinked in surprise. Justus had remained close-mouthed to everyone else regarding where she came from. She gave him a cautious nod and cringed when her neck throbbed.

"And I presume they drugged you there?" he inquired and flinched as he dug into his upper arm with what looked like a pair of pliers.

She frowned at his strange action, but didn't pry. "Yes. Doctor Keene had a special tonic that tasted horrid and made me dizzy. I hated it."

"But you want it," he said flatly.

Revulsion prickled her arms. "No, I don't!" And yet she remembered her dreams of Morningside, and her eagerness for the medicine. Doubt clouded her head, increasing her anxiety.

"You're opium-sick, Lady de Wynter," Rhys said. "I've seen plenty of it in my mortal days when I was a sailor on a trading expedition into the Orient, and you display all the signs: the shaking, sweating, bursts of temper, aches and complaints. You may not have been fond of the Doctor's tonic, which likely contained laudanum, but your body became accustomed to it and demands more." He dug the pliers deeper and pulled out a leaden ball with a groan of pain.

Bethany gaped at him. "You were shot?"

"Such is the fate of highwaymen. Fortunately, I heal faster than most." He dropped the lead ball on the floor and withdrew a little brown bottle from his pocket. After taking a drink, he passed it to her. "Take a small sip, and your suffering will calm. You need to be weaned from the drug."

She opened her mouth to refuse, but her hand reached for the bottle of its own volition and brought it to her mouth. The oh so familiar bitterness made her shudder even as an aching nostalgia and blinding relief washed over her. She passed Rhys the bottle, wanting it as far away from her as possible, but he handed it to Justus.

"I do not understand how this is possible," Bethany said. Was it her imagination, or did the ache in her bones seem less severe? "I wasn't drugged every day. Besides, I'm certain I would have suffered from the addiction sooner. It's been seven nights since Justus rescued me from Morningside." Doubt imbued her own words, since she *had* experienced tremors, aches and mild stomach upset ever since they left.

Rhys shrugged. "How often were you drugged when you were in that place?"

"About once a week. Sometimes more if the doctor decided I was 'overstimulated,' as he called it." Foul memories of being denied the simplest comforts in life flashed before her eyes.

"Once a week is enough to do it," Rhys said. "Your body is on a clock. That's why you felt fine for the last few nights. Then, when you didn't receive the good doctor's tonic as scheduled, your body and mind made the disruption known."

"Oh." She hadn't really felt exactly right, but still, those nights had been nothing close to the torment she'd endured this evening. Even more disturbing was that the truth of Rhys's words became more apparent by the moment. The laudanum was making her feel better, giving her mind and body the calm that

Doctor Keene always insisted upon. And devil take her, she wanted more.

Justus stroked her hair. "God, what I'd do to go back and put my fist through that bloody doctor's teeth. Locking you up and depriving you of books wasn't enough for him. He had to force opium sickness upon you too."

She nodded in grim agreement. "I'd like to put that blunderbuss to use." As the implications of her malady sank in, worry pulsed through her veins as she glanced back at Rhys. "Is it permanent?"

The rogue vampire shook his head. "No, and your escape from the asylum was the first and most important step for the cure. I've given your husband the rest of my laudanum, but you had best try not to ask for it for a few days. Go as long as you can without it, and soon enough, your body will forget about it if given the chance."

Justus looked down at Bethany with pained eyes, though he spoke to Rhys. "Why couldn't my blood cure her?"

Rhys shrugged, then winced as the movement irritated his wounded shoulder. "I don't know. It doesn't seem to do very much for addictions. I met a vampire who was a drunkard in his mortal days and fed his thirst by feeding off other drunkards. I knew another who smoked opium."

The subject was much too depressing for Bethany. She changed the subject. "What made you decide to be a highwayman?"

"My mortal descendants are in danger of losing the family farm," Rhys said. "So I rob from the aristocracy and give it to my poor family so they can pay the outrageous mortgage that my great grand-nephew took out on the property to support his wastrel lifestyle."

"Oh, how terrible!" Bethany said, then realized she could be misconstrued. "About your family, that is. But how wonderful that you still look out for them. You're like Robin Hood."

Rhys laughed. "All I need is my Maid Marianne."

"I am certain you shall find her someday." Bethany liked this vampire. He had an irascible charm, and a kind heart.

"Lord, I hope not." Rhys said with a look of mock horror. "Aside from women naturally being trouble, and I mean that in the kindest way possible, I have no desire to endanger myself nor anyone else with my situation in life. De Wynter here may not be an infamous criminal like I am, but he is a rogue all the same and you, my dear are a fugitive. I do not think I could bear the difficulties you both are enduring."

Bethany looked down at her lap. If it weren't for her, Justus wouldn't be a rogue.

Justus tilted her chin up and kissed her. "I know this must sound ludicrous, but before I found Bethany, I was living only half a life. I enjoyed doing my duty for my lord and we were the best of friends, but something was missing. Even with the peril and hardships we face, the world has more color and I feel like I have a reason to live."

"It does sound ludicrous," Rhys said. "All the same, I understand. But I have my family to think of." His sober expression dissolved into a mirthful smile. "Besides, if I saddled myself to a woman, I could no longer steal kisses from the women I divest of jewels."

They all laughed, and Bethany relaxed against Justus, feeling more at ease than she had since their wedding night. She even managed to eat some bread and cheese from their bag.

"Thank you for helping us," Justus said as he built up the fire.

"No thanks needed. It is past time I did a good deed, though it will do little to blot out my many sins." Rhys tossed Justus a few coins. "You may stay here for as long as you like. I am off tomorrow night."

"To where?" Bethany and Justus both asked.

"Blackpool. Quite the opposite of where you two are bound."

Justus's eyes widened at the distance. "Your family farm is in Blackpool? What is the lord like?"

"A heartless bastard." Rhys's upper lip curled in scorn. "He holds the loan on the farm."

"Good God!" Justus gaped at him. "And you said we were enduring difficulties!"

Rhys nodded grimly. "I imagine he'll catch me one of these days and take my head. I only hope my family is free of him by then." He stretched and crossed the cave to a bedroll in the corner. "Anyway, it is nearly dawn and I need my rest if this blasted arm is to heal by nightfall."

As if his words held magic, Bethany's lids drooped and she yawned.

Justus laid down on their makeshift bed and she cuddled against him gratefully. As he stroked her hair, she peered at the fire and said a silent prayer for Rhys to save his family and avoid the Lord of Blackpool's clutches, and for her and Justus to be welcomed in Cornwall. And most of all, she prayed her opium sickness would go away.

Without Rhys's intervention, who knew what would have happened?

As sleep sucked her into its dark void, one final thought tinged her dreams with worry.

What would the Lord of Cornwall do if he knew she was not only an escapee from a lunatic asylum, but also an opium addict?

Chapter Twenty-eight

When Justus awoke, he studied Bethany. She lay still and relaxed, sleeping deeper than she had in days. Even as relief flooded him at her lack of a tremor, self-recrimination rained upon him that he hadn't realized the cause of her shivers. He'd assumed she'd either been cold, or was overwhelmed with the sensation of being out in the world again. It had not occurred to him that she'd suffer withdrawals from being drugged.

The bottle of laudanum felt heavy in his pocket. He prayed that she wouldn't ask for it too soon, for he didn't know if he'd have the strength to refuse her after witnessing her suffering.

Bethany's eyes fluttered open and she favored him with a smile that made his heart ache. "Where is our gracious host?"

"Rhys already departed for Blackpool." Gratitude welled within for the rogue's aid and generosity even as he worried about the highwayman. Once more he felt ashamed of his previous scorn for rogue vampires, thinking them all to be evil and violent. And though there were indeed plenty of rogues of that ilk, there had been others whose kindness had been instrumental in Justus's and Bethany's survival. He only hoped Rhys would find similar help. Justus knew what tangling with a Lord Vampire on their own territory entailed. Rhys would be lucky to survive. He shook off the concern and focused on his own situation.

"How are you feeling?" he asked, determined to focus on the present.

"Much better." She stretched, her delectable body grazing his before she twined her arms around his neck. "I haven't slept this well in ages. I had the most wonderful dream that you and I were choosing chairs for our library."

Justus smiled at the enchanting mental picture. "There is nothing better than a dream that will come to pass." Though even if the Lord of Cornwall agreed to make them citizens, their accommodations would be meager until Justus found profitable employment. Thankfully, once he Changed Bethany, they would have many years to save their coppers.

Bethany hugged him tight. "I do not know what I'd do without your reassurance. How far did we travel?"

"We're in Devon." Justus fought back the memory of carrying Bethany as she'd shivered and moaned in a delirious sleep. "We could be in Cornwall tonight, though we'd best hurry since Ridley's third in command heard me blurt out our destination."

"Thank heavens," Bethany said. "I pray the Lord Vampire takes us in. And if he doesn't, that he will allow us to pass."

"The Lord of Rochester tells me that Deveril is eccentric, but soft-hearted." He did his best to ease her worry.

"Deveril?" Bethany's brows rose. "The Lord Vampire of Cornwall is the Mad Earl of Deveril? My father ranted about his proxy vote on the Corn Laws and my mother was always trying to invite him to her parties in London when she was on her relentless quest to see me married off. He never came, since he was reputed to be a reclusive madman. Him being a vampire makes sense."

Justus cursed under his breath. "I was not supposed to tell you until we met the man."

"Why not?" Bethany shrugged. "I would know his crest the moment we arrived at his doorstep. I can feign ignorance until then. And while we're on the subject, who is the Lord of Rochester? Much of what you told me implies that he is a noble as well." She gasped as Justus looked at his boots in apparent evasion. "He is, isn't he? How many vampires are there in the nobility?" she asked.

"Twelve, I think," Justus said. "Though it can be difficult to keep track, as some relinquish their titles and others reclaim theirs if their family line is in danger of dying off." He rubbed the bridge of his nose. "We should set off. The sooner we are in Cornwall, the sooner I can make you privy to my world." When he pulled her to her feet, he frowned at the lingering shadows under her eyes. "I intend to Mark you as soon as we pass the county border."

Her eyes widened and she opened her mouth, then closed it and nodded.

"Are you frightened?" Worry speared his heart. What if she was still wary of being tied to him?

"A little." Bethany fidgeted with the sleeve of her dress. "What if your Marking me lands you in trouble? Or if things go unfavorably in Cornwall and the vampires there use me to get to you?"

He hated himself for being relieved even as he was touched that her concern was for him. "If things go unfavorably in Cornwall, I'll need to know how to find you, or at least if you are well. Deveril may imprison me and banish your memories." Not to mention that Justus would also know if she was suffering from opium sickness on their way to Castle Deveril in time to abate her suffering. He never wanted to see her go through that again.

"Why don't you Mark me now?" she said softly.

Justus hesitated. It could be a risk if he was taken by the Devon vampires, but then again, every cell of his being cried out to make her his. The savage instinct was alarming. He'd never Marked a mortal before. "All right," he said and bit his finger.

As Bethany drank his blood, Justus brought forth his power and recited the words. "I, Justus de Wynter, of… nowhere… Mark you, Bethany Mead as mine, and mine alone. With this Mark, I offer you my undying protection. Let all others, moral and immoral alike, who cross your path sense this Mark and know that to act against you is to act against me and thus invoke my wrath, as I will avenge what is mine."

Magic jolted through them like lightning. For a moment Justus could feel every thought and emotion swirling in her mind and he was breathless at her inner beauty. He bent to kiss her and was lost in her embrace.

Bethany moaned and pressed herself against him, tugging at his falls of his trousers even as he pulled up her skirt. He lifted her and impaled her on his hard length. They made love fast and fervent, the Mark between them pulsing in time to the beating of their hearts. Bethany cried out and shuddered, her climax bringing his own like shattering a floodgate.

"Heavens," Bethany breathed, resting her head against his chest. "May I now consider myself Marked?"

He chuckled and set her down. "Thoroughly. But now we've delayed too long. We must go now if we hope to reach Cornwall before dawn."

When they left the cave, a stroke of luck came Justus's way as he spied a fisherman pulling his boat to shore. He was on him in a flash and returned to Bethany, well fed. Scooping her up, he ran faster than he had in several nights.

After only a brief stop in a fishing village for a bowl of chowder and roasted potatoes for Bethany, they arrived at the Cornish border in a little over three hours.

Justus took a deep breath as he surveyed the rolling green hills and jagged seaside cliffs. It was time for them to find out if damnation or salvation awaited them. "We must do what we can to not look hostile. To appear as supplicants."

Bethany reached up beneath her skirts and tore a strip of muslin from her petticoat.

Justus's brows rose. "What in the heavens are you about?"

"A flag of surrender." She picked up a stick from the ground and tied the white fabric to the tip.

Admiration curved his lips in a smile. "That could work."

They crossed the border into Cornwall, Bethany holding her makeshift flag high. "I wish I could see this place in the daylight. It already looks magical."

"It looks about the same as the Devon coast." Justus chuckled. Though, now that she mentioned it, something seemed different. Perhaps it was the hope of safety and home that made the rolling hills seem greener and the rocky storm-swept cliffs more enchanting.

Clouds were gathering over the sea, nearing the shore. If they didn't find shelter or weren't apprehended first, being soaked by rain loomed as a discomforting possibility.

"We should head west and stay on the coast. Castle Deveril is just outside of Falmouth," he said, trying to hide the uncertainty of their welcome from his tone. "I do not know how far we'll make it before one of his vampires takes us into custody."

As if summoned by his words, a vampire crested the hill before them. "Stop, right where you are."

Justus and Bethany froze, the white flag held before her, waving in the sea breeze. The vampire raised a brow at the scrap of white fabric and strolled down the hill to meet them. "A flag of surrender? Now that's something I haven't seen from a rogue." His brown eyes narrowed on Bethany. "And a human companion. That does not bode well."

"I cannot Change her until I'm legitimate, so that she will not be a rogue." Justus sensed other vampires approaching and sank to his knees before they had the idea to attack. "I surrender to you and ask to be taken to the Lord of Cornwall so I may petition him for citizenship."

The vampire nodded. "Ah. You wouldn't be the first. I am Emrys Adair, Second in command to the Lord of Cornwall. And who do I have the pleasure of speaking with?"

Justus inclined his head. "Justus de Wynter, formerly Second in command to the Lord of Rochester. And this is my bride to be, Bethany Mead." He ignored Bethany's nudge on his ribs at omitting mention of their Roma wedding ceremony. It wouldn't be good for Emrys or the Lord of Cornwall to know he'd preempted his whole purpose for being here.

"Bride to be, eh?" Emrys appraised Bethany coolly. "His Lordship will decide about that. Come along."

To Justus's vexation, the vampire placed himself between him and Bethany. She shot Justus an alarmed look, which he answered with the slightest shake of his head. They could not risk coming off as troublesome.

They walked with Emrys up the hill, the other vampires in the distance making a discreet perimeter, who may have escaped the eye of a less seasoned rogue vampire. Justus felt a touch of respect for Deveril's efficient method even as he realized such a strategy would have been his downfall had he not wanted to get caught.

Was it possible that Gavin had lied to him? Or perhaps Lord Deveril was not as welcoming as Gavin had thought. Justus's heart sank as a thousand dismal possibilities flitted through his mind.

Emrys cast them suspicious glances while they walked, as if they'd change their minds on surrendering and bolt at any moment.

Suddenly, tension bled into the air around him as a sense of deep power thudded in his bones. Justus grasped the reason for the sense just as the surrounding vampires melted further into the shadows.

Emrys grasped Justus's and Bethany's arms, halting them as a tall figure emerged from the shadows of a copse of trees.

Justus's eyes widened at his first sight of the Lord of Cornwall. He'd heard the man was tall and unconventional-looking, but the gossips hardly did the vampire credit. At six and a half feet tall, he towered above them. His slender frame conveyed a sense of tightly-coiled speed and power rather than frailty, and his silvery blond hair looked more ethereal than earthly.

"Justus de Wynter," Lord Deveril said in his musical Cornish accent with an unreadable half smile. "I've been expecting you."

"Is that a good thing or a bad thing, my lord?" Justus asked cautiously.

Deveril frowned as if he thought the question to be insolent. "That remains to be seen." He turned to Emrys. "Give me the woman."

Justus lurched forward and was stopped by the two other Cornwall vampires who'd been drawing nearer all this time.

Deveril's eyes narrowed in irritation and he shook his head in a chiding manner. "That is no way to behave to one who you hope to be your lord." His long fingers closed over Bethany's shoulders and she stiffened at his touch. "There is no time for us to walk to my castle, so we must run. I am only ensuring that you follow." He turned Bethany to face him, forced her chin up so he could capture her gaze and whispered, "Sleep."

As her knees buckled, Lord Deveril lifted her into his arms, holding her far too close for Justus's liking. He bit back a possessive growl.

"Now, now," Deveril said softly. "I mean her no harm. You truly should have waited to Mark her, if it means you cannot control yourself." He sighed. "The hour grows late. We shall talk at the castle." With that he took off in a blur, moving faster than any vampire Justus had ever seen.

The sight ripped Justus's heart from his chest. He and Emrys took off after Deveril, keeping pace with each other, but quickly losing sight of the Lord Vampire. He was simply too fast and too powerful, even though as far as Justus had heard, they were close to the same age. With a sinking heart, Justus knew that if it came to a fight between the two, he would lose badly.

When he and Emrys at last stopped, foreboding filled Justus as he looked up at the ancient castle. The dark clouds obscuring the moon engulfed the structure in shadows. Deveril stood before the arched stone entrance, a rusted iron portcullis raised above his head, looking like it could slam down at any moment.

But that sight wasn't nearly as unnerving as seeing his Bethany unconscious and cradled in another vampire's arms.

"How did you know I was coming?" Justus asked in effort to reign in his temper.

"Rochester sent me a letter awhile back, as well as some of your personal effects, should I decide to take you in." Deveril frowned. "Rather presumptuous of him to ask me to provide sanctuary for a vampire he himself exiled. One who has committed a serious crime." He looked down at Bethany. "And who is committing it once again even as we speak. Presumptuous and arrogant indeed, given that Rochester's and my interactions haven't been all that congenial."

"I knew nothing about Gavin's letter," Justus said quickly. "If my presence is not to your liking, we can leave."

Deveril chuckled. "No, you cannot flee so easily. It is still my duty to detain those who violate our laws. Besides, I am curious to hear of what caused a vampire who served as a loyal second in command and valuable spy to one of the most ruthless vampires in England to fall so far from grace."

Justus's gut sank further. His hope for an end to his and Bethany's peril faded by the minute.

Chapter Twenty-nine

Bethany opened her eyes with a jolt. She found herself sprawled in an overstuffed chair beside an unlit fireplace in an ancient castle solar, decorated with paintings and tapestries. Before her mind could dwell on the beauty, she bolted upright, heart in her throat when she realized it was not Justus who sat beside her.

She couldn't suppress a gasp at her first sight of the Lord Vampire of Cornwall in the light. He was abnormally tall and lanky, with hair like spun moonlight threaded with gold. He looked more like a creature from the fey realm, more mystical and dangerous, than a human or even the vampire that he was. A sword hung on his belt and she had no doubt he could unsheathe it before she could blink.

"Ah, h-how do you do, my lord?" she stammered, wishing she had the courage to demand where Justus was.

"Miss Mead," Lord Deveril leaned back and smirked in amusement at her visible relief when she saw Justus sitting on his right. "Lord de Wynter has been telling me about how you two met, and the ensuing disasters that occurred."

Justus's lips tightened in a grim smile. Her belly knotted. He didn't look as if their petition was going well.

"None of it was his fault," she said louder than she intended. How could Justus continue to be blamed for her mistake?

"Oh, I think it was," Lord Deveril said mildly. "Had he not told you what he was, you wouldn't have blurted it to your suitor."

Bethany flinched. Would he then lock Justus up? Or worse, execute him?

"However," Deveril continued, "I understand that no one took your outburst seriously. Furthermore, Lord de Wynter was punished for his crime. And so were you."

Hope bloomed in her chest. "Does that mean you'll allow us to stay?"

The Lord Vampire of Cornwall sighed. "I am not certain yet. Taking in a vampire who served as second to another Lord, a vampire who should have known better than to commit such a dangerous indiscretion… I am unsure whether that is a risk that I want to undertake. Yet to banish him would simply pass the danger to someone else. And then there is you. A human who knows about vampires must either become one or be killed if their memory cannot be erased. Something must be done with you both." He steepled his long fingers and stared at the candle flames. "For the time being, you will remain here as my guests under observation."

Bethany and Justus exchanged knowing glances. Guests certainly meant prisoners.

"A room has been prepared for you and—"

"Oh, there you are!" A beautiful, black-haired woman who looked younger than Bethany entered the solar. She wore a canvas smock splattered with paint. "You did not tell me we had guests."

Bethany blinked at the woman's American accent, then frowned at the intent way in which Justus was studying her.

Lord Deveril, meanwhile, looked almost abashed. "Lydia… this is not a very good time for introductions. Did Emrys not tell you to wait in the study?"

"No. I didn't see him when I came in." Lydia frowned. "Vincent, is something wrong?"

"Bloody hell," Deveril growled.

Justus startled them all by laughing. "When did *you* get married, Deveril?"

"Three years ago," Vincent replied gruffly, though the ghost of a besotted half smile curved his lips when he looked at his wife. "I am surprised you did not hear of it."

"I was on the run," Justus said flatly. "I've missed much that has happened over the last eight years. Though I did hear of the Lord of London's scandalous marriage." He straightened in his seat, his uncertainly replaced with confidence and a touch of amusement. "Tell me, was yours nearly as legally precarious?"

Vincent heaved a sigh. "The marriage itself? No. An incident during our courtship, however, invoked the wrath of the Elders." His stern frown returned. "Which is why I am eager to keep further trouble from my domain."

"Trouble? We're certainly accustomed to that." Lydia perched on the arm of his chair and twirled her finger around a lock of her husband's long silvery hair. "Now are you going to tell me who these people are, and what sort of trouble they bring?"

Vincent sighed and inclined his head toward Justus. "This is Justus de Wynter, Viscount de Wynter, formerly second in command to the Lord of Rochester, and now a rogue exiled for revealing our secrets to a mortal." He turned to Bethany with a humorless smile. "This is Miss Bethany Mead, daughter of the Baron of Wickshire, and the mortal in question. Ah, and she is an escaped patient from Morningside lunatic asylum, though de Wynter insists that she is quite sane."

Lydia's jaw dropped as she stared at Bethany with light brown eyes that appeared gold. "Why were you committed?"

"For telling Lord Tench that Lord de Wynter was a vampire when I was drugged with laudanum." Saying it aloud made it sound even more foolish. "I'd fallen from my horse that morning."

"Oh my!" Lydia breathed. "And you were in there for eight whole years? You poor thing!"

Bethany's throat tightened at such sincere sympathy from a stranger. Perhaps she could sway Lady Deveril into persuading her husband to let them stay. As she observed the sweet, young countess, a thought occurred to her. She turned back to the earl. "Begging your pardon, my lord, but isn't your countess human?"

Lady Deveril laughed, revealing tiny pointed fangs. "No, I am just so young that I do not yet convey that otherwordly power that my dear husband does." She turned those intent golden eyes on Justus. "Why haven't you Changed Miss Mead yet?"

Justus spread his hands in a helpless gesture. "Because if I do so without having a Lord Vampire grant me permission, I'd be breaking the law, and she would be a rogue like me, perhaps worse as she would be illegitimate."

Was it Bethany's imagination, or did the Lord of Cornwall flush?

Lady Deveril grasped her husband's shoulders. "So you'll make them citizens so Lord de Wynter can Change her and wed her, yes?"

"I have not yet decided," Vincent said. "It depends on—"

Rapid footsteps echoed outside the solar before Emrys burst in. "The Lord of Gloucestershire is here. He claims that you are harboring his prisoners and demands that you turn them over to him at once."

Bethany's hope vanished like a dandelion puff in the wind. Squire Ridley had followed them after all. Would the Lord of Cornwall turn them over to him? Ridley would kill them, she had no doubt about that.

"*His* prisoners?" Vincent raised a brow and turned to Justus. "You did not tell me you were both arrested on your way here."

"Only I was arrested," Justus said. "Bethany rescued me from his dungeons."

The Earl of Deveril gave Bethany an appraising look before rising from his seat and addressing his second. "And where is Squire Ridley?"

"Still outside in the courtyard with his third in command," Emrys said. "I told him to come back tomorrow evening, but he refuses to leave until you come to the door."

Vincent's scowl deepened. "I hope it starts raining soon," he muttered before turning to Justus and Bethany. "Follow me."

They left the solar, staying behind the earl and countess until Lord Deveril stopped at a door that opened onto a balcony. "Stay there," he ordered to Justus, Bethany, and Emrys.

The Earl and Countess of Deveril walked out onto the balcony and looked down. "Ridley, old chap," he called out. "I am afraid this is not a good time. It is only three hours until sunrise, after all. Would you come back tomorrow evening?"

"I will do no such thing!" Ridley's petulant shout echoed against the parapets. "You are harboring *my* prisoners. I demand that you deliver them to me at once!"

"And what prisoners would those be?" Deveril sounded bored.

"Justus de Wynter and a blonde mortal woman."

Deveril leaned idly against the stone balcony. "What was de Wynter's crime?"

"He was a rogue trespassing in my lands."

The Lord of Cornwall shrugged. "And this woman's?"

The squire made an exasperated sound. "She shot my third in command!"

Deveril lifted a brow. "Is that not your third standing beside you?"

Ridley spluttered again. "He is healed, yes, but that does not change the fact that she attacked one of my people!"

Deveril glanced over his shoulder. "Lord de Wynter, Miss Mead, come here."

On leaden legs, Bethany made her way onto the balcony, clinging to Justus's hand. After coming this far, all was lost. Ridley and the vampire she'd shot would identify her right away. Something the Lord of Cornwall would not view in a charitable light.

She peered over the edge of the stone balcony and got her first glimpse of Squire Ridley. He was exactly as she'd pictured him. Short of stature, gaudily dressed in a puce surcoat over canary yellow trousers, and a mustache so thin it looked like a caterpillar perched on his upper lip.

"That's the wench!" the other vampire roared, pointing at Bethany. "Peppered me with lead balls, she did!"

Deveril regarded Bethany with an expression that was either amusement or disapproval. "Why did you shoot him?"

"He was coming towards me with his fangs bared. I had to protect myself." She didn't know what else to say.

"I see." Vincent turned back to look over the parapet down at Ridley. "So he showed his fangs to a mortal and tried to attack her. It seems your third was the one violating the law, which caused me to arrange for her to be Changed sooner than I'd have preferred." He gave Bethany a warning glance as he inclined his head toward Justus. "As for Lord de Wynter, he is no rogue. He's a citizen of Cornwall who'd forgotten his writ of passage. So you see, you have no cause to take one of my people."

Bethany clung to Justus, hope blossoming in her soul. Was the Lord of Cornwall truly defending them and declaring them to be his people?

"That chit is no youngling." Ridley pointed. "She looks as human as my breakfast this evening."

"As does my lovely wife." The earl put one long arm around his petite countess, tucking her against his side. "That is the way with younglings."

"You're lying," Ridley spat. "And that doesn't change the fact that the woman broke into my home and stole one of my prisoners."

"A prisoner you were holding for no reason, as he is one of my people," Lord Deveril fired back. "As for Miss Mead's trespassing, which was truly a brave rescue, you should have had the human authorities handle her rather than revealing our secrets to her."

Ridley's beady eyes bulged with rage. "She already knew! That bloody rogue told her. And she's clearly still a human!"

Deveril yawned. "I grow weary of this conversation, Ridley. Take yourself back to Gloucestershire and do not trouble me or my people again."

The Lord of Gloucestershire and his third in command moved forward as if to charge the door. Five Cornish vampires blocked his path wielding swords.

"Do you truly wish to risk a battle with me?" Deveril purred.

The squire's mustache twitched in impotent fury. "The Elders shall hear about this. And this time you will face more than a fine." With a final huff of indignation, the Lord of Gloucestershire spun on his heel and marched off as if he'd been the one to deliver a crushing set down.

Bethany slumped against Justus in relief. He grasped her shoulder and looked up at the Lord of Cornwall. "Thank you, my lord."

"Call me Vincent," Deveril said tiredly. "And I didn't do it for you. There is no way I would relinquish anything to that sanctimonious pipsqueak, not if I want to maintain my authority and the respect of my people and peers. I do not know who he bribed to become a Lord Vampire in the first place. He's barely over a century old."

Bethany placed her hand on the ancient vampire's forearm. "You told him we were citizens. Do you mean it?"

He frowned down at her so severely that she snatched her hand back. "Ridley gave me no choice. I warn you, my decision is on a contingency basis only, provided the pair of you give me no more trouble than you already have. And as for you, you must be Changed immediately, before one of the Elders catches me in a lie."

"Immediately?" she squeaked, overwhelmed by the sudden paradigm shift. Just like that, her humanity would end.

Vincent glowered at her. "I presumed you knew what wedding Lord de Wynter entailed."

"Oh, I do," she said quickly. "It is just that I did not expect to happen so quickly after we arrived. I'd hoped for more time to prepare."

Unbelievably, Lady Deveril laughed. "Oh, sugar. Do not worry. I had far less time than you, and everything was all right." She looked up at her husband. "May I have a few moments to talk with her and offer reassurances?"

Vincent nodded. "I need to take Lord de Wynter to feed and wake up my solicitor to send for a Special License. And Miss Mead looks as if she could do with a bath and a hot meal."

Bethany flushed, realizing how disheveled she must appear… not to mention her odor. Justus bent and placed a tender kiss on her forehead. "I will return to you shortly." Something glimmered in his eyes.

Fear and uncertainty, she recognized.

He'd misinterpreted her words. He thought she didn't want to become a vampire and spend her life with him. She reached out to reassure him, but he and the Lord of Cornwall had already walked away.

Lady Deveril hooked Bethany's arm in hers. "Let's get you cleaned up and fed. I'd already had the servants bring up hot water for me when I finished painting, but you are far more in need of a bath than I."

"Thank you, my lady." She curtsied.

"Please, call me Lydia," the young vampire said. "And may I call you Bethany?"

"Of course." Bethany curtsied, glad to do anything to make this woman happy.

Lydia led her up to a magnificent chamber hung with more even more glorious paintings of landscapes and animals. A monstrous bed with an oak frame and a blue canopy dominated the room. A fluffy gray and white cat bolted up from its perch atop the embroidered coverlet and bolted from the room. A large brass tub sat near the fireplace. Once Bethany sank into the steaming water, she looked up at Lydia. "What did you mean when you said you had far less time to prepare for the Change than I?"

"My throat was slit by a cutthroat in an alley," Lydia said as she scrubbed Bethany's back with a damp cloth. "Thank heavens that Vincent was there. He Changed me immediately."

Bethany jolted so hard in the tub that water sloshed the edges. "Sweet Jesus!"

"I think it was my grandmother's doing." Lydia sounded indifferent as she reached for the bottle of shampoo. "She did her utmost to get rid of me."

"Why?" Her own parents had also wanted her off their hands, but they would never resort to murder.

"My father married a commoner, and they fled to America after Grandmother disowned him." A note of derision tinged her voice, underpinned with disappointment. "When they died, my arrival in England meant the return of the old scandal. Lady Morley abhors scandal. So she convinced Lord Deveril to take me as his ward, thinking he'd keep me tucked away in Cornwall, but instead he brought me to London to find me a husband."

Bethany gasped. "Lord Deveril was your guardian?"

"To my utter disappointment, yes." Lydia handed her the washcloth and a cake of scented soap and averted her gaze as Bethany scrubbed her body. "For I think I tumbled head over heels in love with him the night I first laid eyes on him. And I was bound and determined to make him realize I'd already found my perfect match, though I didn't know that he felt the same until after he Changed me." A dreamy smile crossed her lips.

"I'll have to tell you the whole story another time. Right now, we need to prepare you for your new life as a vampire."

"Yes." The present crashed around her, heavy as a cairn. She dunked her head beneath the water before taking the shampoo. "Does it hurt?"

Lydia nodded. "For a small amount of time, when your fangs grow and your body changes. "But after that, it's wondrous. Colors and scents are more vivid, you can move like the wind, and you will heal almost any injury. Vincent taught me the joy of this existence, which is so odd because he loathed being a vampire before we met. He too was Changed without a choice." Wonder shone in her eyes as she told Bethany about her first nights as a vampire.

And while Bethany learned much of what to expect from her new life, she also knew what was most important: To have the man she loved by her side.

Chapter Thirty

Justus licked the smuggler's blood from his lips and released the man from his trance. Vincent shook another smuggler's hand after accepting a purse of gold and a cask of brandy. They left the cave that Lord Deveril allowed the men to use in exchange for a percent of the goods and profits.

"Thank you," Justus said when they were out of earshot.

Vincent grunted. "If you say that again, I may have to box your ears."

"I am sorry," Justus said. "But you cannot imagine what these past eight years have been like. Constantly on the run with no food or shelter, others always trying to capture or kill me."

"I served in the loyalist army and spent years evading and fighting Cromwell's forces," Vincent said. "I think I have an inkling. On top of that, I recently faced a death sentence over Changing Lydia without authorization from the Elders."

Justus's jaw dropped. "Is that why Rochester suggested I go to you?"

"It damn well better not be," Vincent said darkly. "I was not speaking idly when I say I cannot afford to risk trouble in my domain. However, Lord Darkwood likely recommended me because I have legitimized more rogues than most others. He *mocked* me for it the last time he paid me a visit."

Justus chuckled. That sounded like Gavin. "While he has possibly executed the most."

"Yet he allowed you to live." A sardonic smirk curved Vincent's lips. "I think he is going soft."

"Even softer, now that he married." For that was the second time that Gavin had shown Justus mercy he hadn't deserved. And he'd even told him where to find Bethany. But Justus didn't dare tell the Lord of Cornwall about his misguided and hazardous quest for vengeance.

"He wasn't married the *first* time he allowed you to live." Vincent's words were like a douse of ice water. "But I'm certain losing his heart to that youngling from London had a great deal to do with why he allowed you to live a second time, after you led an ill-advised insurrection against him."

Justus's jaw dropped. "He told you about that?"

"No." Vincent replied airily. "He is not the only one with spies. And this is another reason why I am hesitant to take you."

So he wasn't out of hot water yet. Justus scrambled to keep up with Deveril's long strides while still maintaining the pace of a mortal man. "I swear, my lord, I will never disobey you."

Deveril arched a brow. "You would if I asked you to give up your bride."

Justus's blood froze in his veins. "But you told me to Change her!"

Vincent clapped a hand on his shoulder. "Calm yourself. I was only making a point. You cannot make me a promise you're unable to keep. You are not the first vampire to become reckless because of love, nor will you be the last. I only want your solemn vow that you will be honest with me on all matters, and if there is ever a time where you feel you cannot obey one of my laws or commands, you will tell me."

Justus bowed. "I will, I swear."

"You may start by telling me why you have a vial of laudanum in your pocket."

Justus's shoulders slumped. "They kept Bethany drugged at the asylum. She now suffers from opium sickness, but she is improving. Since she was only drugged once or twice a week, it takes her a few days before the cravings begin to plague her. Another rogue gave me the laudanum to give her a small dose when her suffering is unbearable and to slowly wean her off the substance."

Justus closed his eyes, expecting Deveril to rage at him for throwing yet another complication on the situation. Instead, Vincent replied, "Ah. Now that is the sort of honesty and wise thinking that I expect from my people. Was this rogue honorable, do you think?"

Justus nodded. "In some ways. He is a highwayman, but only because he is trying to save his mortal descendants from having their farm taken away for not being able to pay an unfair mortgage. He'll probably end up losing his head for it, but he is set on his course."

"A highwayman in these days?" Vincent shook his head. "That is indeed the likely outcome. Does he range around my lands?"

"No. We encountered him in Devon, but he was on his way North."

Vincent shrugged. "Then I wish him luck, as he is none of my concern. Shall we visit my solicitor now?"

"I ah, have one more confession." Justus rubbed the back of his neck. "Bethany and I were wed in a Roma ceremony when we stayed in their encampment."

"My, you have had some adventures." Deveril chuckled. "All the same, a gypsy marriage is not valid under English law, so another wedding is necessary."

He had no quarrel with that. "I understand."

They walked through the quiet village and Justus admired the cobblestone roads, the charming brick houses and shops with slate roofs, and the clean sea scent in the air. Vincent walked up to a stately townhouse and knocked.

The solicitor opened the door, looking both vexed and accustomed to visits at three in the morning. However, his demeanor was much improved when he learned that he would be attending to the business of yet another member of the peerage.

"I will secure this license with the utmost haste," he assured Justus with an ingratiating smile that was somewhat off putting with his oversized false teeth.

By the time that business was concluded, it was only an hour before sunrise.

"We'll have to secure Miss Mead her first meal." Vincent sighed. "I usually do not feed from my servants, but given our narrow timetable, I suppose I have no choice."

His words were like a jolt of ice. It was time to Change Bethany. "Yes, my lord," Justus said through numb lips.

Vincent's eyes narrowed. "You look nervous. Have you never Changed a mortal before?"

"No. But it isn't that. It's Bethany… she seems afraid." Justus fought off a wave of dismay. "What if she hates being a vampire? What if she hates me?"

"Unfortunately, neither of you have a choice in the matter," Vincent said sharply. "But I do understand your sentiment. I had to Change Lydia immediately, without her even knowing what I was, much less giving her a choice. I thought she'd despise me. Instead, it was she who taught me the joys of our existence."

Justus frowned in confusion. "Why did you have to Change her so fast?"

"A thief slit her throat." Fury blazed in the vampire's blue-gray eyes. "It seemed a random attack at the time, but now I am not so certain. I think Lydia knows something about it, but she seems reluctant to tell me."

"You had to Change her or let her die." Justus couldn't fathom having to face such a situation and being forced to act so quickly. However, he knew he would have done the same as Vincent. Suddenly, he didn't feel so uneasy about Changing Bethany. At least he'd had a chance to tell her what her new life would entail.

When they returned to Castle Deveril, Bethany walked toward him, her hair clean and shining loose over an ivory gown that was a little snug and so short that her bare calves were revealed. When she embraced him, the scent of wildflowers teased his senses.

"I am ready," she whispered and rose up on her toes to kiss him.

"Are you certain?" he whispered against her lips.

"Yes." She linked her arms around his shoulders. "Even if we did have a choice, I realized I want to share my life with you in every way. As a wife and as a vampire. I need you more than I need the sunshine." The love in her eyes stole his breath/

Heart in his throat, Justus scooped her up like a groom preparing to carry the bride over the threshold. Perhaps that was exactly what he was doing. "Where do we do this?" he asked Vincent.

"I'll take you to your room." The Lord of Cornwall gestured for them to follow, his countess at his side.

They were led to an ornate tower room with no windows, so they'd be safe from the daylight. A large four poster bed with a cornflower blue coverlet beckoned them.

"I hope this is suitable," Lydia said as she walked the circle of the room. There's a wardrobe, wash basin, writing desk, and several lamps and candles.

"After sleeping in hovels, caves, and crypts, this is heaven, my lady," Justus assured her.

Vincent cleared his throat. "Would you like us to stay, or leave you in private?"

"If you could give us a few minutes…" Justus said.

Lord Deveril nodded. "We shall return with sustenance for her."

One they were alone, he sat Bethany on the bed. She looked up at him with wide, fearful eyes. "Lady Deveril told me that it will hurt."

Justus took his place beside her and ran his hands through her hair before tucking it over her shoulder. "I would take your pain were it possible. You are so brave."

She tilted her head to the side. "Do it now, before I lose my courage."

Hunger flared in his gut at the sight of her creamy neck. Saliva filled his mouth in remembrance of her taste. Justus pulled her into his arms and sank his teeth in her soft flesh. She cried out and tightened her arms around him as he drank in deep pulls.

He continued to drink until her pulse slowed to a thready rhythm. Praying that now was the right time and he hadn't killed her, Justus withdrew from her neck and bit his wrist.

"Drink," he whispered, pressing his wound to her lips.

At first, she swayed, motionless and pale. Justus steadied her and said a silent prayer. When her hand grasped his arm and her mouth latched on the wound, he thanked the fates with all his soul.

She sucked his blood in greedy gulps until his head swam with dizziness.

"Enough," he said, but it took some gentle coaxing to get her to release him.

Bethany whimpered in disappointment before falling back on the bed. Her bosom heaved as she panted with heavy gasps, her pulse now rapid and strong. Justus grasped her hand, threading his fingers through hers as he tried not to panic.

Had it been like this when he was Changed? It had been so long.

When Bethany clapped a hand over her mouth and moaned in pain, some of his recollection returned. He did remember that part. Growing new fangs hurt like the devil.

"Oh, Justus!" she cried, "It hurts!"

He laid down on the bed beside her and took her into his arms. "I know. Don't be afraid to cry. It will pass and I will never leave you."

She sobbed against his chest, her hand clenching his in a grip that grew strong enough to give him a twinge of pain. Her other hand knotted in his jacket, agony radiating from every shudder and spasm of her body.

Unable to bear her suffering, Justus pulled the bottle of laudanum from his pocket. "Take a bit of this." He had no idea how much it would help since vampires typically recovered from the effects of strong drink or cannabis rapidly, but he would do anything to mitigate her pain.

Bethany shook her head, teeth clenched. "I can do this. The last thing I need to be is an opium-addled vampire like the one Rhys met."

Vincent's shadow fell over them. "Take it," he commanded. "Had I had some on hand to give to Lydia when she was Changed, I would have. The drug will wear off fast anyway."

Bethany regarded Vincent and Justus in turn with a stubborn glare and pressed her lips together so tight they turned white. Heart-rending moans still emitted from her, but she averted her face from the little brown bottle.

Justus sighed and brushed her hair from her face as she thrashed and moaned, desperately wishing there was something he could do to take the pain away.

After a hellish eternity, Bethany's tremors subsided and her free hand slid down to clutch her belly. "I need…" she whispered. "I want…"

Vincent nodded. "It's time."

He left the room and returned quickly with two vacant-eyed chamber maids. "Treat them gently, or you will not survive this night," he warned.

Lydia led one of the maids to the bed, grasping the woman's wrist and holding it towards Bethany's mouth. "Your first meal."

Bethany shook her head and started to turn away, but then her eyes glowed lightning blue and her mouth opened to reveal her tiny pointed fangs. With a groan of hunger, she bit down on the maid's wrist, moaning in pleasure as she drank.

Color returned to her cheeks, and her breathing evened out as she fed.

"No more," Justus said, cupping her jaw.

She groaned in protest, but withdrew from the maid's wrist. Lydia healed the wound and led the servant from the room.

Vincent urged the other maid forward. "Now for you."

Justus drank as little as possible, restoring the strength he'd lost from Bethany's transformation. After healing the puncture marks, he looked up at Vincent and Lydia. "Thank you."

Vincent nodded curtly. "It's nearly dawn. You both should rest. Tomorrow we have a youngling to teach, your fealty to swear, your presentation to my people, and of course, a wedding to plan."

Justus's mind swam with the impossible schedule. Something so different than his constant nights of running and searching for food and shelter.

When the earl and countess left them, Bethany rolled over to face him. "Oh, my heavens…" She stroked his cheek. "You're so beautiful."

"I was thinking the same about you," he replied, dizzy with relief that she'd come through the Change.

Her lips parted as her eyes studied him and then peered over his shoulder at the room. "The world looks so different. So much more vivid. Is this how you've always seen it?"

His gaze scanned the room before returning to her face. "In some ways, yes. In others, no. Without you, the world was rather dull."

She twined her arms around his shoulders and pressed her lips against his. "Oh Justus, I'm so happy. We finally have a home. We can finally be together."

"Home." The word was thick as honey on his tongue. "You know, in all my years as a rogue, I never even tried to find one."

She frowned. "Why not?"

He kissed her again. "Because there is no home without you."

Epilogue

Twelve nights later

Bethany turned twice in front of the mirror, breathless with excitement at the sight of her white satin wedding gown encrusted with pearls. Two vampires known as the "Mad Sisters of Cornwall" had sewn it for her.

Lydia grinned over her shoulder. "You look like a fairy princess."

"Thank you." Bethany blushed. "You truly shouldn't have gone to this expense." She'd only recently learned that Lord and Lady Deveril were mortgaged up to their ears because of the fine Vincent had to pay the Elders for Changing Lydia without their sanction. A regular vampire needed permission from his lord to Change a human, but a Lord Vampire had to gain the Elders' approval. Vincent could have been sentenced to death, but instead the Elders made him pay them one hundred thousand pounds. Thankfully, they'd live long enough to pay off the mortgage on their castle.

"Nonsense," Lydia said, adjusting Bethany's veil. "All I had to do was trade them a painting they'd been coveting. Just wait until you see your wedding gifts."

Bethany's flush deepened. "Oh, you shouldn't have. You and Lord Deveril have already done so much for us." Vincent had given Justus a job as an assistant to Emrys, sold them a cottage— which Justus had been able to purchase with his money that the Lord of Rochester had returned to him— and made them welcome among the vampires of Cornwall.

All very much at their peril. Only two nights after she was Changed, the Lord Vampire of Edinburgh, who was one of the Elders, arrived to investigate Squire Ridley's claims that Lord Deveril was harboring a rogue vampire and a mortal woman who was an escaped lunatic. It seemed Ridley had read the papers and made the connection.

Bethany had been certain that all was lost, but Lord Deveril had coolly presented Edinburgh a letter from the Lord of Rochester recommending that he allow Justus and Bethany to live in Cornwall because with Bethany's father being such a prominent figure in politics, it wouldn't do for her to be recognized. No mention was made of Justus being exiled, or Bethany being committed to an asylum all these years.

The letter had been signed by a man named Gavin Drake. A name Bethany found to be as familiar as the wax seal, though she couldn't place it. It had been too long since her days among Rochester's Society members.

Edinburgh had handed the letter back to Deveril with a grunt. "Damn it all, I knew that wee bugger had dragged me down here for nothing. I've known too many lordlings like him. Always making trouble for their own amusement. He'll think twice about that after I pay him a visit on my way home."

Bethany and Justus had linked hands under the table, lips compressed to hold back sighs of relief.

Vincent had covered his mouth to hide his smile. "Care for another glass of brandy, my lord?" He'd given the Elder two whole casks from his stores.

"Aye." Edinburgh accepted the snifter with gleaming eyes. "Though this Frenchie swill is not nearly as good as Scots whiskey. At any rate, watch out for Ridley. He seems to have taken a dislike to ye. If he does anything out of line, file a report immediately." He took a deep drink of brandy and licked his lips. "Och, I am so bloody tired of these squabbles. I cannot wait until I retire."

Vincent and Justus both gaped at him. "You're retiring?"

"Aye." Edinburgh rubbed his brow. "I've held my post for five centuries. I want to do something else for a time." He regarded Lord Deveril over the rim of his glass. "I dinna suppose ye'd be interested?"

Vincent reared back in his chair as if a cobra had appeared on the table. "Good God, no!"

"Pity. Despite the trouble you got yerself intae the other year, ye've done a fine job ruling over a larger territory than most." Edinburg set down the glass of brandy that he clearly enjoyed despite his complaints. "Ah well, we're to interview the Duke of Burnrath in a few months. I think he's a wee bit young to be an Elder," he chuckled at his pun, "but he's held one of the largest cities in the world for a long time."

"Ian as an Elder?" Vincent took a deep drink as if he needed fortification to contemplate the notion.

"I think it would suit him," Justus said. "He's certainly staid and stuffy enough." He paled at the Lord of Edinburg's glare. "I mean, he is qualified."

"But his wife..." Vincent shook his head. "That is right. You never met her."

Bethany's eyes widened as she grasped the connection. "We admire her novels." She remembered Justus's amusement when she'd told him she'd enjoyed the Duchess's work. Her Grace was a vampire, and her husband must be the Lord Vampire of London.

Bethany had spent the remainder of Edinburg's visit in rapt awe at the enormity of her new world. Every night, some new secret had revealed itself. She wondered if she'd discover that someone else she'd heard of or even met was also a vampire.

Now that the Elder had departed and all was peaceful in Cornwall, Bethany was more than ready to be Justus's wife at last. She grinned at Lydia, happy to have at last found true friends and a home with the man she loved.

After Lydia and her maids had finished with Bethany's wedding gown and hair, they left in the Deverils' coach for the church. It was a small ceremony, attended by half the vampires of Cornwall, but Bethany barely noticed them or even the vicar. She only had eyes for Justus. After eight years of misery and isolation, they were together at last. Sometimes, in her cell in Morningside, Bethany wondered if had she known what would have happened after Justus had first proposed to her, if she would have said yes.

Now, as Justus slipped an antique ring on her finger, she knew she would have paid any price for this moment.

When they were pronounced man and wife, he kissed her until she was breathless and wished they'd opted for a private ceremony.

Bethany forced a polite smile as the guests offered congratulations, when all she wished was for her and her husband to return to their seaside cottage with its bookshelves they were just starting to fill, and their soft, downy bed.

"Justus," a husky voice interrupted her musings.

Bethany bit back a gasp when she recognized the Baron of Darkwood. She remembered her mother shoving her at him and his cold hostility when they'd danced. Darkwood was the Lord Vampire of Rochester, the vampire who'd been Justus's closest friend. The vampire who'd sentenced him to exile.

Justus didn't seem to mind anymore. "Gavin!" he exclaimed and embraced Darkwood.

"How are you faring?" Gavin asked, his usual harsh features softened with wistful regret.

"Much better than the last time we spoke," Justus answered with a grin.

"You found your lost love." Gavin turned to Bethany and bowed. "My lady, you cannot imagine how I've wished to see you here with Justus at this moment. And how much I regret all the suffering you both have endured, how I wish I had done something sooner…"

"It is quite all right." She extended her hand and he took it. "If you hadn't found out that I'd been taken to Manchester, Justus never would have found me in the asylum. And if it weren't for your letter to Lord Deveril, we may not have been welcomed." Not to mention the fact that Lord Deveril, Justus, and herself could have been subject to the wrath of the Elders.

Lord Darkwood lifted her hand and brushed his lips over her knuckles. "You have a generous heart, Lady de Wynter."

"And you seem to have a forgiving one, for the trouble we have caused," she returned.

Darkwood smiled. "The credit belongs to my wife. I did not know I had a heart until she uncovered it." He turned and grasped the hand of a slender, dark haired woman beside him.

She'd been so quiet that Bethany hadn't noticed her. "Allow me to introduce you to Lenore, my baroness."

Lenore gave Bethany a shy smile. "I've heard so much about you."

"I can imagine." Bethany chuckled, remembering how Justus told her of how he'd kidnapped Rochester's bride in his quest for vengeance when he'd thought that Rochester had killed Bethany.

Lady Darkwood's smile broadened. "You should have seen the look in his eyes when Gavin told him that not only were you alive, but he'd also tracked down your location. It was an extremely difficult task, as your parents did not want anyone to know where they tucked you away. You must be very brave and strong to have survived being imprisoned so long. Gavin felt terrible about the whole unpleasant business. He'd assumed you'd been taken to live with one of your relatives. We had no idea that you'd been committed until Justus wrote us a letter last month."

"And I had no idea that the Lord Vampire of Rochester had anything to do with my rescue." With that, the letter he'd written to the Lord of Cornwall, and the carts full of Justus's books, furniture, and other personal possessions, it was clear that the Baron of Darkwood was doing his best to make amends for his role in their separation. "I'd love to hear the whole story of how you met Lord Darkwood." It was apparent in the way the two looked at each other that Lenore had indeed been instrumental in the softening of the vampire's heart.

"And I would love to hear about how you met Lord de Wynter and the adventures you encountered on your way to the altar." Lenore touched her sleeve. "But you have a wedding night to enjoy, and we have to return to Rochester. We'd like to come for another visit in a month or two, if that is agreeable with the Lord of Cornwall. I know Gavin is eager to renew his friendship with Justus, and I would very much like to befriend you."

Despite Lady Darkwood's outward timidity, there was a quiet strength and compassion in her large dark eyes that made Bethany want to reach out to her and pour out all her secrets. "I would like that too."

Bethany peered over Lenore's shoulder and met Justus's gaze. The heat that flared in his gaze ignited a fire in her belly.

In tandem, they excused themselves from their conversations and said their farewells. When they rode off in a curricle beneath a shower of rice, Bethany looked closer at her golden ring set with a ruby. "Ever since I saw you wearing my locket, I wished I'd had something to keep you close to me as well."

"The ring belonged to my grandmother. I'd meant to give it to you the night I was to call upon your father." Justus smiled. "All this time I'd thought that Gavin had seized my personal effects to keep for himself. Instead he'd saved my things to return them to me."

She rested her head on his chest. "He is much kinder than I was led to believe."

"Indeed. And I've known him for over a century." Justus flicked the reins, urging the horses to trot faster.

"Do you think you'll ever want to return to Rochester? To your estate?"

"I'm not certain. I truly enjoy it here in Cornwall, and Lord Deveril is much less prickly. My manor in Rochester is in shambles anyway. I'd left it like that to keep people away, but I don't really miss it. Our cottage is much more cozy and the people and vampires here are friendlier. And since I'm not as well known around here, the vampires are more free with their information. I am resuming my old role as spymaster already." His lips curved in a mischievous smile. "For example, have you heard that the Lord of Blackpool's niece was kidnapped by a rogue vampire?"

"No!" Bethany gasped. "Do you think it is our friend, Rhys?"

"Undoubtedly," Justus said. "Blackmail could suit his ends. I cannot help but admire his boldness."

Bethany shook her head. "Oh, he's going to get himself killed."

"I'm not so certain about that. Rhys struck me as very resilient and clever," Justus said as the curricle turned into the drive leading to their cottage.

When their stable boy came to claim the horses, Justus lifted her from the curricle and carried her into the cottage.

Bethany's eyes widened at the pile of books that were stacked on their dining room table. "Where did these all come from?"

"I do not know." Justus set her down and they approached the stack.

A letter sat upon a copy of *Beowulf.* Justus opened it and read. "A wedding gift from the people of Cornwall and Rochester."

Bethany's throat tightened at the generous gift. "We have our library at last!"

Justus pulled her into his arms. "And the time to read them all."

As Bethany pulled him down for a kiss, her heart overflowed with joy. At last, their story had a happy ending.

About the Author

Formerly an auto-mechanic, Brooklyn Ann thrives on writing romance featuring unconventional heroines and heroes who adore them. She's delved into historical paranormal romance in her critically acclaimed "Scandals with Bite" series, urban fantasy in her "Brides of Prophecy" novels and heavy metal romance in her "Hearts of Metal" novellas.

She lives in Coeur d'Alene, Idaho with her son, miscellaneous horror memorabilia, and a 1980 Datsun 210.

You can be follow her online and keep up with her latest news and releases at http://brooklynannauthor.com as well as on twitter and Facebook.

Keep in touch for the latest news, exclusive excerpts, and giveaways! Sign up for Brooklyn Ann's newsletter!

Books by Brooklyn Ann

Historical Paranormal Romance

Scandals With Bite series

1.) Bite Me, Your Grace
2.) One Bite Per Night
3.) Bite at First Sight
4.) His Ruthless Bite
5.) Wynter's Bite
6.) Coming soon

Urban Fantasy Romance

Brides of Prophecy Series

0.5.) Tesemini (prequel)
1.) Wrenching Fate
2.) Ironic Sacrifice
3.) Conjuring Destiny
4.) Unleashing Desire
5.) Coming Soon

Heavy Metal Romance

Hearts of Metal series

1.) Kissing Vicious
2.) With Vengeance

3.) Rock God
4.) Metal and Mistletoe
5.) Coming Soon

For the most current list of Brooklyn Ann's books as well as news about upcoming releases, visit http://www.brooklynannauthor.com

27027115R00174

Made in the USA
Columbia, SC
24 September 2018